WHEN

WE

WAKE

by Karen Healey

LITTLE, BROWN AND COMPANY
New York   Boston

WHEN

WE

WAKE

Little, Brown and Company

Hachette Book Group
237 Park Avenue, New York, NY 10017
Visit our website at lb-teens.com

Little, Brown and Company is a division of Hachette Book Group, Inc.
The Little, Brown name and logo are trademarks of Hachette Book Group, Inc.

The publisher is not responsible for websites (or their content) that are not owned by the publisher.

First Paperback Edition: March 2014
First published in hardcover in March 2013 by Little, Brown and Company

Library of Congress Cataloging-in-Publication Data

Healey, Karen.
    When we wake / Karen Healey.
      p. cm.
    Summary: "In 2027, sixteen-year-old Tegan is just like every other girl—playing the guitar, falling in love, and protesting the wrongs of the world with her friends. But then Tegan dies, waking up a hundred years in the future as the unknowing first government guinea pig to be cryonically frozen and successfully revived. Appalling secrets about her new world come to light, and Tegan must choose to either keep her head down or fight for a better future."—Provided by publisher.
    ISBN 978-0-316-20076-9 (hc) / ISBN 978-0-316-20077-6 (pb)
    [1. Science Fiction.   2. Australia—Fiction.]   I. Title.
    PZ7.H3438Whe 2013
    [Fic]—dc23

                                                                    2012028739

10 9 8 7 6 5 4 3 2 1

RRD-C

Printed in the United States of America

For the wonderful friends
who live in wonderful Melbourne.
And for Melanie Reese, who doesn't.

CHAPTER ONE
Yesterday

My name is Tegan Oglietti. One of my ancestors was a highwayman, and another was a prince. Two were Olympic medalists, three were journalists, half a dozen were chefs, a whole bunch were soldiers, and a lot were housewives who didn't get a quarter of the credit they deserved.

I've been thinking about inheritance a lot lately, about what we make, about what makes us, about the legacies we give those who come after us. Well, I would, wouldn't I?

We all begin with our past.

That last day, I was running late for the train, and I almost didn't stop to say good-bye. But Mum called me into the kitchen, where she was working on an experiment for her little restaurant.

"Ricotta and beef ravioli," she said, waving a laden fork at me. "Open your mouth."

I did. The pasta was light and silky, and although I prefer

cheeses with more flavor, I had to admit the ricotta added something to the texture.

"Good?" said Mum, quick dark eyes moving over my face.

"Good," I said through my mouthful. "Contributing to global destruction with the production of heat-trapping methane gases, but really very tasty. Tasty destruction! Now can I go?"

"Mm," she said, eyeing the liqueur bottles lined up beside the microwave. With any luck, I'd be coming home to a spectacular dessert. "Oh, wait." She hooked an arm around my neck and hauled me back, kissing my cheek. She smelled like herbs and flour, the warm smell that meant home. "There. Now you can go and save the world."

I laughed, kissed my fingers to the photo of Dad hanging on the kitchen wall, and ran out the door, rubbing the pink lip gloss off my face. Alex would be waiting, and she would want the complete goss report before we met Dalmar at the station.

Smart, intense Dalmar, who cared about the environment and domestic violence and famine. Handsome, talented Dalmar, whose skin was smooth and dark, whose eyes were round and a deep, rich brown, like new-turned soil. Perfect, perfect Dalmar, who'd been my brother's best friend for eighteen years, and my boyfriend for one day. The climate-change protest was going to be our official first date, and I was already planning our wedding.

My name is Tegan Oglietti, and on the last day of my first lifetime, I was so, so happy.

≈ ‡ ∞

I'll tell you the whole story.

You might wonder why I bother; you already know the facts. But one thing I've learned over the past months—maybe even before—is that facts aren't enough. It's not enough to know; you have to *believe*. It has to be personal. So here I am, giving you my memories and my feelings and my words. My soul, if you like. It's the only thing that still belongs to me, and there were some times, bad times, that I doubted even that.

But I know the Father was wrong. No one can take your soul from you. You have to give it away.

Here's my soul. I'm giving it to you.

I hope you're listening.

≈ ‡ ∞

Alex opened the door before I could knock, her grin wide on her narrow face. She was wearing what she called her protest uniform—long red peasant skirt, leggings, heavy boots, and a bright shirt under a sleeveless vest covered with buttons. STRAIGHT NOT NARROW. WOMEN AGAINST WAR. RIGHT IS MIGHT. UP THE UNIONS. I could see placards with more meticulously lettered slogans leaning against the wall and tried not to grimace. Those things were heavy, and I'd been hoping not to lug one around all day. But for once, Alex had concerns other than saving humanity from itself.

"I got your text," she said. "Tell me everything, from the beginning."

"Fourteen billion years ago, the universe expanded," I said, jumping out of Alex's reach. She'd stopped boxing, but she still had a mean right hook, even when it was just for fun. "Okay. Okay. He came around to my place yesterday, and I said, 'Owen already left for Tasmania,' and he said, 'I know. I want to talk to you.'"

"Oh my god, Teeg," Alex breathed. "We're running late, but tell me as we go."

Alex swung her battered satchel over her head. I knew from experience that the bag might contain anything from a couple of muesli bars and a bottle of water to fireworks, a complete set of lock picks, and a collapsible crowbar. She picked up two of the signs and thrust them at me, shouldering the rest herself.

"Do I have to?"

"Yes, lazy," she said, and called a cheerful good-bye to her foster mother.

"It's just that it's so freaking hot."

I already had heat rash, prickly red bumps on the backs of my knees, and it was only September. Mum said that when she was my age, Melbourne's spring had been long and wet and cool, hitting the nineties only in November or even December. The superstorms and bushfires hadn't been so bad, either.

But it was 2027, and things were getting worse—which is why Alex and Dalmar were so keen on this protest. I mean, they were always up for a march or promoting a petition from a stall on Swanston Street, but this time the Prime Minister was attending the rally. I didn't think she'd actually do anything about the climate, but it was an election year, the youth vote was up for grabs, and Dalmar had some cautious hopes.

He had a lot of hope, Dalmar. I think that's why I fell in love with him. It was all those conversations in the garage, where, between practices, he tried to get Owen involved. In anything, really.

"We're going to inherit the world, and everything needs to change," he'd said. "Adults don't care, so we have to make them care, or replace them."

Owen called him obsessed, which was pretty hilarious because Owen was the single most obsessed person I knew. His whole life revolved around music, usually to the exclusion of minor things like environmental collapse, or the horrific state of refugee camps in the Horn of Africa, or his little sister. I started playing the guitar to spend more time with Owen, but I ended up listening to Dalmar. I learned to care.

To be honest, I cared more about Dalmar than things like climate change. One was right there, in the extremely awesome flesh, and the other was slow and terrible and felt far away. I cared, but not like Dalmar and Alex did. Still, it's not like I betrayed myself and my own ideas to get closer to a beautiful boy. I just couldn't resist his hope.

"So he said, 'I want to talk to you,' and *you* said..." Alex prompted.

"And *I* said, 'Oh, really?' like a total idiot."

"Hah!"

"But it doesn't matter, because then he took my hand—"

"Oh my god."

"—and said, 'Tegan, I've been thinking about you a lot, and if you say no, I will understand, and it won't ruin our friendship, but would you like to go out with me?'"

Alex stopped in the street. "Seriously?"

I grinned. "Just like that." Every word he'd said was written on my brain in blazing letters of gold.

"And then what?" she demanded.

"Classified." My whole body was buzzing with the memory.

"Teeg, I will kill you and sink the corpse in the river."

I snorted. "What river?" The Yarra ran through the city, but you couldn't hide a body in that shallow brown flow.

"I will dig a river and fill it with my tears, because I will be weeping from the betrayal of my best friend not giving me every damn detail!"

"We kissed," I said. "Well, I kissed him, and he kissed me back. In the front hallway."

"Oh wow. That is the best."

"Then Mum walked in and said, 'Oops,' and walked back out, and Dalmar said sorry and I said sorry at the same time, and then we went up to my room, and seriously after that is classified."

Alex pursed her lips and nodded. "Acceptable."

"He said I was beautiful," I said softly. I could feel a tingle in my lips, the ghost of Dalmar's kisses. We hadn't done much, just held each other and talked and laughed. The talking and laughing we'd done for years, but after so much waiting, the touch was all new, and it was like a drug, making me giddy and calm at the same time. I didn't want to pick apart something so special with Alex, much as I loved her. Let it be just for us, Dalmar and me.

"You *are* beautiful," Alex said. "I wish I had your boobs."

"You want my backaches?"

"Well, maybe not," she conceded. "Or your red nose."

"I burn so fast," I sighed, and scowled at the tip of said red peeling nose. Dalmar had kissed that spot last night, I remembered, and the frown smoothed out.

"Haaah, look at you. You're so in love!" Alex spun around in the street, signs and all, wide skirt flaring up around her hips. "You and me and Dalmar and Jonno have to do something. A couples dinner. Couples bowling!"

"Um," I said. I didn't like Alex's boyfriend that much. He was one of those pretentious guys who thought conversation was all about being smarter and more important than everyone else in the room. And he talked down to me all the time, just because I was the youngest. But Alex thought Jonno was hotter than summer at the beach, and I had to be supportive. "Can I keep Dalmar to myself for a bit?"

"Of course, yeah. Want me to get lost at the rally?"

I hesitated. I really did, but... "I don't want to be that girl, you know?"

"Please, I know you'd never abandon me for a guy. I'm offering! We go together; I conveniently get lost in the crowd; oh no, where is Alex? Gosh, it's just you and Dalmar, holding hands.... You can make out all you want."

"Gross," I said. "In public?"

"Whatever, lovebird. But tonight, you and me are still up for some exploring, right?"

"Right."

So the satchel was holding the lock picks and the collapsible

7

crowbar, and probably a couple of flashlights, too. Alex's version of exploring meant breaking into abandoned buildings, underground tunnels, and the occasional construction site, ferreting out the secrets of the city. It was a great way to spend a few hours, and not something I thought my mother ever needed to know about.

It was nearly midday, and we were flagging in the heat. Like most 2027 Australians who weren't sun-loving beach bunnies, we tried to avoid the outdoors between eleven and three in the hotter months, when it seemed as if the sun was maliciously beaming right through the hole in the ozone layer and setting us aflame. I was slathered in a thick layer of SPF 70 sunscreen and wearing dark sunnies and a big floppy hat, and with all that, I knew my nose would still be redder by the end of the afternoon.

But the Prime Minister was meeting the petitioners on the steps of Parliament House at noon, so our sun-shunning habits had to adjust to her schedule.

My pocket beeped. My heart jumped.

"Dalmaaaaaaar," Alex cooed.

"If you do that when he's here," I warned, and fished out my phone. She was right, of course; the message was from him.

TRAIN DELAYED, TEN MINS LATE XXX

It was a perfectly ordinary message that he could have sent the day before yesterday, or any time in the three years we'd been friends instead of my big brother's preachy best friend/best friend's annoying little sister.

Except for that postscript of kisses.

For once, the flush in my cheeks owed nothing to the sun. I ducked my head under my hat and silently thanked Alex for her mercy as she pretended not to notice a thing.

Not that it mattered. When Dalmar stepped off the train and met us on the platform, I think the whole world could have seen how I felt. But for me, the rest of the world wasn't there. Just Dalmar, with his easy stride and wide smile.

I know Alex was talking, but I can't remember a word. I've tried, I really have, but it's all just buzzing.

He leaned into me, and we touched fingertips. It was a game we'd come up with the night before, finding how little we could touch and still be in contact. We were seeing who could hold out longer, but eventually he gave in and held my hand. He had bass-player calluses. He'd built them up fingering those thick strings, and now they were rough, stroking down the side of my little finger. Nothing in the world had ever felt that good.

"I missed you," he said, relieving me of the placards.

"I missed you, too," I replied, and leaned my head against his free shoulder.

A narrow hand landed in the small of my back and shoved. It was Alex, her other hand on Dalmar's back. "We've got to catch a train, lovebirds," she grunted. "Next platform, move move move."

Dalmar laughed. "You should be a general, Alex."

9

"No way, man. Make love, not war." She darted up the escalators before us, multicolored curls bouncing on her shoulders.

We made it to the platform in time to catch the train to Parliament Station. The car was full of people dressed in Earth Punk fusion; I felt completely underdressed and sweaty in my shorts jumpsuit with a nonmatching long-sleeved cotton bolero thrown on at the last second to try to stop my arms from burning. Dalmar, with his orange safety vest catching the lights in the car, and Alex, with the badges on her protest uniform, fit right in. The train car was loud with debate.

I caught a glimpse of the golden statue of the goddess Mazu, who watched over the shallow remnants of the Maribyrnong River that dribbled by the Buddhist temple. She might bring us good luck today. Mazu was the protector of the sea, after all, and rising oceans were probably one of her concerns.

But I wasn't Buddhist. Instead, I silently asked the Virgin Mary, Star of the Sea, to intercede on our behalf.

Prayer concluded, I let the train's motion sway me against Dalmar where he stood braced against the yellow pole. "I wrote you a song," I whispered in his ear, resisting the urge to kiss his earlobe.

"Really?" He slipped his hand from mine and draped it over my shoulder, pulling me close.

"I'll play it for you tonight," I promised. "Just so you know, nothing good rhymes with *Dalmar*."

"Far. Car. Tar. Star. Bizarre?"

"Help!" I sang, making up the lyrics as I went along. "I need

Dalmar. Help! He's so bizarre. Help, you know I need Dalmaaaar. Help!"

"You and your Beatles," Alex said.

"Best musicians of their century," I said, as I had many times before. "And ours. And all the centuries to come."

"Let's make sure the species *has* centuries to come," Dalmar said.

As the train jerked to a stop, we stepped out together, into the future.

≋ ‡ ∞

I don't remember if it hurt.

There are questions I get asked a lot, in therapy, at school, and even at the compound, when the girls loosened up enough to talk to me. *What do you remember? What did you see? How did it feel?*

I'll tell you the whole story. Even the embarrassing parts, even the bits where I behave like an enormous loser.

But I can't tell you if there was any pain.

The truth is, it all stops with us pouring out of Parliament Station and up the steep steps, with Dalmar's arm around my shoulders and Alex grinning at how cozy we were together. I was thinking of finding a quiet place to kiss Dalmar, and wondering whether Alex could be talked into letting me do some free-running practice before we broke into whatever abandoned hulk she wanted to explore. I was thinking about whether Owen might bring me something back from Tasmania, and if Mum might be whipping up my favorite raspberry macarons, and if Dad would be proud of what I was doing today.

And then it all stops. The final memory of my first life is a freeze-frame of me leaning against Dalmar on the way up the steps.

But when Marie thought I was ready, I saw the same footage everyone else did.

It's awful phone video, not even a real camera. Nothing like the superclear footage you guys have of everything now. But you can still make it out easily enough if you know what to look for.

There's the Prime Minister in a blue skirt suit standing under a shady canopy, speaking to the protesters, saying pretty things that aren't quite promises. There's the dark-haired girl high on the steps, just visible in the corner of the screen. There she is, falling down. There are screams as the crowd starts to realize what's happened, and someone shouts, "It's a sniper!" and then the camera turns to the sidewalk as the unknown videographer runs away.

Memory loss is a perfectly normal trauma reaction, Marie says, but it still feels weird. Watching that footage doesn't spark a thing. It could be a perfect stranger dying on the steps of Parliament House.

But it was me.

I woke up one hundred years later.

And then things really went to hell.

CHAPTER TWO
A Hard Day's Night

There was light in my eyes and soft murmuring at the edge of my hearing, like a radio cycling through stations. Bits of the conversation became clear, then faded out again.

"—activity indicates conscious interaction—"

"—report to General—"

"—my patient. I'll talk—"

"—press conference in—"

The noise went away altogether, and the light brightened. I tried to blink it away.

Eyelids. I had eyelids, and a face, and a neck and a chest. I tried to sit up, my hands flailing weakly at something soft. I felt like a fish out of water, flopping and struggling to breathe. Once, when he was home on leave, Dad took me fishing, and I caught one, and then I screamed and screamed when I realized the fish would die.

"It's all right," a voice soothed. A woman's voice, I thought, with a faint accent I couldn't place. "You've been sedated. It's wearing off."

"Can't see," I choked. "Only light."

"Your vision should clear soon. My name is Dr. Carmen. Do you remember your name?"

Did I? "Tegan," I said, relieved. "Tegan Oglietti. What happened?"

"Your date of birth, Tegan?"

"December 17, 2010."

There was a slight pause, then, "And today's date?"

"Ummm. September 23. Did I miss the rally? Where're Dalmar and Alex?"

"We'll get to that in a moment," Dr. Carmen said. "For now, I just want to check on you. Your communication centers and memory seem fine. That's very good!"

Something stung my toes. I kicked automatically.

"And you've got good nervous responses. Can you feel this?"

The stinger hit my ankle. "Yes! Stop it!"

"Don't panic, Tegan. It's okay. Please say yes every time you feel something."

I obeyed as the stinger moved up my body, down both arms, and finished between my eyebrows. The steady motion-and-response calmed me down; it also gave me time to think.

"Am I in a hospital?" I asked tremulously. "Is my mum here?"

14

A shadow passed through the light, and I blinked harder. "I see something!"

The shadow paused, hovering in the middle of my vision. "Keep blinking," she advised, and I did until the shadow resolved itself into a blurry face. I could make out dark, short hair and pale skin and not much else.

"I can see you," I said. "But not very clearly."

"It might take a little while for full vision to return," Dr. Carmen said. "But your responses are great, Tegan."

"What happened?" I asked again, with more force. It hadn't escaped me that she hadn't answered any of my questions.

Her face moved to one side and then down. She'd sat down next to the bed, I figured after a moment. Her accent was weird—like a little touch of American mixed into a normal Australian accent.

"Tegan, I'm afraid I have bad news," she said, and my stomach tightened into a knot. There'd been an accident. Someone had set off a bomb. There'd been an earthquake.

"This is going to be very hard for you to hear, but I want you to listen to as much as you can. Do you remember going to the rally?"

"Yes," I whispered. "We were on the way. Who's dead?"

She ignored that, as she'd ignored the other questions. She was following a script, probably from a book called *How Soft-Voiced Doctors Break Bad News*, and she was going to stick to it, whatever I said.

"Well, a sniper was waiting to attack the Prime Minister. I'm afraid that—"

"Just tell me who's dead!" I shouted. "Dalmar? Alex? Who did the sniper hit?"

There was a pause. "He hit you, Tegan," she said very calmly. "The bullet tore through your heart, left lung, and right kidney. Bone fragmentation damaged most of your other internal organs."

I sucked in a big gulp of air, and she hurried into the silence left by my shock.

"You were declared dead in the ambulance on the way to the hospital. But you'd signed up for the donation program, do you remember?"

The bright yellow cards declaring that in the event of my sudden death, I was donating my body to science. I'd signed up the day I turned sixteen, with my mother's proud signature on the form. It could mean giving up my eyes, my skin, my kidneys to someone who could use them better. Or it could mean being used for experimentation or dissection by med students who needed corpses to study. It wasn't as if it would matter to me once I was dead. My soul would go to heaven, so my body might as well be of use to someone.

But none of those things had happened, right? Because I was here, wherever here was.

"I remember," I whispered. "I was dead? I died? But I'm here!" This couldn't possibly be heaven.

"Legally, technically, yes, you died. But as you say, you're here. Most of your organs were too hurt to be donated, but your brain and spine were undamaged, and you were moved to the hospital within minutes. You were a perfect candidate for a new treatment. A cryonic treatment. Do you know what cryonics is?"

"Freezing dead people," I said automatically. There had been some talk in the news about advancing techniques, but I hadn't known they'd actually gone ahead with experimentation.

"Exactly. So—"

"That's what you did?" I gasped. "Where's my *mum*?"

"You can think of it as being in a coma," she said. More and more of her face was swimming into focus now. "A sort of frozen coma that lasted a long time."

Dr. Carmen paused, waiting for the obvious question, but my mind was whirring, and I missed my cue.

"It's 2128, Tegan," she said. "I'm sorry, I know that must be difficult to hear. You've been in stasis for just over a century."

It felt like running headfirst into a brick wall—a pain so huge it was hardly pain at all.

My vision hadn't cleared enough to make out expressions yet, but Dr. Carmen's voice was soothing. "Tegan, I realize that it won't feel like it yet, but you're a very lucky girl."

"Shut up," I told her.

She did, while I concentrated on breathing.

"I want to be alone," I said, and prayed that she'd give in.

I had to get out of there. I had to find Dalmar and Alex. I had to get in touch with my family.

But most of all, I had to find out what was really going on.

≋ ‡ ∞

Of course I didn't believe her. Would you? Think about waking up to a complete stranger saying, *Hey, surprise! It's the future!*

Marie says that not believing her was a defense mechanism, and also a perfectly normal traumatic response.

But I don't know. I still think it was rational to assume that she was lying.

I mean, come on. She told me I was lucky.

At the time, I was just relieved that telling her to get out was apparently on-script. The blurry shape of Dr. Carmen stood up. "Of course, Tegan."

"And stop calling me Tegan," I added viciously. "I don't know you. We're not friends. What's *your* first name?"

She hesitated, and I got the feeling she was leaving the prepared speeches behind for the first time. "It's Marie," she said.

My middle name. Huh. "Okay, Marie. Thanks for the info. Get out."

Something smooth and slim was slipped into my hand, and I jumped.

"It's a...well, like a bell," Dr. Car—Marie said. "When you want anything, or if you want to talk to someone, just squeeze it three times, and they'll come. All right?"

"Fine. Bye, Marie."

I heard a chiming, and then a swish, and I lay there, blinking hard and counting down the seconds as the room gradually became clearer around me.

When I was eleven, I spent three days in the hospital with an infection that needed IV antibiotics—thankfully, it wasn't a drug-resistant strain. This place smelled like a hospital, all right, that clean industrial smell. But it didn't sound like one. I couldn't hear anyone moving back and forth, or talking in the corridors. There was no beeping machinery or rattle of wheeled beds being rolled over linoleum floors.

I slid my legs out of the bed and stood. The soles of my feet felt tender against the floor, but I could support my weight on them. Well, that was proof against the whole revival thing, right? Surely my legs wouldn't hold me up if I'd actually been out of it for a hundred years.

I was wearing a loose blue thing, sort of like a really wide tunic dress, made out of some material I didn't recognize. I wasn't game to just strip it off, but the neck was wide enough for me to pull it out and look down at myself.

There were lots of little white scars on my chest and stomach, but I'd expected that and braced myself for it. What really shocked me was a much smaller thing.

My legs and underarms and, in fact, all the skin I could see were completely bare. I didn't go in for all that shaving-plucking-waxing stuff. Someone had done it to me while I was asleep.

I mean, I had those scars, so they'd probably been a lot more intimate with my body than just shaving my legs, but for some reason the idea that someone had removed all my body hair while I was unconscious really grossed me out.

When I took my first step toward the door and automatically reached to push my hair over my shoulders, I discovered that it wasn't only my body. My questing fingers found only the soft, bare skin of my scalp.

The bastards had taken my hair. Eight years of growth, just gone.

My fists clenched. I was suddenly more angry than scared,

which, let me tell you, is a much better response when you wake up in a hospital bed with no hair, no underwear, and no memory of what got you there. Being frightened had threatened to make me slow and stupid; being furious made me move.

I wanted to throw the alarm thing at the wall, but instead I put it carefully on the bed, with a hand that trembled with control, and tested the door. It wasn't locked, and I could see no one moving down the dimly lit corridor.

So I walked out.

The corridor was long and silent and completely empty of people.

It was also almost completely dark. Lights turned on overhead as I padded along and turned off behind me. There were other doors evenly spaced on each side, but I wasn't brave enough to test any of them yet.

To be honest, I was thinking about Alex's games and how many of them involved long halls, flickering lights, and monsters jumping out of nowhere. I didn't have a grenade launcher or a flamethrower. I didn't even have Alex's right hook.

I kept close to one wall and walked fast, ready to take my chances with one of the side doors if I heard anyone coming.

No one did, and that didn't make sense. What kind of hospital didn't have a nurses' station or full-time lighting? My skin prickled under what I was almost certain was silent scrutiny. There had to be security cameras somewhere.

Twelve doors down was a door striped in red with a picture of a flame above it.

It was way too obvious of an exit. What I needed was a window—something that would give me an idea of the lay of the land, or possibly even an escape route in itself. I'd dropped from a story up a couple of times, when security crews had come to investigate the lights Alex and I were flashing around their construction sites. I wasn't the best free runner in the world, but I was confident I could safely do it again.

I opened the door to the left of the fire escape.

There was no window there, just an empty trolley bed with a mattress, and equipment I didn't recognize. I backed out, crossed the hallway, and tried the door on the right.

There was no window there, either. But the bed was not empty.

On the white mattress lay a naked man, several years older than me, maybe twenty-one or twenty-two. It was hard to tell, with all the wires and tubes attached to him. His bare chest rose and fell, and his eyes were open, but his face was slack and quiet.

There was no curiosity or alarm in his face. He was staring directly at me, and nothing about him said he registered my presence at all.

I could have stayed there for a few minutes, gaping like an ill-mannered jerk, but my ears picked up the sound of some-one's voice in the corridor. The man's room was a dead end; I had to get out.

Obvious escape or not, I ran for the fire door.

In the dim light, concrete stairs stretched upward; I was apparently on the bottom floor. I pounded up two steps at a time. The feeling of air rushing over my bare scalp was weird, and running without a bra was really uncomfortable, but my muscles worked fine.

I was hitting the zone, where everything was smooth, efficient motion. Other fire doors flashed by on the landings, but I wasn't interested in going back inside.

What I needed was the roof, and eight floors up, I found it.

Gasping for breath, I burst through the roof door at pretty close to my top speed and stumbled two steps to a clumsy halt that wouldn't have hurt so much if I'd been wearing shoes.

The sky was dark, but there were a ton of lights; under them, the roof was bright as noon and almost as hot. It was a flat, skinny rectangle, edged with a low concrete wall. That would have been easy to deal with, but inside the wall, there was a wire fence taller than I was, except at the narrow gap left for the fire-escape ladder. There were lights showing the roofs of other buildings, close by and lower. I was way closer to the ground than I'd thought—maybe only two or three floors up, which meant that most of the building was underground.

And standing by the fire escape, the obvious exit, was a man in a uniform with a long weapon in his hands, spinning to stare at me.

I took off.

"Halt!" he called behind me. Something whistled past my ear, and I dodged behind an air-conditioning unit, teeth gritted.

Keep moving, I thought. *Keep momentum.* My flying strides eating up the concrete, I charged at the corner where the wire fence made a right angle.

I loved right angles.

I was trying not to remember all the times I'd tried this trick and had to bail out, for Alex to laugh hysterically at me (and, one time, help me to the emergency room). Free running is half body, half mind. If either one quits on you, you can't pull it off.

I'd never tried the trick with someone shooting at me, but my timing, for once, was perfect. I popped up the fence right-left-right, using my momentum to push off and up. In fact, I had so much speed I nearly went straight over, but some frantic grabbing at the top turned into a decent grip, swinging me around and down to stand on the edge, facing back along the length of the roof.

The man in uniform was aiming directly at my face. "Halt!" he bellowed again, just as another man burst out of the fire door.

"Don't shoot!" he shouted, and then, "Tegan! Stop!"

I jumped off the roof.

I was two stories up, I was wearing very little, and I'd never done a drop that high onto a hard surface. Even if I rolled to take the impact, it should have really hurt, but my brain was busily pumping out endorphins, and I couldn't feel much. As it was, my right forearm, which hit first, went numb and then throbbed. There was no stopping to assess the damage, though. I was up on my bare feet again, seeking out shadows.

Ahead and behind me, sirens sounded.

I darted between buildings, listening for shouts and foot-steps as well as I could over my own frantic heartbeat. If I could get far enough away, or find a good spot to hide, I might be okay.

All I had to do was make it to someone who'd let me borrow their phone.

There were voices ahead. I flattened against the wall and edged back around the corner.

Voices ahead again, and coming closer. But on the other side of the narrow alley was a door, and if luck was still with me, I could make it there in time.

I darted across, praying for deliverance, and yanked at the door handle.

The good news was, it wasn't locked.

The bad news was, the room was full of people.

≈ ‡ ∞

They'd been looking toward the front of the room, where a small, dark-haired woman was speaking at a podium. But as I burst in, they all turned in their seats to stare at me.

"Who the hell is that?" someone muttered.

"Tegan?" the woman at the podium said, sounding stunned.

"That's *her*," said someone else. "The Living Dead Girl!" And then I was surrounded by people, all of them loud and excited and shouting questions at me.

"Tegan, what's your opinion of Operation New Beginning?"

"Tegan, what do you think of the twenty-second century?"

"Tegan, are you proud of what you've helped achieve?"

"Tegan, do you think it's acceptable to add revivals to an already overpopulated society?"

"Tegan, are you looking forward to our dead diggers coming home?"

"Tegan—"

"Tegan—"

"Tegan!"

I shrank against the wall, staring at them, unable to register details or tell them apart. They were just a blur of strange clothes and outlandish hairstyles. A swarm of small things swooped in, buzzing around me like mosquitoes. I shook my head back and forth, and stared into one, watching the tiny camera lens. Something zipped past my eyes, and I shrieked, slapping it away and stamping on the horrible thing as it hit the ground.

They stopped shouting all at once, apparently appalled at this destruction.

"Out of my way!" someone sounded through the hush, and shouldered her way through the pack, hair flying, elbows akimbo. "Can't you see this girl is injured? This press conference is over! Leave my patient alone!"

I recognized her voice and clung to it as the one real thing in the nightmare.

"Marie?" I asked, too scared to be ashamed at the way it came out like a sob.

"Yes," she said, turning my hand over carefully. "Oh, Tegan, what happened?"

"I ran," I said, distantly aware that the pain in my arm was getting worse. Men in uniforms were filing into the room and herding out the journalists. Some of them were still shouting questions as they went.

"Sit down," Marie said, and got me into a chair. "I'll fix this up. Nothing's broken; you're all right." She pulled out a little black pouch and sprayed something on my arm.

There was blood on the floor. Blood from my torn feet, from my scraped arm. The endorphins and adrenaline were fading, and my body was telling me I'd hurt it a lot more than I'd had time to feel in that wild flight.

Sore as I was, I still tensed all over when someone else came through the door. It was the second man on the roof, the one who had told the guard not to shoot.

"There you are, Tegan," he said.

Marie stiffened, too, and didn't look up. "Colonel Dawson, please wait in the hall," she said.

"I need to—"

"*I* need to establish my patient's physical health," Marie said.

The colonel stared at the back of her head, still bowed over my hand, then at me.

"Well, then," he said, forcing good humor into his voice. "I'll see you later, Tegan. Unless—"

"Get out!" I yelled, my voice squeaking with the strain. The door closed, leaving Marie and me alone in the big room.

The journalists had made it feel small and crowded. Those mosquito machines, buzzing around me. They were only cameras and microphones, I thought, nothing to be scared of. But they'd been picking up every detail of me—my shaven head, my torn skin, my fear.

"Those people," I said. "Their clothes. Their tech." I couldn't make myself form longer sentences.

But Marie seemed to understand. "We meant to introduce you to change gradually," she said. She sprayed my feet and shook her head. "A big dose of culture shock . . . that wasn't supposed to happen." She looked up at me, and I found myself inspecting her face, concentrating on the details to keep myself steady. Marie had thick, straight, blue-black hair in a tight bob, creamy skin, and high cheekbones. There was no fold in her eyelids, but fine wrinkles spread from the corners of her dark brown eyes. As far as I could tell, she wasn't wearing any makeup. She was maybe my mum's age, maybe a bit younger.

"Marie," I said, "is this really the future?"

She took my good hand in both of hers, looking steadily into my eyes. "I'm sorry, Tegan," she said, sounding so, so sad. "It really is."

CHAPTER THREE
I Am the Walrus

One of the many things the twenty-second century has gotten right is painkillers.

I didn't feel a thing as Marie picked all the tiny bits of grit out of my scrapes, washed them all down with something that smelled revolting, and sprayed on something else that turned into a thick layer of dark brown gunk.

"It's artificial skin," she explained. "You had something like it in your time, but this is better. It'll prevent infection while the skin underneath heals. Not that there should be any infection; you're on a lot of immunoboosters. We were worried about today's diseases. Let me have a look at your shoulder."

"What's Operation New Beginning?" I asked as she gently rotated my upper arm. "Ow!"

"Sorry. Just a muscle strain and some bruising, I think. Operation New Beginning is a project researching and experimenting on the revival of the cryonically frozen. Like yourself."

"So this is your job? You do this all the time?"

"No," Marie said. "Well, it is my job, yes. But you're the first successful human revival."

I thought of the blank-faced man in his hospital bed. An unsuccessful revival?

"So there's no one else," I said. My voice felt tight and dry, but I could feel tears sliding down my cheeks. "Alex and Dalmar—were they okay? The sniper . . ."

"They were fine, Tegan. The sniper was aiming at the Prime Minister, but he was an amateur. He panicked after he shot you and didn't try again. From the records we have—" She sat back on her heels and looked at me uncertainly. "I'm a body doctor, you know, not a psych specialist. You'll need to talk to someone qualified."

"No," I said. "I don't want people poking in my brain."

Marie's face went even sadder. "Tegan," she said, "you signed your dead body over to science. And you're the first revival who can actually answer questions; maybe the only one for some time. I'm afraid you won't be given much choice."

I would have run again, maybe, if I hadn't been so sore and shocked. As it was, I just sat in that chair, too numb to even think of escape.

That morning, I'd been in love and loved. I'd had family and friends, and an idea of my place in the world. That night, I'd lost everything.

It was kind of a lot to think about.

≈ ‡ ∞

29

They put me in a room—a room with a real bed and an attached bathroom. They gave me real clothes to wear, and some books and a stereo. The stuff was all weirdly familiar and therefore looked suspiciously like things that had been hauled out of a museum and set up to make me feel more comfortable. The old stereo still worked, and they'd found some CDs, which, by the way, were an outdated medium well before my time. It was an odd mix—some Elvis Presley, some Dusty Springfield. A lot of European classical. Some disco rubbish I listened to only once, and a few Broadway musicals.

No Beatles. No guitar so that I could make music of my own.

No computer to give me that large dose of culture shock, the one I'd already had.

No windows.

I spent most of the next three weeks grieving.

Actually, that's a lie. I've spent the last two and a half months grieving. I reckon I'll do it for the rest of my life—every time I see or hear or smell something that reminds me of the life and the people I used to have.

But for those first weeks, it took up a lot of my time. I was grieving for the people I'd lost and the experiences I'd never share with them. Alex and I weren't going to spend a gap year volunteering in South America. Dalmar and I weren't going to have sex. Owen wasn't going to play at our wedding. And Mum would never, ever feed me again. On top of my own grief, I had to deal with theirs; I thought they must have felt something like this when I died, so fast and violently, and that was almost more than I could stand. It was bad when Dad died, but losing everyone at once was much, much worse.

For the first week, I cried. I also yelled a lot, threw books around, swore at Marie, and then apologized to her over and over for being so horrible.

"I'm not like this," I kept saying. "I'm not really like this."

"It's all right," Marie would tell me. "It's all right." Every now and then I'd catch her scrawling notes on something that looked like a shiny piece of paper, but she actually seemed to care. Colonel Dawson and the other doctors just asked their questions and took their notes openly.

Some of the questions were really dumb. Like Colonel Dawson asking me when I'd learned free running, sounding slightly offended that I'd managed to surprise him. He explained that it wasn't in my file, and I nearly laughed in his face. Like I was going to tell my mother that I was practicing getting through gaps, throwing myself over rails, and jumping down steps at high speeds. Alex must have kept that secret, even after my death.

And that was good for another hour-long crying session, right there.

They were also doing a ton of tests, and a lot more of them when the yelling stage faded. They wheeled in various machines and got me to look into screens and said *hmm* a lot. I had to wear a silvery headband thing when I went to bed—it wasn't uncomfortable; it was just sort of weird, especially on my scalp, which was all prickly with the new hair growth. (Dawson said that they could easily remove the hair if I liked. I didn't like.)

On my twentieth day underground, I asked Marie how she'd brought me back to life.

She put her shiny paper down and told me.

It got really complicated, really fast. I'm not trying to protect the project or keep your grandma on ice or anything when I say that I can't give you the full details of how a successful revival works. It's just that between protein chains and gene therapy and cloned replacement organs, I completely lost track about ten minutes in.

One thing I do remember, because it's just so freaking weird, is that when I died, they pumped me full of something derived from tardigrades. Never heard of them? Neither had I. But they're also known as water bears and moss piglets. They look like really tiny fat caterpillars with little feet. You can probably find them in your sink. In fact, you can find them everywhere, because these little guys are amazing survivors.

They're fine under meters of solid ice, or on top of the Himalayas, or in boiling water. Despite being, you know, *water* bears, they can survive drought and dehydration for up to ten years.

They can even survive in outer space, which is about as hostile as it gets. If you were blown unprotected out of an air lock into the void, you'd survive for about two minutes, tops. You'd have mild injuries after ten seconds: solar-radiation burn, swelling skin and tissues. Then you'd get the bends as bubbles of inert gases started to form in your bloodstream. After about twenty to thirty seconds, you'd black out. Your saliva would boil off your tongue. You'd have nothing to breathe, but your lungs might try anyway, which is when you'd get lung damage from the vacuum. All this time, you're burning or freezing; your body can do a pretty good job of regulating internal temperature, but it can't hold out long against direct sunlight or its lack, when there's no atmosphere to smooth things out.

Two minutes unprotected in space and you're absolutely dead.

Tardigrades hung out in space for *ten days*. Then a bunch of them came back from their trip, thawed out, and had perfectly healthy little tardigrade babies.

Marie explained how they do it, and it has something to do with a special kind of sugar and anhydro-something, and seriously, I wasn't taking it in. But essentially, tardigrades can suspend their metabolisms. When they encounter something that's just too much to deal with, they curl up, shut down, and wait for things to get better.

And it turns out that's the kind of thing you should reproduce in humans if you want to be able to freeze them before their brains die and thaw them out later at a point when you can repair their injuries.

So I partially owe my second life to unbelievably hard-core bugs.

But I also owe it to a lot of people and a lot of coincidences. Traffic had been cleared for the Prime Minister's visit, and the nearest hospital was right up the road, so the emergency workers got me there fast. On the way, they called Dr. Tessa Kalin.

Dr. Kalin was the head of an experimental cryonics unit working with a tardigrade solution. She and her team were there, and three days earlier they'd been granted ethics approval to use human subjects. I wasn't the ideal specimen for their first go, but I was on hand, and I'd consented. They didn't know how to reverse the freezing process, or even if what they'd done would one day result in me breathing again.

But I sure wasn't going to start breathing again *without* the treatment, so they tried anyway.

And, eventually—thanks to Marie and her team and a lot of tireless work and so much money poured into army medical research that it makes me really uncomfortable to think about it—I did.

You don't have to believe in miracles to think that all those people in the right place at the right time with the right knowledge add up to something amazing.

Marie and her team fixed the many, many things that would have killed me, got me breathing again, and registered brain function. Then I was put in an induced coma for a while, so that my immune system could be boosted and my muscle regrowth stimulated, while the media became increasingly interested in demanding results from the program.

It was no wonder why Marie called me Tegan when I woke up. I'd been her patient for months, and the first one in a long time who was capable of responding to her own name.

"But why?" I asked Marie. "Why is the army even doing this?"

It was a good sign, I suppose, that I'd stopped being too miserable to be curious.

Marie lit up all over. "There are so many applications for cryorevival. Widespread civilian use is sadly a long way off—both the cryostasis and revival process are prohibitively expensive, for one thing, and revival is almost exclusively experimental at this point. But the army is very interested in the potential use for trauma victims, people who experience massive wounds and bleed out quickly without brain or spine injuries. You see—"

"Soldiers," I said. "You're going to bring soldiers killed in action back to life?"

"I hope so. Eventually. Yes."

She had to stop then. I was crying too hard to listen, but, this time, I was smiling, too.

≈ ‡ ∞

My dad was a soldier, you see. I don't remember him very well, because I was only seven when he was shot in East Timor, but Owen did. We had his picture in the kitchen, and his ashes in the jar, and his medals. We had him watching over us from heaven. But we didn't have him.

It was the one thing Alex and I couldn't agree on. I didn't like war, but I thought it was sometimes necessary, and of course I supported our soldiers. Alex was very antiwar, and sometimes, when she forgot how I felt about it, she was antisoldier, right in front of me. I got up every Anzac Day for the dawn remembrance ceremony, while Alex, who was normally an early riser, stayed pointedly in bed until noon. Dalmar's mum and dad had fled several wars before they arrived in Australia, so he wasn't that keen, either. But they weren't going to stop being friends with Owen and me for loving and missing our dad.

They might have thought differently about cryonics being used to revive dead soldiers.

But I was proud to be a part of it.

≈ ‡ ∞

I can't believe I was such an idiot.

≈ ‡ ∞

"So when do I get to leave?" I asked Colonel Dawson the next morning. Dawson didn't look like much of a military man, being sort of skinny with a zillion wrinkles in his olive skin, but he was clearly in charge. The other military doctors were all captains or lieutenants, and then there was Marie, who was *Doctor* Carmen, thank you very much, and only military by association.

"We can talk about that later," he said, and his eyes flicked up and away from me.

I blinked at him. I didn't actually want to leave right away, but something about his evasion made me nervous. "What if I said I wanted to leave now?"

"Well, Tegan, I'm afraid that legally you don't necessarily get to make that decision."

"Wait a minute," I said. "I signed my dead body over to science. That doesn't mean I signed over the rest of my *life*."

Dawson cocked his head, like a bird eyeing a worm it was thinking about eating. "Tegan, you make it sound as if

36

we're monsters. Are you unhappy with the care you've received?"

"No, it's okay. I just... I don't want to stay here much longer. I never see anyone my age."

"You're under a lot of stress," he said. "It will get easier." He sounded as though he meant it.

"When are you going to let me out?" I groped for something stupidly far away, just so that he could reassure me. "Like, in a *year*?"

He should have laughed at my ludicrous suggestion. Instead, he looked very serious. "There will probably be a fairly lengthy transition period—for your own health and safety as much as anything."

Ice settled in my stomach. "I don't want that. I want to leave now."

"Tegan, where will you go?"

"That's up to me," I told him.

"Don't be so childish."

Wow.

I didn't like him, but I didn't think Dawson was evil. Patronizing, and with no idea how to talk to teenagers, but not really a bad man. After all, he was in charge of a project trying to save soldiers' lives.

But you could have asked anyone in the progressive movements of my time and they'd tell you that there were plenty of mostly okay people doing bad things, thinking they were right. People like Alex and Dalmar came up with all sorts of ways to deal with those people, to force them to change what they did.

I hadn't been as into it as they were, but I'd paid attention all the same.

What I needed was leverage. And I was the only leverage I had.

"I'm on a hunger strike," I said. "Effective immediately."

He stared. "Tegan, what—"

"And I'm going on a talking strike, too," I interrupted. "As soon as I'm done with this explanation. When you want me to stop, you'll come and ask me what I want, and when I tell you, you'll do it." I smiled at him, as wide as I could. "That's all."

"If you would just explain your wishes, I'd be happy to consider them," he said patiently.

I said nothing.

"Communication is essential to negotiation," he tried. "Surely you can't expect me to proceed without more data."

I picked up the book I was halfway through—a really good supernatural romance that was published only fourteen years after I died—and started turning the yellowed pages.

After a while, there was the soft click of the door closing behind him.

I didn't eat lunch. I didn't eat dinner. I didn't say a word to anyone for the rest of the day.

The hollow in my stomach ached and would get worse, but I knew two things. One: They needed me. They wanted me healthy, if possible, but talking, for sure.

And two: They hated surprises. Dawson had been thrown into a complete tizzy when I'd jumped off the building because it wasn't in his plans. It was time to give him a lesson in just how surprising Tegan Oglietti could be.

≈ ‡ ∞

Marie came in with my breakfast the next day, and I knew that was no coincidence.

"Please eat, Tegan," she said. "I want you to be well."

I shook my head.

People came and went all day. So did food. I was getting dizzy, and it was harder to read, even though I was getting to the bit where the banshee was going to have to decide between saving her boyfriend and obeying her queen. So I started singing the Red and Blue Albums in my head, in the correct song order. I got stuck on whether "Lady Madonna" came before "Hey Jude" or after, and then decided it didn't really matter. I drank a lot of water, sipping it slowly; death was no part of my plan.

It was pretty peaceful, really, though I could hear my mother's voice complaining about all the food I was wasting by turning it away.

But I knew she'd approve if she knew all the details. No way she wanted me helpless in this bunker for a "lengthy transition period."

≈ ‡ ∞

On the fourth day of the hunger strike, Dawson came back in.

"The Department of Defence does not bow to the whims of

39

teenagers. You either start cooperating, young lady, or you'll be made to cooperate."

He stared at me for a while.

I stared back. I wasn't reading or singing inside my head. I was mostly napping, now that the gnawing in my stomach had given way to a floating emptiness.

"You're seriously retarding our progress. Do you want to be the one who tells children that their mother or father won't come back from the war, because Tegan Oglietti won't talk to us?"

I flinched.

"Dr. Carmen will not return until you eat," he said. "She's very disappointed in you."

I started crying big, fat tears that dripped out of the corners of my eyes and down my face onto the pillow, pooling around my neck.

Dawson looked vaguely satisfied. "Now, be a good girl, and have something to eat, and she'll come back," he said.

I closed my wet eyes and drifted back to sleep.

≈ ‡ ∞

On the fifth day, Dawson tried to bribe me with a guitar.

My fingers ached for it, but I locked my mouth shut before I let anything out.

Hail Mary, full of grace, I began, and went through a decade of the rosary before he left the room.

Pray for us sinners now and at the time of our death.

≋ ‡ ∞

On the sixth day, I tried to get up and go to the bathroom. I passed out instead.

I woke up in bed, with something that I recognized as an IV poked into my arm. Light brown fluid was flowing through it, and I felt much stronger.

Dawson and Marie were standing at the foot of my bed. Dawson looked grim. Marie looked nervous and hopeful.

"All right," Dawson said tightly. "What do you want?"

≋ ‡ ∞

Ringo is my favorite Beatle. He wasn't the best drummer in the world, and he definitely wasn't the best singer or songwriter. He was the last one to join, when they kicked out their original drummer, and he was sure they were going to replace him, too. And he was left-handed, playing a right-hand drum set. The other Beatles laughed at most of his compositions because they sounded like other popular tunes. But he stuck with it, with all of it. He invented lots of incredible fills to get around his hands, and he wrote "Don't Pass Me By" and "Octopus's Garden," and he sang "With a Little Help from My Friends," which is one of my top-ten favorites.

At his funeral, everyone talked about what a great musician Ringo was. And he really was. Not because he was particularly gifted, but because he never gave up.

I'd learned to be good at the guitar without any of the natural musicality that Owen had, and I'd gotten decent marks at school without being supersmart like Dalmar, and I'd kept going with free running, even though I wasn't naturally athletic like Alex.

Talent is great, but persistence is totally underrated.

≋ ‡ ∞

"I want to live outside the compound," I said. "I want to go to school." My voice was cracked and scraggly from disuse. I sounded at least seventy years old. Or a hundred and seventeen, ha-ha.

A muscle in Dawson's jaw jumped. "Your demands are unacceptable."

"I'm going back on my hunger and talking strike, effective—"

"I need to talk to some people," he said furiously, and marched out. He sure looked like a military guy then, back straight, jaw set.

Marie lingered, under cover of checking the IV. She bent over me and fluffed my pillow. "I hope you know what you're doing," she whispered.

I gave her the faintest ghost of a wink.

She carried a tiny smile out with her.

I lay there and contemplated my toes. There was a limit to how far I could push this. I didn't want to make them so angry with me that they gave me up as a dead loss and tossed me out into this strange new world. And I really didn't want to sabotage or delay Operation New Beginning. Bringing back soldiers was good work, and helping out was the right thing to do, even if I didn't want to do it at the expense of my freedom.

It was so nice to have energy and a clear head. If I was honest with myself, I wasn't positive I could go without food again.

Dawson came back after a couple of hours, Marie beside him.

"I have a counterproposal," he said. "You will continue your participation in Operation New Beginning as an outpatient, undergoing daily interviews and testing. You will give us your full and complete cooperation. You will go to a school that we select. You will take part in carefully selected media opportunities, which we will supervise. And until you become a legal adult, you will live with Dr. Carmen."

I sat up in bed and looked at Marie. She nodded, that tiny smile hovering at the edge of her lips.

"Dr. Carmen has generously offered to take this role as your guardian, and you will be under her supervision and authority, which you will respect," Dawson continued. "I want you to understand just what sacrifices taking you into her home will entail on her behalf." His expression said, quite clearly, that he would never let me within five hundred meters of his home.

"I don't want to get tested every day," I said.

"Twice weekly," Marie said before Dawson could open his mouth. "We do need that data, Tegan. I know you don't want to imperil the project."

"No, I don't. Twice weekly is okay. And I want to be able to talk to the media by myself."

"No unsupervised media," Dawson said. Not like he was an

adult telling an unruly kid what to do. Like someone explaining something to—well, not an equal, but a not entirely stupid subordinate. "Sections of this project are highly classified. If you don't agree to this condition, I can't let you out."

I paused, thinking of the blank man in his hospital bed, but for only a moment. After a month underground, I needed to get out. I needed to see sun and breathe unrecycled air, or I wasn't sure what would happen inside my head.

I needed to see what this new life had in store for me.

"Agreed," I said, and held out my hand.

Dawson shook it with no hesitation. "I'll get the lawyers to draw up the contract," he said. "And you will not pull any stunts like this again, however justified you think your actions are."

"Hey, that wasn't part of the deal," I said, and smiled at him.

Wonder of wonders, he smiled back.

And that's how I strong-armed the Department of Defence into letting a girl with no legal existence have a life.

≈ ‡ ∞

I'm pretty sure they're regretting that now.

When they find us, I imagine they'll make me pay for it.

≈ ‡ ∞

It turned out the army base was in Williamstown, where there'd been a smaller navy base in my time. I'd lived in the next suburb over, in Newport. I'd walked along Hobsons Bay and tossed spare bread for the ducks and black swans. I'd watched the huge container ships drift past, and smiled at the gray navy ships bristling with radio masts and gun barrels. There had been pleasant houses with big gardens and lots of glass windows to let in light and air and a view of the bay.

Now the houses turned inward, windows smaller and shaded. The green colonial vegetation was gone, too delicate for the harsher sun and strict water restrictions. What gardens remained were Australian natives or gene-doctored plants, made to withstand the droughts. The sea was higher, swallowing the estuary and a good chunk of what had been the waterfront.

And the black swans were gone, another great extinction that humanity added to the list.

You'd think the changes would make me sad, but, except for the heat and the swans, it was okay. It's easier if you treat the past like another country. You can tell yourself you've moved, and it's just been a while since anyone got in touch. And after so long underground, the freedom was exciting. I felt like someone in a fairy tale who'd won herself a prize through her own bravery and perseverance. And I was going to help people. I was going to bring soldiers home.

We drove past all of that and went on, over the bridge that had replaced the West Gate, closer to the city proper. The houses there had changed, too, gleaming with their own newness.

When I first saw Marie's house, I had no idea where she was going to fit me. It looked as new as the others on the block, and really, really small—a little one-story building that was maybe about the size of my old living room, in the middle of a largish section.

She pulled out keys for the security door.

"People still use keys? I was expecting some infrared wand thingy."

"It's hard to hack a physical lock," Marie said, which just went to show that she'd never had a best friend like Alex teaching her the lock-picking ropes. "But the house is electronically protected, too." She whispered something under her breath, and the inner door swung open at her touch. "There. The house computer will recognize you now."

≈ ‡ ∞

It turned out I didn't have to worry about Marie finding a place for me. The visible part of the house was only the hallway and the kitchen. A pretty big kitchen, with a lot of shiny equipment that my mum would have loved. To the side of the door was a flight of stairs leading down to the rest of the house underground, where Marie and I would live like wombats in a burrow, hiding from the sun.

That was my first clue that this new world was even more different than I'd imagined.

For the next fortnight, I did my psych interviews and checkups like a good girl, and the rest of the time, Marie put me through an intense catch-up curriculum on history and technology and social customs.

I'd wanted to go to school right away, but I didn't know enough about really basic things, like how to use a "computer," which is what all those plastic sheets were that the medical staff had been scribbling on. Yeah, I know, you were laughing at me the whole time I was describing them, right? Well, whatever. To me, a computer was a bulky screen with a processor inside and a mouse and keyboard, or maybe a book-sized thing you flipped open and rested on your lap, or, if you didn't mind a tiny screen, part of your phone.

It definitely wasn't a thin sheet you could fold or crumple into your pocket, or open to full size and shake rigid and then scribble all over with a stylus, or type on with a keyboard application, or gesture at. Marie taught me the most basic universal signs and then let me train my computer in how I wanted it to work. It occasionally suggested new moves, and I nearly always took its advice.

I named it Koko, after that gorilla that talked in sign language, and if it's possible to love an inanimate thing, I loved that computer. Koko put me back in touch with the world.

≈ ‡ ∞

Here's another thing people ask a lot: What happened to your friends and family after you died?

They assume I just looked that up right away. I mean, why wouldn't I? Information is everywhere, and even in my time, there was a lot available. But you're forgetting that formats change, files get corrupted, servers crash, and data goes missing. And there's so much information that it can take a while to unearth anything, especially the lives of ordinary people from a hundred years ago. I didn't have a lot of spare time, and I didn't have much inclination to search. I had moved to another country, and people from my old home didn't get in touch anymore; that was how I wanted to handle it.

I wanted to remember them as they were. Not discover who they had become after time had worked on them and passed me by.

≈ ‡ ∞

Anyway, it took me about a week to climb a decent way up the computer learning curve, and that was just one thing. For most of you, all the stuff that you do every day, you learned how to do without thinking much about it—buying books or music or movies, cooking, putting out the garbage, doing laundry, taking showers. I had to relearn all that in two weeks, concentrating hard the whole time.

I bet you wouldn't be laughing if you'd had to deal with computers from my time. You'd have loved the showers, though. No auto timers to cut the water off, no need to account for every drop in the weekly ecobudget. Future showers are depressing, though I know Alex and Dalmar would have approved.

They would have approved of the toilets even more.

In the base, where they were trying to limit my culture shock, I'd had a bathroom like one from my time, with a flushable toilet and warm water to wash my hands. But Marie's toilet was a box bench built into the wall, with a seat, and a hole, and some sort of container positioned under the hole. There was no cistern. There was no flush button.

The first time I went to use it, I had no idea how to.

While I was still staring, Marie knocked on the door.

"I forgot to say," she said when I opened it, "humanure wasn't widely adopted in your time, was it?"

"No," I said, then, "I've heard of it, though." Dalmar had once enthusiastically explained the concept, but the idea of using my own poo as compost had made my face curdle, and he'd changed the subject fast.

But there was no escape from Marie's ten-minute lecture on how to use the hole toilet. To my relief, Marie didn't keep a garden. Instead she put the collection container on the curb every week with the food scraps, and it was taken away, mixed with everyone else's manure and food scraps, and turned into compost for the big farms on the city outskirts. Marie got a tax deduction, and we all got to eat food grown in human poo.

Culture shock. It's the little things.

≋ ‡ ∞

It was pretty cool, though, once I got over the shock. Dalmar would have been thrilled to know that something so practical and Earth-friendly was in widespread use, and it made me happier to think that some part of the future he'd been working so hard for had actually happened. Alex would have been more pleased about the social changes that meant that people could basically marry anyone who consented and love whoever they loved without fear.

I so badly wanted both of them there to see what they'd helped bring about.

Anyway. Sentimentality aside, I got used to the house computer responding to verbal commands and stopped groping for light switches whenever I entered a room. I even worked out how to watch things. Marie had a huge archive of documentaries and old movies.

But her music archive was nonexistent. She had some tracks, sure, but they were all called things like "Rain on Summer River" or "Windy Evening." I thought they might have been nature songs, but they were exactly what they said: the noise of rain hitting flowing water, the sound of air moving through branches. There was even one called "Long Train Trip."

When I asked Marie about it, she looked embarrassed. "I like to listen to white noise while I work," she said. "I find music distracting."

"You don't listen to music for fun?" I asked.

"I used to, before I moved to this house." She smiled. "Perhaps you can reintroduce me to the pleasure. I'll set up a monthly allowance for you on my account. Shall we make it eight hundred?"

I did a rough conversion in my head—inflation was another thing to get used to. That was about fifty dollars, or what I could easily spend on music in a couple of weeks.

"Sixteen hundred?" Marie guessed, watching my face. "The amount doesn't matter. I just have to tell the store something."

"Sixteen hundred is fine," I said. "Thanks."

I blew it all twenty minutes later. Well, I had to. On top of the new music I wanted to try out, the complete Beatles catalog was supercheap, and there were three extra John tracks that John and Yoko's estate had released after I'd died.

When Marie knocked on my bedroom door that evening to tell me she was going to the supermarket to pick up a few things she'd forgotten on the weekly order, I tore myself away from the White Album and told her I'd go, too.

"I can, right?" I said.

"Oh, certainly," she said, and touched her EarRing. That was another thing I had to get used to, mobile phones as jewelry. Look, just assume I didn't know anything, okay?

"Tegan will be coming with me," she said to the person on the other end, and then cut the call. "Zaneisha will discreetly escort us there and wait in the car," she explained.

Sergeant Zaneisha Washington was one of the two soldiers assigned to my protection detail. I was pretty sure I would like her, if I could get over the embarrassment of having my very own bodyguards. I didn't want to be discreetly escorted. But I really wanted to get out of the house, so I kept my mouth shut and nodded.

≈ ‡ ∞

If I'd ever thought about food in the future, I'd imagined that it might be, like, pills and potions and stuff, but food was still food. I didn't know many of the brands in the supermarket, and

I didn't recognize a few ready-to-heat dishes, but the only real difference was that there was absolutely no meat for sale.

There were plenty of vegetables and breads and even a small fish section. That was pretty much what Marie had been feeding me, and it's not like I objected to fish and lots of fresh, tasty veggies—but when I saw the lack of meat at the supermarket, I realized it wasn't a choice.

"Can you buy meat?" I asked.

I meant, was it even *possible* to buy meat, but Marie looked really taken aback. "Are you a meat eater?" she asked. "Red meat?"

"I was," I said, feeling embarrassed. I'd been happily eating her food all this time. It wouldn't be a hardship to keep it up.

"We could get some meat," she said, frowning. "But it's taxed so heavily.... And I'm not sure there's a supplier in our neighborhood. It might have to be a special treat, Tegan."

"It's not a problem," I said quickly.

"And people do talk.... It's—well, I don't care about fashion, but the ethics of the time have changed. I should have covered this in more detail, I'm so sorry—"

"It's okay! Honestly! I was thinking about giving up red meat, anyway." This was mostly a lie. I'd thought about it, to the point of realizing it would probably be a good idea, but I had the disadvantage of a mother who did incredible things to steak.

"Oh, but I don't want to increase the culture shock. If you're used to it...let's see. All right, it looks as if there's a supplier two suburbs over. We could go past on the way home."

I was shifting in my shoes, wondering how I could get her to drop the topic. Most people weren't paying us any attention, but a slim man with dark skin and reddish locks was giving me a disapproving look when his face suddenly changed. "Tegan!" he said. "Tegan Oglietti!"

And then everyone was looking at me. Marie's hand shot up to her EarRing and then came down on my shoulder.

"I'm Carl Hurfest, Melbourne Media Collective," Red Locks announced, stepping close to us. His bumblecam whizzed out of his jacket pocket and hovered by my face, right on the border of the sixty-centimeter legal boundary. "Tegan, just a few questions."

"No comment," Marie said. She'd abandoned our shopping basket, and we strode toward the exit.

"What's your position on Australia's No Migrant policy, and do you think it's fair that the dead be given a loophole?"

"Tegan has no comment," Marie repeated.

I hadn't even heard of a No Migrant policy, so it was easy not to comment on that. The rest of the crowd was pressing around us, happy to let Hurfest ask the questions while they waited avidly for my replies.

"Do you think it's right that the army paid so much for your revival while the families of civilian freezies still grieve for their loved ones?"

There was a murmur of disapproval from the crowd. I thought it was directed at Hurfest, and maybe his use of *freezies*, not at me, but I just wanted them all to go away and leave me alone.

Through the mass of bodies, I saw Zaneisha, a tall woman in

a casual suit that probably wasn't fooling anyone. She'd pushed open the glass door of the supermarket and paused just inside, watching. One hand was out of sight, probably holding a sonic pistol. If she needed to down the crowd fast, she could, but packed in and shifting around as we were, she'd find it hard to pinpoint the shot. Marie and I could end up with ruptured eardrums and vertigo along with everyone else.

Besides, Hurfest wasn't threatening me with anything but his tiny bumblecam, and I wasn't sure how to deal with that.

"Don't you think you have an obligation to speak to the people of Australia, Tegan?" he said. "They paid a great deal for you with their tax dollars."

That hit a nerve. "I'm a person, not property," I snarled, and then, remembering, "No comment!"

Hurfest's smile sharpened, like a shark scenting blood in the water. I'm a city girl, and I don't know much about sea predators, but I could tell that smile was trouble.

"Your father was a soldier killed in action, wasn't he? Do you think only the army should have this technology?"

"Leave the girl alone," an older lady told him.

Hurfest ignored her. "What do you think about the allegations of the Inheritors of the Earth?"

"Never heard of them." I knew I should shut up, but his voice was burrowing into my ears, and his horrible little camera kept buzzing around my face. There was no way to stop it from getting a good shot, short of smacking it out of the air. Which was assault on private property, Marie had explained to me, and not the kind of legal trouble I needed. "I mean, no comment."

We'd reached the door. Zaneisha reached out, and Marie's grip on me was replaced by a much stronger one. The bodyguard hustled me through the door and into the parking lot.

"They say you should commit suicide!" Hurfest shouted after us. "They say the real you is already dead and that what's left is a soulless husk!"

I tried to turn, to yell something back at him—I wasn't sure what—but Zaneisha forced my head down and shoved me into the back of the car. Marie scrambled in behind me, and the door slammed.

"What's the Thingy of the Earth?" I asked.

"Do your seat belt up," Marie said.

I did, scowling. "Don't you think this should have come up before?"

"They're a fringe group, nothing to worry about. They have extreme religious beliefs; a cult, really." She tried to smile. "If it helps, Intelligence says they stress it would be sinful to murder you."

"They just think I should kill myself." I sank back into the seat. "Well, gee, thanks for keeping me informed."

"It was impossible to cover ineffective cults with all the other things I've had to teach you," she snapped back, and then winced. "I'm sorry, that was ungracious—"

"Ugh, whatever." I snorted. "I'm sorry that your pet project isn't house-trained. That's what happens when you pick up strays."

"You're not a stray," she said. "I know that was unnerving, Tegan, but please don't snap at me."

I turned away and stared out the window. "We're not going home," I said after a while.

"No," Marie said.

After several trips to the base to get poked and prodded and subjected to *really annoying* questions, the route to Williamstown was beginning to seem horribly familiar. I hadn't said anything too bad, I thought . . . but I had talked to the press. Two weeks after signing a contract that said I wouldn't do that without prior approval. "How much trouble am I in?" I said.

Marie gazed at the gates of the base as they opened for us. "Probably quite a lot." She met my eyes. "I can't tell you everything, Tegan. But I promise I'm on your side."

CHAPTER FOUR
Things We Said Today

When Colonel Dawson walked into the meeting room where Marie and I were sitting on uncomfortable stools, he was clearly really, really pissed off, and just as clearly trying not to show it.

He pulled his computer out of his pocket, shook it rigid, and looked at me. "Tegan, you broke our agreement." His voice was tightly controlled.

"I'm sorry."

"Sorry may not be good enough," he said, and twisted his fingers at the computer. My face filled the screen, and I winced. My hair looked terrible. Almost two months' growth had turned it into shaggy black waves standing out in all directions, unstyled except for my amateur snips in front of the mirror. The little caption across the bottom of the screen named me as TEGAN OGLIETTI: LIVING DEAD GIRL.

"That is an awful nickname," I muttered.

Dawson tapped his finger in the air twice. "—person, not property," my voice snarled.

"A stirring statement from Tegan Oglietti in this exclusive interview," Hurfest's voice said.

I stiffened. I hadn't given him an interview.

A caption flashed under an image of an older woman in a military uniform, identifying her as Keiko Nakamura-Chang, president of the Returned and Services League. "Ms. Oglietti has performed a great service to the armed forces of Australia," she said solemnly. "The RSL has seen too many of our fellow soldiers die and be suspended in the hope of eventual revival. Ms. Oglietti is a symbol of that hope, so soon to be realized. We thank Ms. Oglietti for her sacrifices and for her commitment to the principles of comradeship and loyalty that all Australians hold dear."

That didn't seem so bad to me. What was Dawson worried about?

A new face flashed on the screen, and a man with long dark curls was identified as Charla Flamdt of Second Chances. He was beaming at the camera, tears gleaming in his eyes. "As I've been saying for weeks, Tegan's amazing recovery is an inspiration to all of us who work in cryonics advocacy. I'm so glad to hear from her own mouth that she's a firm believer in the inherent personhood of cryonic survivors. Companies that are funding the suspension process in return for an agreed term of labor after revival are engaged in indentured labor. Australians are entitled to the basic human right of a second life."

58

Huh. The politics of cryonics were obviously a little more complicated than I'd thought.

"But not all commenters are so pleased by Tegan's revival," Hurfest interrupted, and a third face flashed on the screen, identified as THE FATHER. Unlike the others, he was speaking from an outside location, face partly shaded by a wide-brimmed hat. I could make out dark eyes on a pale face, and a strong jawline. "This poor girl is a victim," he said. "She is a victim of humanity's godlessness, of its meddling in matters it was not meant to touch. Death is a divine mystery, not a medical conundrum. The real Tegan Oglietti is dead. Her husk may proclaim that she is a person, but she has been separated from her soul, and her body is desecrated by this supposed resurrection."

I gasped.

The Father stared out of the screen, dark eyes appearing to fix on my own. "Tegan, if you are watching this broadcast, I'm praying for you. I pray that you have the courage to return to God, and to the death and everlasting life he decreed for you."

"The Father of the Inheritors of the Earth," Hurfest said. "Well, there you have it. Three people, three opinions. What do you think? Leave your thoughts and tubecasts in the comments."

The picture froze on the Father's serene face, a small smile lightening those deep-set eyes.

≈ ‡ ∞

Of course I had given the state of my soul some thought. If you grow up thinking that your soul is going to heaven and eternal happiness, where you get to help and guide your loved ones left behind, the whole New Beginning thing was a shock. Like, where was my soul when I was dead? Was it waiting with my body all that time? Was it in heaven and then it came back when I started breathing again? Had it been in some sort of not-quite-real place?

I wrestled with the idea for a bit, and then I decided it was probably one of God's mysteries that I wasn't meant to actually understand, like how exactly bread and wine became the body and blood of Christ or how a virgin conception worked.

Until the Father, I'd never considered the idea that my soul and I might now be separated.

I knew that it wasn't true. But I didn't know how I could prove it.

≈ ‡ ∞

I stared at the Father's face, thinking about arguments I might make, until Dawson pulled my attention back to more worldly matters.

"The 'cast has millions of views already," he said quietly. "Most of the comments are assuming you're aligned with their cause and are praising you. The rest are ... not so kind. This is exactly the kind of situation we were hoping to avoid by controlling your media presence very tightly, Tegan. But you broke the contract with this interview."

I jumped to my feet, no longer concerned with concealing my fear. "I didn't do an interview! I said that one thing, and the rest was all no comment. Ask Marie if you don't believe me. It was just one thing! It wasn't even about the project!"

"It only takes one thing," Dawson said. "I didn't place a media ban on you only to protect the project. These people will twist anything, and they jump on any weakness. You'll find yourself saying things you never intended and could never have meant. I'm getting a lot of pressure from my superiors to bring you back inside."

"You can't," I said frantically. "I just got out. I'll go crazy. You can't—please, please. I am a person; I'm not property. You promised me."

"My lawyer—" Marie started.

"Dr. Carmen, lawyers won't be necessary. I managed to get Tegan a second chance."

I sucked in a deep breath and sat down again.

"Tegan is starting school next Thursday," Marie said anxiously.

"And if I didn't think boredom was a trigger for trouble, that wouldn't be happening," Dawson said. "But I imagine the Elisabeth Murdoch Academy will keep you busy. Your alma mater, I believe, Dr. Carmen?" He didn't wait for Marie to reply but waved a finger in my face. "And from now on, you'll have a bodyguard with you at all times whenever you leave the house. No more waiting in the parking lot."

I opened my mouth, but Marie gripped my shoulder tightly.

"That's nonnegotiable," Dawson said. "You're a public figure—a largely celebrated one—but we've received threats, and we're going to take them seriously."

"You didn't tell me that!"

"We didn't want to scare you," Marie said.

"But I think you can handle it," Dawson said. He folded his arms and stared down at me. "Am I wrong?"

I *knew* he was manipulating me. But I couldn't stop the automatic surge of pricked pride. "Of course I can."

"Good. Then you'll do what your bodyguards tell you. And no more surprises."

Which just went to show, he still didn't know me very well.

≈ ‡ ∞

Still, with only a few days left before I started school, Dawson didn't need to worry about unscheduled trips to the supermarket. I didn't have the time. I had never worked so hard in my life.

It helped that Koko automatically recorded and organized everything into searchable mind maps and knowledge trees, but it was still a lot to cram into my head. Marie started teaching me slang along with the history and customs lessons, but I was more dubious about that. A mum-aged person teaching a teenager slang?

On the final day, I got a security seminar from Zaneisha, who put me through protocols (never walk through doors first, basically), communication codes, and a dangers briefing. The Inheritors of the Earth weren't on that list—as Marie had said, they were counted as low-risk.

High-risk groups included the Australia for Australians crew, who had also taken exception to my claim that I was a person.

They'd decided I was an immigrant from the past, and therefore, according to Australia's No Migrant policy, an illegal immigrant, who they didn't seem to think were people at all. They were campaigning to get me deported. Working out where I should get deported *to* didn't seem to have bothered A4A; "anywhere but here" was their guiding principle. They were armed and fanatical, and had killed at least two dozen "foreigners" in the Northern Territory this year alone. Two of the victims had legal visas for short-term visits. Three of them had been Australian-born.

A4A wore black masks in their tubecasts and ranted on-screen about how I was a fake Australian, taking up resources that *real* Australians couldn't spare. And they scared the shit out of me.

Zaneisha finished the afternoon with a pop quiz, including a couple of questions she hadn't actually covered in the session.

"If anyone threatens you with a weapon and tells you to get into a vehicle, what would you do?" she asked.

I thought back to the one compulsory self-defense class I'd taken at school. You were supposed to give someone your wallet if you were mugged—your money wasn't worth your life. "Cooperate," I said confidently.

"No. Scream. Run in a zigzag. Draw as much attention to yourself as possible."

"Uh," I said, "what if they shoot me?"

"Anyone who wants to get you into a vehicle probably wants you alive, so they won't risk it. Or they want to get you somewhere quiet where they can kill you very slowly. At least if it happens on the street, it'll be fast."

My eyes bugged out so hard it actually hurt.

Zaneisha nodded soberly, and then her EarRing chimed. "Ah. Ms. Miyahputri is here. I wanted to teach you some self-defense, but we've run out of time. After you start school, inshallah."

"Inshallah," I echoed weakly. Self-defense sounded like a really, really good idea. Why had I spent all that time practicing guitar instead of taking up boxing, like Alex? "Are you sure you can't just show me a few—"

Marie bustled in. "All done?"

"Yes, ma'am," Zaneisha told her. No matter what Marie said, she couldn't get Zaneisha to call her anything but ma'am or Dr. Carmen.

"Well, Bethari's here, Tegan. Let's go and say hello." She smiled. "Or *geya*."

We went upstairs, Zaneisha trailing us unobtrusively, and found a girl my age sitting at Marie's big golden table, a cup of tea steaming gently in front of her.

Bethari Miyahputri was the daughter of one of Colonel Dawson's army colleagues, and she also went to Elisabeth Murdoch. She was supposed to be my guide to the school.

I hesitated in the doorway. Marie, who could be ruthless when she wanted, nudged me through.

"Geya," I said, the slang greeting sitting awkwardly on my tongue. "I'm Tegan." They were the first words I'd spoken to someone my own age since I woke up.

"Hello," she replied, turning toward me. Bethari was a really pretty girl with light brown skin and a few dark freckles sprinkled over her cheeks. Her nose was long and turned up at the end. She was wearing a flowing dress made of purple memory fabric and a gorgeous yellow-patterned headscarf. "I'm Bethari."

I scrubbed my hands on my linen drawstring pants, wishing I'd had a chance to do some shopping.

"Um, so, thanks for agreeing to do this," I said. "It's really kooshy of you."

Bethari's thin eyebrows jumped, but her face returned to polite blankness. "You're welcome," she said.

Marie beamed. "Why don't you show Bethari your room, Tegan, and I'll prepare a snack? You girls don't need us old ladies standing about."

Zaneisha's expression remained absolutely impassive, but I had the feeling she disagreed with this assessment. "Sure," I said. "Come downstairs."

We walked down the spiral staircase in absolute silence. My skin was crawling all over with embarrassment.

"So, this is my room," I said.

Bethari barely glanced around. "It's nice," she said, sitting carefully on the edge of my bed.

It *was* nice, though I still wasn't used to having no windows. A skyshaft to the surface let in natural light, but it wasn't the same.

Still, the decor was good. The furniture was all matching blond wood. Marie had let me choose prints to make and hang, and I'd mostly gone with landscapes of urban decay that reminded me of clambering through old buildings with Alex. On the nightstand was an iron statue of a stylized woman standing half submerged in a cresting wave, long hair hanging down her back and flowing over her breasts to become the sea. Her features were obscured by rust, and it was hard to tell whether she was rising from the ocean or falling into it, but I liked the shape of her head, and the strength in her outstretched hands. I'd seen the statue on the tubes when Marie was teaching me how to use Koko, and she'd bought it as a surprise.

The prints of my family were tucked in my nightstand drawer. I didn't want them on display.

Bethari was just sitting there, like a breathing statue, eyes fixed unwaveringly on my face.

"Uh," I said. What did people *talk* about in the future? Well, school was standard. "What's your specialty at Elisabeth Murdoch?"

The school was one for talented students, and everyone was supposed to have a specialty that they trained in. Marie's had been biology, and she'd assured me that I'd love the training and attention from the specialty teacher.

"Journalism," Bethari said, and pinched her mouth closed again, as if every word was costing her money.

I had no idea why Marie thought I'd be friends with this snobby, closed-off girl, but I hadn't had high hopes to start with. Most friend setups, in my experience, turned out pretty badly. It was the people you met by accident who worked out.

≈ ‡ ∞

I met Alex when she was the girl in the seat opposite me on the train, crying behind her tattered book.

I ignored her sniffs for a little while, and then I put my hand out flat in front of her, palm up. I didn't touch her. That didn't seem right, somehow.

"Are you okay?" I asked.

The girl lowered the book, and for the first time I saw what had been done to her face. She had a big purple bruise right up her jaw, and half hidden behind her tangled fringe, her left eyebrow had a cut that was crusted over with red-black blood.

The fresh marks stood out over a pattern of pale yellow-and-brown bruises, like the ones I built up over soccer season. Someone had been beating her for a long time.

"No," she said. She was so direct about it, looking me straight in the eye, that I just let the next words spill out of my mouth.

"Who did that?" I asked.

"Foster parents," she said. "Do you have any painkillers?"

I rummaged around in my backpack, fighting the sway of the car as we went under the West Gate Bridge, and found some ibuprofen. She swallowed two of the pills dry. When she tipped them into her mouth, her long sleeve rode back, and I saw the sores wrapped around her wrist, red and raw.

I gasped.

"Oh yeah," she said, and looked absently at the marks. "They tied me up the first time I ran away."

"Where are you going now?"

"Anywhere."

"Come home with me," I said. I was twelve years old, and I'd just started taking the train home from soccer practice by myself. I didn't know what to do, or what to say in the face of something this awful. But I was horrified, by the cruelty, by her matter-of-fact reaction to it, and I wanted to fix it. "You can stay with us. My mum's really nice."

She looked me over, taking her time, assessing the threat, and happy to let me know she was doing it.

"Okay," she said finally, and put the book on the seat beside her. "I'm Alex."

"Tegan," I said, and from then on—even though she didn't stay with us long and went to live with a different, much better set of foster parents, even though we argued and teased each other a lot, even though she grew up and got political and hated soldiers and dragged me to rallies when I would much rather have been home with my guitar—we were friends.

≈ ‡ ∞

I didn't think things with Bethari would go so well.

"That's a pretty headscarf," I blurted, grasping for any topic at all.

But that, of all things, got a reaction. Bethari's hand rose protectively to her head. "I wear this as a symbol of my faith," she announced. "I'm Muslim."

I nodded.

"And no matter what my mother said, I need to know right away. Do you have a problem with that?"

"Of course not," I said.

She was still watching me, and I realized that she wasn't being unfriendly. She was being careful.

"A hundred years ago," she said, "not many of your people were very accepting of Islam."

"Oh," I said. "It's so good that that's changed."

Bethari's eyebrow popped up.

"No, I mean it!" I said. "My boyfriend was Sunni Muslim. People always assumed stuff about him. They said things—he hated it. It was awful."

"You had a Muslim boyfriend?" she asked, probably not meaning to sound so disbelieving. "What was his name?"

"Dalmar," I said. "He'd just... he'd be so happy things are better now. I wish he could see it." And then I had to stop and duck my head to hide the tears, my face burning with just how stupid I must look. Upset over a guy who had been dead for forty-six years, who'd had a long and successful political career, and who married a woman he'd described as "the true love of my life."

A woman who wasn't me.

≋ ‡ ∞

Okay.

I totally lied to you about not looking up my friends and family. It was the first thing I did as soon as I knew how to use Koko. I searched for everything on record, and I regret that more than almost anything else.

I wish I *had* chosen to remember them as they had been.

It's just hard, all right? It's hard, even when they had really great lives, like Dalmar and Alex did. Because they had those great lives without me—and feeling that way is stupid and petty and gross, but it's still hard.

It was much, much worse when I found out about Owen. But that's not relevant, and I don't want to talk about it.

But I'll tell you the truth from now on. I really will.

≋ ‡ ∞

"Were you with Dalmar long?" Bethari asked after a strained moment.

"One day." I gulped.

"Oh." In my peripheral vision, I could see her hands twisting, the first nervous motion she'd made. "Well, was he pretty?"

My head came up. She was smiling, looking as uncertain and uncomfortable as I did.

"Yes," I said, and a great big bubble of laughter rose from my stomach and out my throat, shattering into high-pitched giggles. "He was so pretty!"

She blinked at me, but it was the kind of infectious laughter you can't resist, and she started giggling, too. "I can't believe you said *kooshy*," she snorted. "That's what people were saying when I was a ween."

"A ween?" I cackled. "What's a ween?"

"A child! A wee one!"

"A kid?"

"Kid!" she howled, and we collapsed on my bed. Every time one of us started to slow down, the other would whisper "kooshy!" or "ween!" and we'd be off again.

Finally, I sat up, wiping tears from my eyes. "You have to teach me some better slang."

"I will, if you teach me yours," Bethari said. "Hey, who's that?"

I followed her eyes.

On the back of my door was a print of that famous picture of John and Yoko. She's wearing a black top and blue jeans, lying on her back with one arm raised. He's totally naked, and curled up around her like a comma to her exclamation mark. Her expression is calm, unsmiling. His is passionate as he presses a kiss to her cheekbone. Her eyes are open. His are closed. But they curve into each other; her arm is around his back, her hand just visible at his side; his leg is lifted over her body, his arm wrapped around her head. The photo emphasizes their differences and their connection.

John was murdered on the day that photo was taken, and *Rolling Stone* put it on the cover of their next issue.

After I died, I was on some covers, too.

"It's John Lennon and Yoko Ono," I said.

"Were they friends of yours, too?"

I wasn't sure if she was joking. "No. John was in the Beatles. You know the Beatles?"

"Is that a . . . oh! A band, right?"

"Right," I said, relieved.

"They had the song about the daydream believer?"

71

My relief vanished. "That was the Monkees. Totally different. Imitators put together to capitalize on the Beatles' success—do people really not know about the Beatles anymore?"

Bethari shrugged. "How much do you know about the music a hundred years before your time?"

I buffed my nails on my boring pants. "1927? That was the year of one of Stravinsky's operas. *Oedipus Rex*, I think. It was the year *The Jazz Singer* was released, the first talking movie ever, and it was about music. Al Johnson? No, Jolson. And it was the year *Funny Face* first played in New York; it had opened in Philadelphia earlier, to terrible reviews, but the revised version ran on Broadway for two hundred and fifty shows."

Bethari began to laugh again. "I think I can guess your specialty."

"Music is universal," I said. "And thank god. Um... about the journalism..."

"Don't worry. Mami told me you're under a lock clause. She made me sign one, too. I won't 'cast a thing." She sighed mockingly, her face suddenly alive with self-deprecation. "Kept away from the biggest scoop of my career. It's so facebreaking."

"Oooh," I said. "New word."

"Right! Let's see. You don't want to break your face—um, do something embarrassing or humiliating. If you break someone else's face and they deserve it, that's cool, but they'll probably be angry, like, 'That bazza broke my face. I'll get him.' And if people know something embarrassing about you, that's facebreaking."

"Like you not being able to scoop everyone with the Living

Dead Girl because your mum said so," I said, filing *bazza* away for later.

"Is that really what you call yourself?"

"God, no. I'm Tegan. Teeg."

"Teeg," Bethari said. "Okay. Tell me more about these Beatles, Teeg, and then I'll give you the ontedy on everyone at Elisa M."

"Ontedy?"

"Oh-en-tee-dee. News. Gossip." She frowned. "And I think you could do with some education. Not *everything* has changed for the better."

I rolled off the bed and snapped Koko open. "Sounds like a plan. Prepare yourself for a musical awakening."

When Marie came in with a tray of sliced apples and carrot sticks, I was showing Bethari pictures of my family while we worked our way through the Red Album.

For the first time in a lifetime, I was truly happy.

CHAPTER FIVE
Hello, Goodbye

We gave Bethari a ride to school the next day.

"I was thinking," she said, even before she scrambled into the car. "You should try out for stunt squad! I bet you'd make a great flyer."

"For what?"

"The cheerleading team! I'm a flyer, too, but I'm a bit tall. You'd love it! It's like your free running thing, only you do the tumbles in the air."

I made a face. The tumbles she was talking about were the tricks everyone associated with parkour: big, flashy movements that I, unfortunately, didn't have the strength or conditioning to pull off. I could fit through tiny gaps like no one's business, but I wasn't going to be doing spinning fan kicks anytime soon. "I'm a free runner mostly, not a tricker. Elisa M has cheerleading?"

"Elisa M has nearly everything," Bethari said. "Except amazing boys and girls who want to experience all that I have to offer. For that, I go extracurricular."

"Don't screw the crew?" I asked.

"Good phrase! Yeah. You're going to get lots of offers, you know. Have you seen the stuff about you on the tubes?"

Hurfest's interview had turned me off tubecasts for a couple of days, but I'd peeked afterward. It had gone past politics now. There were people judging my fashion sense, rating my hotness level, and wondering if dating me would be necrophilia. "A little bit," I admitted.

"Everyone *loves* you. Watch out for the famers." She saw my expression and went on before I could ask. "People who sort of harvest celebrity by hanging out with people who are famous. Famous plus farmers, famers, see?"

"Got it. Not everyone loves me, though. There's Australia for Australians, and—"

"Ugh, those drongles! Actually, that might be even a good thing, you know? Them ranting at someone coming back from the *dead* might just wake people up to how stupid the No Migrant policy is."

She'd told me a little bit about the policy last night, among her other efforts to fill me in on some of today's politics, but I hadn't gotten it all straight in my head yet.

"So, it's no migrants at all, right?"

"That's right. Short-term visas only—study visas, or for, you know, holidays and stuff, if you're rich enough to afford the air-fuel tax. No one gets residency, no one gets citizenship."

"But people try to come anyway?" I asked. It seemed like in

my time, every third story on the news was about the refugee crises and illegal immigration. Every second story had been about the climate. Bethari had shown me some of that stuff on the 'casts here, too, but it was quieter.

I'd assumed that was because the problems weren't so bad.

"Oh, they try," Bethari said. "Usually they get caught and stuck in one of the refugee camps in the North."

"Like a detention center?"

"Like a camp," Bethari said patiently. "Tents, shared toilet blocks, no unsupervised access to food or water. Surrounded by barbed wire and fully armed soldiers. They're breaking Australian law by coming. So they end up in huge prisons."

"I didn't see anything about that on the tubes!"

Bethari shot a wary look at Zaneisha, who was impassively navigating behind a laden tram. "It's on the media lockout list," she said quietly. "A few years ago, a guard smuggled some footage out that showed the conditions in the camps, interviews with the residents, that kind of thing. Every 'caster who played it—and some of the ones who even *linked* to it—was subject to massive fines or voluntary shutdown for three months." Her fingers made quote marks around *voluntary*.

It was hard to believe. "If it's so bad, why do people still come?"

"Because Australia's a land of opportunity," she said flatly, and then sighed. "Because what they're leaving is worse. The oceans are rising, and there's less land to live on. Freshwater's drying up, and people are fighting over it. It's not great."

"Oh," I said. This wasn't what I'd expected, not with the special toilets and timed showers. Surely people had done their best to prevent that kind of thing. I must have looked depressed, because Bethari nudged me.

"Don't worry about that right now, though. Worry about the famers."

"Gosh," I said. "Thanks."

≋ ‡ ∞

Army secrecy must have worked, because no reporters were waiting for us outside Elisa M's door. Elisa M's honor code strictly prohibited recording or 'casting students without their permission, but it would be impossible to stop my fellow students from letting the world know that the Living Dead Girl was now one of their classmates, even if they couldn't record me directly. Bethari had said the process would probably start about ten seconds after I walked in the door.

She was wrong. With Zaneisha in front of me, it took a whole twelve seconds after we entered the building before Bethari's computer beeped at her.

"And we're off," she said, waving to a passing friend.

"I hate you," I moaned, and tried not to notice the kids looking at me, looking away, and suddenly getting very interested in their computers.

It was stifling hot in the corridors, and Bethari had already warned me not to expect too much from the air-conditioning in the classrooms. Apparently schools statewide were held to a ninety-degree standard. By the time we hit the third floor, I was sweating in my white linen skirt and black tank top. Bethari had looped a patterned scarf around my hips to provide some color, but I really needed to go shopping.

Zaneisha indicated a seat in the back corner and stood directly behind me.

She wasn't the only bodyguard in the room. The kids at this school were obviously rich, and some of them—or their parents—were important enough for around-the-clock security. Two men and someone whose gender I couldn't pick traded glances and shallow nods with Zaneisha. Their charges ignored the byplay.

One of them, a tall boy in a red jumpsuit, detached from his group of friends and sauntered toward us. "Heeey. Tegan, right? What's it like to be dead?"

"I don't know," I said. "I'm alive."

He smiled at me, perfect teeth flashing. Literally—they were inset with some sort of device that was blinking colored patterns at me.

"Go away, Soren," Bethari said.

"I missed you last night, Bethi. The party wasn't the same without you." He turned to the group behind him. "It was no fun without Bethari, was it?"

They assured him that it wasn't.

"It never is," Bethari said. "But I don't drink, and I don't take breathers, and your bangers get a little rowdy for me."

"Bangers?" I said.

"Parties," she told me.

Soren turned his glittering smile back to me. "You should definitely come to the next one, Tegan. What's your specialty?"

"Music."

"Well, there you are," Soren said triumphantly. "We always have music at my bangers." He leaned in. "My specialty is journalism, like Bethi. You won't mind if we 'cast our little occasion, will you, Tegan?"

"Is this a famer?" I asked Bethari, voice clear.

She grinned. "Soren is our *best* famer."

Soren's eyes went tight. "Maybe next time, then," he said, and drifted back to his group. They giggled and whispered to one another.

I wondered what they could possibly say about me. I wasn't rich. I had no famous relations. I was just some weird kid with awful hair and dull clothes, a celebrity for being dead.

I stared at my computer and tried not to mind.

≈ ‡ ∞

Okay.

I know this is shallow, but in my time, I was really good-looking.

Not, like, model-hot, 'cause I've always been short, but I was noticeably pretty, and I knew it. Clear skin, high cheekbones, symmetrical features, and huge, dark eyes. I had—still have—big boobs for my size, which didn't fit the ultraslender ideal, but sure attracted attention. Conditioning for free running kept me slim and muscled, and I had long, black hair, which was sort of my trademark. I could leave it loose or tie it up in one of those casual knots that usually took me ten minutes to get just right, or throw it into a fancy style for special occasions.

Boys like Soren used to like me because I was pretty, not because I'd been a corpse and was now a pseudocelebrity. It wasn't until that first morning at Elisa M that I wondered if I just wasn't attractive anymore.

And I was shocked by how uneasy that thought made me.

≈ ‡ ∞

So, right then, when I was feeling ugly and insecure, he walked in, and the air emptied out of my lungs. My vision narrowed to that familiar form as he scanned the classroom and sat down at the front of the room, slouching a little in his seat.

Then I was standing in the aisle behind him with no memory of how I'd gotten there.

"Dalmar," I whispered, and reached for his shoulder. My hand was shaking. "How did you get here? Dalmar?"

Zaneisha appeared at my side. "Tegan..."

"No!" I said, and ducked away from her, reaching for his arm. "Dalmar! Dalmar! Look at me!"

He did.

The face was so close: strong cheekbones and full lips with the exact curve of those that had kissed my bare skin. The perfect shape of his naked skull was the same, and the shade of his skin like rich earth. But this close I could see the differences—

the three freckles Dalmar had had under his left eye were missing, and this boy had a wider, flatter nose. His eyelashes weren't as long, and his eyes were a different shape and much lighter, golden-brown instead of a brown so dark it was nearly black.

And the contempt in those eyes was chilling. Dalmar had never looked at me like that.

"My name is Abdi," he said in a lilting accent that was nothing like Dalmar's Australian English. "I don't know this *Dalmar*."

"You look just like him," I said, because my brain was still coming back from a century ago.

It was the worst thing I could have said. The contempt in his eyes deepened.

"I am Abdi," he said definitively, and turned his face away.

That hurt so much that it shot through my haze. I looked up. The classroom was packed, thirty people at least, and every person in it was staring at me. Soren was gleefully typing something into his computer. Bethari was looking at me and wincing.

I'd just completely lost it in front of my new classmates.

And, oh god, worse—I was a white girl who'd called a black boy by the wrong name and insisted he looked just the same. Like he was interchangeable. Like he wasn't a person in his own right.

"Bazza," someone whispered.

Facebreaking, I thought, the word like little splinters of glass in my head. The school day hadn't even started, and I had broken my face into bits.

"I'm sorry," I told Abdi. "I'm really—oh, *god*."

And then I ran away.

Even in the future you have to have a place to put your cleaning supplies.

My eyes were tearing up, but as I rushed out of the classroom and down the corridor, I could still make out the mop symbol on the little door. I yanked it open and ducked inside.

The air in that little room was even hotter than it was in the corridor, and it was dense with the scent of pine and lemon. I crouched on the floor, wrapped my arms around my shoulders, and tried to rock myself into something resembling calmness.

I had just done something awful *and* made a fool of myself in front of all my new classmates. I tried reminding myself that worse things could happen, and, in fact, several of them had happened to me, but it wasn't that helpful.

I started going through the Blue Album in my head, my failsafe, surefire calm-downer, but it all turned to mush, and the repetition of one name, over and over, to the beat of "Hey Jude." *Dal-mar. Dal-mar.*

Dalmar, Dalmar, Dalmar, who'd been truly mine for only one day. Who'd married someone else, who'd forgotten all about me except as a tragedy in his youth. He'd gotten white-haired and fatter and happier over six decades.

But to me, he was the boy who two months ago had kissed my earlobes and whispered words of love into my palms, and ghosted his calloused fingers just above the surface of my arms, so that the hairs there had shivered and my skin tightened, trembling. I thought I'd seen him again. I'd been ready to accuse the government of lies, conspiracy, and deception. I'd been ready to march up to Dawson and slap the truth right out of him, to hold them all accountable for their horrible misdeeds.

But that boy wasn't Dalmar. Dalmar was dead.

I remembered again the dislike in Abdi's stare. I deserved it, but I was glad his eyes weren't the same color as Dalmar's. I couldn't have borne it if Dalmar's eyes had looked at me with that chilling contempt.

I could hardly bear it now.

"I really suck," I muttered.

"Suck what?" a voice said from the darkness before me.

The only reason I didn't scream was because the voice sounded genuinely puzzled and interested in my reply. Still, I jerked backward, nearly biting through my tongue.

"It's an expression," I said. "Uh, I thought I was alone in here."

"Nope," the voice said. "I'm here, too. Hi. Lights on."

I had to blink hard in the sudden flare of brilliance. When I could see again, I was staring at a slim girl my own age, with shaggy, light brown hair and skin a few shades darker than mine. She was wearing a purple dress that reached to her knees and cuffed leggings under it that went halfway down her calves. She was sitting in the lotus position, bare feet resting casually on her thighs, and the light was coming from her computer, which was draped over her shoulders like a cloak. "I'm Joph," she said. "What does 'I suck' mean?"

"I'm Tegan," I said. "Teeg. It means that I'm a terrible person."

Joph thought about that. "You don't look terrible, Teeg."

I began to laugh. I couldn't help it. Of all the weird conversations I'd had over the previous weeks, including the one where Marie told me I'd been dead for a hundred years, this was a really strong contender for the weirdest.

"It's okay," Joph said. "You can stay here with me." She gestured at her tiny domain as if it were a gift she was presenting.

"I'm not sure that would work," I said. "But it's tempting." I was beginning to suspect that some of Joph's serenity came from less-than-natural causes. I'd thought her eyes were black, but closer inspection showed a ring of light brown around the edge of the iris. Her pupils were really dilated.

There was a scratching noise outside. "Teeg?" Bethari called. "Can I come in?"

"Is that Bethi?" Joph asked. "Stellar." She gave me another of those beatific smiles.

"Sure," I called back, and wriggled a little closer to Joph to make room.

Bethari edged around the door, not opening it more than necessary, and then stopped when she saw I wasn't alone.

"Ah," she said. "I should have known." She shook her head at Joph, who waved amiably back. "How do you feel, Teeg?"

"Stupid. Stressed. Embarrassed. Facebroken."

"Well, you're getting the vocabulary down." She smiled at me.

"Yeah?" I said, unwilling to smile back. "What does *bazza* mean?"

Bethari hesitated.

"That's a racist white Australian," Joph said helpfully.

"Right," I said, and slumped down again.

Bethari shot Joph a glare, then shrugged at me. "I could explain to people. About Dalmar. I mean, they might understand why you did it."

"No," I said. I couldn't bear the thought of people pawing over my memories of him, the same way they'd pawed over my image in that interview, endlessly dissecting every word I'd said and gesture I'd made, making judgments about who I was and how I felt.

≈ ‡ ∞

Ironic, right? Here I am, serving up all my memories on a platter, just begging you to listen, to discuss, to make your own judgments.

So ask yourself—if I wouldn't do it then, why now?

Is it really so important that you understand where I'm coming from?

I think so. But you'll have to decide for yourself.

≈ ‡ ∞

Bethari wrapped her arm around my shoulders. "I know it probably doesn't help," she said, "but everyone says stupid things that hurt people."

"As stupid as that? I thought things were better here, but it looks like I brought the bad with me."

She didn't say anything to that, just hugged me closer.

"How did you find me, anyway?"

"Zaneisha's standing guard outside."

Of course she was. I groaned. "Does she hate me?"

"Who can tell?" Bethari said. "Her face never moves."

"You're helpful," I told her.

"Was I helpful?" Joph asked, my sarcasm apparently passing her by.

I laughed. "You were, actually."

"Oh, good. I like you, Teeg. You want pop, scene, color, you come to me."

Bethari's face scrunched up.

"What's pop, scene, color?" I asked, just to poke her. As if I couldn't tell Joph was talking about drugs, even if I had no clue which ones she meant. In a century, they'd probably come up with dozens of new ways to fry your brain and a hundred new names for all of them.

"Let's just say Joph's specialty is chemistry," Bethari said.

Joph's smile was slow and sweet. "If you wanted one, Bethi, I'd give you a freebie, too. For old times' sake."

"The past should remain in the past," Bethari told her, and then she clapped her hand over her mouth. "I'm so sorry," she said through her fingers.

"It's okay," I said.

She took her hand away. "Well, at least that's proof that anyone can say something stupid."

"If only you'd said it in front of your new classmates on your first day at school," I said, but I did feel better. If even self-possessed Bethari could make careless mistakes without thinking, I could forgive myself for putting that look in someone's eyes.

Maybe. In a while.

Whether Abdi could forgive me was another matter, but one I had to face. Besides, it was steaming hot in that janitor's closet. My top was sticking to my skin, and I was pretty sure that Bethari had to be sweltering under her headscarf.

"Come and visit me anytime," Joph said as we got up.

"You're coming to class," Bethari said firmly.

"I can learn in the closet," she protested. "The school network works here."

"Classroom," Bethari said. "Socialize with your peers."

"Aw," Joph said, but she got up anyway. "I guess I'd better. When was the last time I was there?"

"Last Wednesday. You fell asleep."

"Might do that some more," she said thoughtfully. "Naps are nice."

"Get," Bethari said, and shooed her out the door. I had the satisfaction of seeing Zaneisha's eyes widen a tiny bit at Joph's unexpected appearance, before Bethari closed the door again and we were together in the hot dark.

"I have to tell you something about Abdi," she said, her breath tickling my ear. I could hear her fidgeting beside me, the shushing sound of her light dress as it whispered over her body. "He's not Australian."

"Oh," I said, meaning *so?*, and then caught up. "Wait, but the No Migrant thing—"

Bethari nodded. "He's here because someone from this big tubecasting company saw him singing in Djibouti City, and they sponsored him on a Talented Alien visa. Talented Alien is weird—it's all, 'oh, look how nice and generous we are, training some of you people, but don't forget, you can't stay!' As soon as he graduates, he's gone. And people are nasty, you know? We're mostly okay at Elisa M, but even some of the people here call him a thirdie, or talk about how No Migrant should mean no one should be coming in for any reason."

I didn't need to ask the meaning of *thirdie*; she'd explained that last night. It meant someone from the developing world. Someone from nations that didn't pursue low-emissions energy, or restrict cattle-herding, or heavily tax large families who consumed more resources and pressed against the world's already enormous population.

"So . . . oh crap. He thought me calling him Dalmar was part of that?"

"Maybe. I really think that if I explain—"

I shook my head. "He sings?"

Bethari snorted. "No. That's the thing. He was sponsored because he sang, and he entered Elisa M with a music specialty. But he showed up the first day with a flute. He's good with it, but it's not what he's famous for. I guess he didn't want to be exploited."

I could definitely empathize with that point of view. I wasn't very keen on being used myself, and people like that Soren guy were obviously eager to use me.

"Okay," I said. "Time to get this done. Let's go."

My second apology went like this.

Me, pretending not to notice half the class openly staring at me: "I'm really sorry about that. I made a stupid mistake."

Abdi, barely looking up from his computer: "Okay."

He didn't look as if it was okay, though; he looked as if he was bored of the situation and wasn't planning to be my bestie anytime soon.

I sat down and got on with my day. The right edge of Zaneisha's lips creased slightly, which I interpreted as wild joy that her charge was finally in the place she was supposed to be.

I'd read about the school's teaching methods in the infocasts, but it was different seeing them in action. Most of the actual teaching was done on the tubes, and students could access them whenever and wherever they chose. Assignments had to come in, and assessments had to be made. But other than that, students could do pretty much what they wanted, when they wanted.

Bethari was squashed into a beanbag in the corner, chatting with a red-haired boy as they went over a statistics assignment. Soren and his cronies were playing a game in the corner that had something to do with physics, and at least a quarter of the class was listening to music, either routed through their Ear-Rings or under cover of sound shields. Joph wasn't even the only one napping.

At my old high school, the teachers had ranged from angry-at-everything to nice-but-useless to occasionally-pretty-cool. None of them would let us eat in class, much less sleep or play. I liked learning, but I'd always found school to be a long grind, and some days it had been slow torture waiting for the minutes to tick over and for my real life to start again.

Maybe I could get used to Elisa M.

I wasn't staring at him or anything, but I did notice that Abdi wasn't listening to music, taking a break, or interacting with anyone. He was staring into his computer, working steadily.

The classroom facilitator, Just-Call-Me Eden, gave me the rundown on the school's policies of everything, but before I could get any work done, I had to have access to the school network. She frowned at Koko and muttered for a while, then enlightenment struck. "Oh!"

"Oh?"

"This computer is in kinder-mode! No wonder I can't get you in."

My computer was set up for babies. My cheeks burned. A huge drawback of pale skin is that everyone can see you blush.

Eden leaned over and tried a few commands until she got the hang of my model. "All right, Tegan. Spread your fingers here, and repeat after me."

I did. "I identify myself as Tegan Marie Oglietti, registered owner of this device, and I authorize adult mode interaction."

My fingers buzzed. Koko's screen went dark, then lit up again. Then six different kinds of music started playing, all at top volume. To make matters worse, Koko was blasting the noise through my EarRing. I clawed off the mobile phone and dropped it on my desk, but the sound continued.

I saw Eden's lips form the word *mute*, but her voice was swallowed in the cacophony. I caught fragments of other voices as I frantically waved my hands in the *go quiet* gesture.

"—satisfying your partner? Try Dr. Tantric's—"

"—memory fabric! Your cut, your way! Hafiza's—"

"—Danish prince with access to ten billion kroner. Dear friend—"

Koko wasn't paying attention to my gesturing. Her screen was shooting 3-D images at me, overlaying them in a complex collage of color and form, and when I lost my head and folded her over, trying to enclose the images inside, they just switched to her "back." Even scrunched into a ball, the computer chattered and flashed.

"Quiet!" I yelled. "Oh my god, shut up."

Most of the class was laughing or cringing. Eden was no help whatsoever, and Bethari was still struggling out of her beanbag.

It was Abdi who got there first, while I was squashing Koko against the desk in a futile attempt to stifle her shouting with my hands.

He put a hand on my shoulder. "I assert my rights as outlined in the Advertising-Free Zones Act 2098," he said clearly, right into my ear. "Repeat it."

Voice shaking, I did.

There was stunning, miraculous silence, and the images winked out. Koko showed the cheerful glow of her start mode, peaceably awaiting instruction.

"What was that?" I whispered.

It had been to myself, but Abdi heard me. "Advertising," he said quietly. "It can be a shock. If you're not used to it."

"Yes," I said. My hands were trembling, too, and I sat down before my knees gave out. "Thank you."

He examined my face. Those light brown eyes were expressionless, but his mouth was pursed. "You're welcome," he said finally. "I will see you in music."

He returned to his seat at the front of the class and went back to ignoring me as steadily as he did everyone else in the room.

Joph lifted her head from her arms. "What happened?" she asked. "Did something just happen?"

I was wondering that myself.

CHAPTER SIX
Revolver

Fortunately for my state of mind, Bethari and I were doing only a half day at school. The whispering stopped, eventually, and by the time Bethari got up and nodded at the door, I was almost in a decent mood again.

I even remembered to let Zaneisha go out the door first.

"Gregor's bringing the car around," she reported in the corridor. "Media waiting at all exits."

I sighed, but I'd been expecting it. Bethari looked intrigued.

Zaneisha continued. "Head down, don't make eye contact, ignore the bumblecams, and—"

"I know. No comment."

Master Sergeant Gregor Petrov was my other bodyguard. He smiled more than Zaneisha, but I got the feeling he was laughing at me and my inevitable confusion. He was waiting just inside the door and nodded at Zaneisha as we got close.

"Go," Zaneisha said, and for the second time that day, the world exploded into noise and color.

This time, I knew what to expect. The journalists weren't allowed onto the school's private property, but nothing stopped them from shouting questions from the street. Their bumble-cams swarmed above them, no doubt getting pixel-perfect shots of my face. I was concentrating on looking blank. I'd never really tried to cover up my emotions before, and it was harder than I'd thought to pull my frown into a neutral line and smooth out my forehead. Maybe Zaneisha could give me lessons on that, too.

I saw Carl Hurfest's red hair but managed not to give him the finger or stick my tongue out for the cameras, which filled me with pride. One of the journalists, in plain linen wear much like mine, was standing at the back of the crowd. He stood out because of his calmness. He probably thought he could entice the shy Living Dead Girl to him as if I were a stray cat.

Good luck, buddy.

Whatever their tactics, shouting or standing back, they weren't going to let up. And what Dawson had said was true; it took only one slip. Now that they knew I could be caught, they were going to do their very best to catch me.

I couldn't blame them, but I could hate them, and I did.

"Is that Abdi Taalib?" I heard someone say. "Abdi! Abdi! What do you think of Tegan?"

"We have reports that there was friction between you and Tegan this morning. Any comment?"

"But you later assisted her. Are you two friends?"

"Do you have a lot in common?"

"What's your connection?"

Twisting in Zaneisha's grip, I caught one glimpse of Abdi. He was standing in the doorway, looking horrified beyond belief.

But his voice was clear, that lilting accent distinct over the hubbub. "We have no connection." Then Zaneisha shoved my head down and hustled me into the car. Bethari ducked in behind me, the door slammed, and for a long, lovely moment, everything was silent.

I fumbled on my seat belt and slumped against the seat as Zaneisha started to move the car, and the flock of bumblecams fell away behind us. "I hate journalists."

"Thanks," Bethari said.

She didn't sound offended, though, so I waved my hand. "I'll hate you later. You're not one yet."

"Of course I am," she said, blinking at me. "Didn't you look at my 'casts?" She reached for her computer.

Bethari's tubecast node was an interesting mix. There were a few reviews, of music and fashion, with a lot of focus on head-scarves and shoes. A lot were opinions on other news stories, all of them sharp and pithy. There was a big category called NO MIGRANT? NO WAY! that had gathered a lot of comments, some of them really nasty. And there was a small section of arty vid-casts, taken on a bumblecam that swooped around Bethari's cheerleading squad as they somersaulted and soared, behaving as if gravity were an occasional inconvenience instead of an undeniable force.

There was absolutely nothing about me.

I made a mental note to check out the node later in more detail. But right then, what I really wanted was gossip.

"So," I said, drawing out the word slyly, "what's the ontedy on Joph? She seems to like you a lot."

Bethari rolled her eyes. "Ex-girlfriend."

"I thought you didn't screw the crew?"

"I don't now. It was awkward after we broke up. She has a knack for home creation, which is fine and everything, except then she started spending all her time in her lab. She missed dates, she was acting like a total spacer, she slept through class or just didn't bother to turn up, and I swear she was lying to me. So I broke it off. We're pretty much friends again now."

"Wow. Her parents didn't notice?"

"Oh, they're thrilled. Chemistry firms are dying to recruit her."

"Wait. Drugs are legal?"

"Well, sure. Why—oh! Right. Yeah, about forty years ago. They're tested and controlled, subject to advertising and enviro standards, like everything else. Perfectly legal for sixteen and up. I don't take them, of course, but I don't care if others do." She shrugged. "It's just that she's the smartest person at Elisa M, and now she spends most of her days drifting around looking at the pretty colors."

"So you try to look after her?"

Bethari snorted. "I don't want to be anyone's mother. But . . . I don't know. No one's really worried about Joph, you know? Just what she can do. She's a genius; she could do anything, but instead she's going to waste all those brains on making happy pills? That's not right." Her voice firmed. "I'm going to be the most viewed 'caster in the world. My content's going to make people think, make them change. I want that No Migrant policy gone."

"But if Australia really can't support all those people..."

Bethari's face was fierce. "Australia has the resources to support every single person in those camps. Rising oceans, rising populations, diminishing food production, and a wealthy world superpower won't accept *any* refugees, because people are clinging to what they've got and refusing to share? That's disgusting."

She reminded me, right then, of Dalmar. Not his looks, but his quiet passion for justice. And Alex, too, who was anything but quiet, who thrust herself to the front of every protest and happily talked to strangers on the street, getting people who tried to avert their eyes to see her, to see the issues.

I was fine throwing myself off heights or jumping narrow gaps, but I really envied that kind of bravery.

"I'm so glad you're my friend," I told Bethari.

"Me too," she said, and we hugged in the backseat, stretching our seat belts to their limits.

As I sat back, a little bit teary, I saw the church over Bethari's shoulder.

I hadn't seen the Catholic basilica on the way to Elisa M. I'd been so stressed about school that I hadn't paid attention to anything out the window.

But I saw it now—the dome, the earthy yellow-gray of the sandstone it was made from, nestled between the skyscrapers on either side. Although no sunlight could reach it through its tall neighbors, the stone seemed to glow with its own warm radiance. I didn't think about it; I just lunged for the back of Zaneisha's seat and stuck my head into the driver's section.

"We have to go back!" I said. "I want to go to that church!"

Zaneisha's jaw twitched, but her gloved hands were immobile on the wheel. "That's not in my instructions," she said.

Bethari was leaning over the backseat to catch a glimpse of the church. She turned around. "Are you denying Tegan her right to free worship, as outlined in the Constitution of the Republic of Australia?" she inquired. She didn't sound angry; she sounded politely curious.

"I'm denying Ms. Oglietti her wish to walk into an unsecured area with no notice," Zaneisha said, equally polite.

"That's fascinating," Bethari said, yanking me out of the gap between the front seats. I fell back, watching the way Bethari's pretty face sharpened, like a fox on the hunt. Her computer was in her hand, squished into a tiny ball and held through the gap. It wasn't quite a bumblecam, but I was sure it was recording just as well; Bethari would have the best media apps. "Sergeant Washington, would you like to tell my viewers more about your opposition to the free worship of Ms. Oglietti?"

"No comment," Zaneisha said automatically, then, "Put that away."

"Are you also in favor of suppressing the free media?" Bethari asked innocently.

"I could confiscate that computer under the Media Safety Act and have your credentials revoked."

Bethari flinched, but her voice was steady. "I could report the confiscation to Media Monitor," she said.

Muscles jumped in Zaneisha's jaw, but at the next set of traffic lights, she reached for her EarRing. "Gregor. Change of plans. Ms. Oglietti's going to church."

Bethari settled back and grinned at me as we made the turn.

Okay. Maybe I didn't hate *all* journalists.

≈ ‡ ∞

I'm not actually a very good Catholic. I was baptized, of course, and I went to Mass regularly for a while. But Mum and Owen and I stopped doing that after Nonna and Poppa died, except for Christmas, Easter, weddings, baptisms, and funerals—although one thing about a big Italian family is that you have a lot of those.

I was also never much for the church's position on women's rights or equal marriage (the Fourth Vatican Council fixed most of that, but back in my time it was pretty horrendous). But I definitely have faith. I believe in an eventual life after death, because the alternative is just too awful. And I've felt something, from time to time, a warm presence that felt to me like Divine Grace.

I'd been confirmed in the church, too; my full name is actually Tegan Marie Mary Oglietti.

Yeah, Marie Mary. I know, but I was thirteen and going

through a stage of really loving the Virgin, and I wanted her name as my confirmation name, even if it meant I had it twice. I still think she's pretty awesome; she got this big job and she did it very well, even though you've got to think her parents and her fiancé were a bit side-eyed about the "virgin pregnancy" deal.

≈ ‡ ∞

The second I stepped into the church foyer, my right hand reached automatically for the holy water in the little niche beside the door, and I dabbed it on myself: forehead, heart, left shoulder, right shoulder.

Bethari had opted to stay in the car, joined by a grumpy Gregor, but Zaneisha had insisted on accompanying me in.

"Should I do this?" she asked, gesturing at the holy water.

Well, goodness gracious me. Something I knew that this future woman didn't.

"It's okay," I said, trying to smother my smugness. It's not like I would have been any more at ease in a mosque. "You don't have to do any of the things I do."

She nodded infinitesimally, eyes tracking every exit and entrance. Being a bodyguard had to be exhausting.

I avoided the center of the nave and the woman replacing the flowers beside the lectern there; I wasn't interested in Jesus on his crucifix behind the main altar. They had a side altar for Mary, though, and I went down to say hi, past the Stations of the Cross depicted on the wall, my steps echoing through the silent space. She was wearing blue and white, and for once she wasn't holding baby Jesus; she was just being herself, inscrutable and watchful.

I went to my knees. "Hello," I said to the perfect stone face. "How are you?"

Mary didn't reply.

"I was thinking about what that Father guy said," I told her. "I don't think them bringing me back was a miracle. I mean, I'd rather be alive than not, you bet. And I think it was people who did it, not God. But I don't think it's God's exclusive territory, either. If it was, they wouldn't be *able* to do it. And I don't feel evil or soulless. I feel like me." I gulped. "Only sadder. And lonelier. It's hard."

Zaneisha would probably have been a lot more comfortable if I'd talked to the Blessed Virgin in my head, which was one of the reasons I was doing it out loud.

I mean, I mostly liked Zaneisha. I just resented that I couldn't go anywhere without her.

"Marie's good. And I like Bethari a lot, and her friend Joph seems okay. But none of them get it, you know? They don't really understand what it's like to be from somewhere so different. I bet Abdi does, but I screwed up, and he doesn't want to talk to me."

Mary didn't seem to think she needed to comment. I felt the tears stinging at my eyelashes and tightened my jaw. "I just wanted to say hi," I said, but that was a lie. What I wanted was to feel God, to be certain that I wasn't some sort of fake person walking around with a borrowed face and voice, thinking I was a real girl.

I was 99.9 percent sure I had a soul. But 0.1 percent can keep you up at night.

After a while I decided that no matter how hard I prayed, there would be no choir of angels or tongues of flame to declare my soulfulness. Still, I stayed on my knees and watched that unmoving face.

"Ms. Oglietti?" Zaneisha asked eventually, and then, though her voice didn't change, "Tegan?"

"I'm okay," I said. The kneeler was padded in memory fabric, and it snapped back to fullness as I got up. There was no dimple in the cloth to show I'd ever been there. "Let's go."

≈ ‡ ∞

We were almost to the big carved doors when Zaneisha said, "Stop," her voice so absolutely commanding that I did what she said without asking why.

My instincts don't usually work that way.

"There's an Inheritor of the Earth outside," she said. "Gregor's taking care of it."

Fear whooshed into my head like a train into a station, but stronger and louder was the whistling sound of my rage. "I want to talk to him," I said.

"No," Zaneisha said flatly. She had her sonic pistol in her hand. "Let me do my job."

Since her job was keeping me alive, maybe even to the point of taking a bullet for me, it was hard to argue with that.

"He's coming in," she said after a moment. "Can't stop him. He's citing freedom of worship."

"I—"

"No." She hustled me backward until we were behind one of the columns holding up the vaulted roof. "Stay," she said, pressing herself against me from the other side so I couldn't go anywhere if I wanted to. All that muscle against my back was reassuring. I wriggled my face out a little bit so that I could see. The memory fabric of Zaneisha's dress had gone hard around us, ready to redistribute any kinetic force.

Like a bullet.

Gregor came in at a fast walk, stepping sideways. His pistol wasn't out, but his hand was hovering right by it, and his eyes were fixed on the door. He edged toward us without ever seeming to look in our direction, taking a position where he could watch both us and the door.

The entrance of the Inheritor was something of an anticlimax. He was an elderly man with olive skin, long reddish hair, and a beard that was fading to white. He wore loose, undyed linen trousers and a long top made out of some kind of light cotton. He walked slowly into the foyer without touching the holy water. He was favoring his left side, and I wondered if he was hurt. But his eyes were sharp as he peered around the nave.

I recognized him by the way he stood; he had been the man holding back while the reporters swarmed toward me. Not a journalist after all, but an Inheritor.

"He followed us here," I said. My fear was getting stronger, blood thrumming in my ears.

"I know," Zaneisha said. "And we didn't see him, which means he might be a professional, which means stay put."

"That's far enough, sir," Gregor said, his deep voice burring. "Any farther and I'll consider it a threat to my charge's safety and act accordingly."

The man ignored him, staring at me instead. "I don't want to hurt you, child."

"Then leave," I suggested. Zaneisha pressed me a little harder against the stone. I'm sure that if she could have spared a hand, she would have shoved my face back behind the column.

The man wasn't moving. "Don't you see what's happening here?" he asked me. "You yearn for a place of holiness. You wish this false consciousness to reconnect with God. You want to rejoin your soul."

"My soul is right here," I said over Zaneisha's warning hiss.

"You should understand that you must shape yourself according to God's plans. To everything there is a season and a time for every purpose under heaven. A time to live, and a time to die. Your time came. What persists is an affront to God, and you must put it to rest."

"You want me to kill myself."

"You're already dead," he said, infinitely gentle. "Child, ask yourself why these godless men of science brought you back. Have you not wondered?"

"It was a godless woman of science, thank you very much,

and they're doing it to save the soldiers," I said, but my heart stuttered. I had wondered, in the nights that dragged on forever, when not even Paul McCartney's most soothing melodies were able to drive the questions from my head. The argument that I was a good candidate sounded all right until you considered all the many people in the century in between who must have gotten themselves frozen the right way, with the right injuries.

Many of whom would know how to handle themselves in this time a lot better than I did. Many of whom were actually the soldiers they were trying to save.

He shook his head sadly. "They mean to use you, child, to further their ungodly ways. God created mankind in his own image. In the image of God he created them; male and female he created them. God blessed them and said to them, be fruitful and increase in number; fill the Earth and subdue it. God gave us this world. But the greed of your masters exceeds his bounty. Ask. Ask them about the Ark Pro—"

There was a sound so loud it was no sound at all, and his chest exploded into chunks of red.

The stone walls were ringing.

Gregor, his weapon out, was carefully approaching the downed man. There was no need for caution. That limp body wasn't going anywhere. He hadn't used the sonic pistol; he'd gone straight for the gun on his other hip. Lethal force.

"You killed him," I said.

"He was reaching for a weapon," Gregor said.

"He didn't have a weapon!"

Gregor turned to Zaneisha. "You'd better get the ween out of here. She's about to go hysterical."

I was *not.* "You killed him," I repeated. "You shot him. How could you do that? He was just an old man; he said he wasn't going to hurt me, and you killed him." My voice climbed until I almost shrieked the last words. I hugged the stone column, leaning on it for strength, as my vision began to gray out at the edges.

"That was an order, Sergeant," Gregor said, and Zaneisha pushed me away from the column and toward the door. We had to skirt the corpse as we went, and I saw the pool of blood inch out from under him. There were thicker pieces in the pool.

"Did I look like that?" I asked. "Was I all limp and bloody? Were there bits of me everywhere? Oh my god, Zaneisha, this is a church; he shot him in *church.* Did I look like that?"

"Don't look," Zaneisha ordered. "Shhh, Tegan, you're safe. It's fine."

"I know I'm safe—that isn't the point. I was safe in there. What was he talking about? What weapon? Did you see a weapon?"

She shot me a troubled look, so fast I nearly missed it, before her face smoothed out again. "Don't worry about it," she said, and pushed me into the backseat.

Bethari looked up from her computer to smile at my return, but her eyes widened as she saw me. "What—?"

"Gregor killed him."

"Killed who? Are you okay?"

"The Inheritor! I'm fine, I'm fine."

"One of those religious nuts? Did he attack you? Oh, Tegan! Are you okay?"

"He was talking; he was just talking."

"What did he say?"

"Seat belt," Zaneisha snapped from the driver's seat.

Bethari had to help me get it on.

"He shot him in church," I said. I hiccuped twice and burst into uncontrollable tears.

But underneath that genuine grief and horror, I was thinking. *Ask them about the Ark Pro—.* Ark Pro what? Ark Professional? Ark Protectorate? Ark Project? Ark Procedure?

Don't worry about it, Zaneisha had said.

Too late. I was worried.

Wriggling closer to Bethari, I whispered, "Something's wrong. I need your help."

If I haven't screwed up her future forever, Bethari is going to be the best journalist in the world. She didn't flinch. She just curved around me and turned her mouth close to my ear, out of Zaneisha's sight.

"What do you need?" she breathed.

"A computer," I whispered back. I wanted to do some hunting around the tubes, and I wasn't stupid enough to do it on my army-issued computer. I loved Koko, but I didn't trust her not to spy on me.

Bethari pulled me tighter into her arms, and I felt her hand shift in the tight space between us, concealed from view. A moment later I felt the cool, flat square of a tightly bound computer slip behind the scarf around my waist. Using my sobs as cover, Bethari twisted it securely inside.

"One condition," she said quietly, ostentatiously patting my hair for Zaneisha's benefit. "You have to tell me everything."

"You bet."

≋ ‡ ∞

I wish I hadn't said that. I'm sorry I dragged her into it, and I hope that telling this story will make them let her go.

Listen to me, you liars.

By the time I'm done, you won't have any secrets left that she could reveal.

CHAPTER SEVEN
Here Comes the Sun

Instead of pulling up outside our house, Zaneisha went for the driveway of the house across the road, where she and Gregor were quartered. I was dragged out of the car and into the house so fast, I swear my feet didn't touch the ground. I was surrounded by people in uniforms.

"Are you injured?" someone asked brusquely, shining a light into my pupils.

"No."

"What's today's date?" he persisted, clipping something to my finger.

"It's the seventh of October. I'm fine," I said. "Where's Bethari?"

"Ms. Miyahputri is being escorted to her home. Clench your fist for me."

And then Marie burst through the crowd and dropped on her knees beside me.

I'd never seen her so unsettled; not when I'd crashed into a press conference barefoot and bleeding from jumping off a roof, not when I'd starved myself, not when I'd opened my mouth to the horrible Carl Hurfest and got myself threatened with reconfinement. Her pupils were huge, nearly taking over the dark brown of her eyes, and her hands were trembling as she reached for my wrist. She checked the finger clip-on thingy, then looked into my face.

"I was worried you'd been hurt," she said.

"I'm fine," I repeated, and forced myself to say the lie that might keep me free from suspicion. "I didn't even see that guy go for his weapon, but Gregor must have. He kept me safe."

"All right. Do you want to go home?"

I nearly said *How?* Home was a century away. But Marie had one lock of hair sticking up from her normally smooth, thick bob. She looked a bit like a cockatoo, feathers ruffled to scare off a threat.

"Let's go home," I agreed, and let her guide me across the street.

We were escorted by armed guards every step of the way.

Once the guards had gone through the house, looking for I-didn't-ask-what, Marie politely shut them all out and asked me to stay in the kitchen while she went downstairs.

I was shaking, and the cup of tea she'd handed me was warm and smooth in my hands. I sat there holding it, without sipping it, willing the warmth to sink into my bones.

When Marie returned, she was carrying a picture of a woman I'd never seen before.

The woman was short and plump, with skin much darker than Marie's and eyes turned up at the ends in a permanent smile. She was wearing something light and yellow that glinted and sparkled around her, and the light of humor in her eyes made her seem solid and touchable, not a two-dimensional image pressed onto a lifeless frame.

"This is Chelsea," Marie said.

"She's pretty," I said, for lack of any other comment.

Marie smiled. "Isn't she? We were married for nearly three years."

Were? "Oh."

"She died," Marie said. "She was shot and killed six years ago, in our old house. The police said it was a robbery gone wrong. They found him. He went to jail. Afterward, I moved here. I couldn't live there anymore."

It hit me like the times I'd judged a landing wrong and knocked all the air out of myself instead of rolling with the impact. Marie smiled at me, but her eyes were glassy with unshed tears. I straightened up from my place leaning against the kitchen wall. This wasn't a time for slouching.

"I'm sorry," I said at last, aware that it wasn't enough. Nothing I said could be enough.

"I know the project's important to you for personal reasons, Tegan. I wanted to let you know about mine. I was already working on Operation New Beginning when Chelsea was shot. Afterward I kept thinking, if I'd worked faster, if we'd made more breakthroughs... It's silly, of course. Chelsea had been dead for hours by the time I got home. I could never have saved her."

"Is that why you invited me to stay with you?" I asked. The words popped out before I could think about them, but when I did, they made sense. Taking in a girl who was revived out of her sorrow for the woman who had been murdered—it was poetic, sort of. And tragic, too. But I wanted to be myself, not a prop in someone else's poetic, tragic story.

"Perhaps a little. Mostly it was because I liked you, and I thought you should have a better deal than what Colonel Dawson was offering." Her fingers tightened on the picture. "Chelsea would have liked you, too. She loved music and musicians. And you'd lost so much. I wanted you to be with someone who had lost someone. I thought I might understand, if only a little. I wanted to help. If I could." Her frightened face said, all too clearly, that she didn't think she was doing a good job.

I crossed the floor and hugged her, with the picture still cradled in her hands. She was all bone and muscle, strength hidden by her conservative clothes and quiet looks, and she returned the hug with interest, making my ribs creak in protest.

"You do help," I said, and summoned a cheeky grin. "Even if it's only a little."

She gave me a proper smile and stepped back with another shaky laugh. "I didn't even ask, how was your first day of school?"

I made an executive decision not to mention mistaking Abdi for Dalmar, hiding in the janitor's closet, or turning the classroom into a spam zone. "It was okay. My basic math and literacy skills are all right, but I have to take lots of remedial classes in history and science. The remedial physics lessons look interesting. What's a Salten Duck? Can we really make starships?"

Marie relaxed even further. "Salter's Duck. It's an old way of converting wave power to electricity. A fairly inefficient method, not often used."

"And the starships? Really?"

"Theoretically," she said, turning Chelsea's picture in her hands. "It would be a huge resource investment, though, and no one would elect a government willing to throw that much money at something so distant. The closest potentially inhabitable planets we've discovered are twenty to thirty light-years away. A ship using our fastest current technology would take several hundred years to reach them, and no crew could survive that long."

I wasn't a science nerd like Dalmar, but I'd seen enough movies to know what the solution should be. "Couldn't you use cryonics for that? Sleeper ships."

Marie laughed. "We're a long way from that. It would be hard to find volunteers for such a mission when I haven't even—" She pressed her lips together.

"Brought anyone else back yet?" I guessed.

She sighed. "Yes. I don't know why, but none of my other patients are responding nearly as well as you are. There's something on the neurological side that doesn't respond properly, and we're having trouble narrowing it down."

I thought again of the man in the bed, of his slack, incurious face.

"That's classified, please, Tegan," she said. "I shouldn't have told you even that much, but you deserve to know."

"The other people, the, um, unsuccessful revivals. Were they all volunteers like me?"

"Of course," she said, looking slightly shocked. "Anything else would be unethical. They have a great deal of trouble finding me viable subjects, however."

Which reminded me of the question the Inheritor wanted me to ask. *Why me?*

Well, a lack of viable subjects was a good answer. I was right on the verge of asking Marie if she knew anything about an Ark Pro-something, but the question stayed locked behind my teeth.

I really wanted to trust her, after all she'd said and done for me. But when it came right down to it, Marie was working for the army. If the Inheritor's reference had been to something dodgy, I didn't want the army to be alerted to my search.

"I'll get dinner started," Marie said. "Or, well, a late lunch, I suppose."

"I should do some assignments," I said, and made myself smile as I went downstairs, Bethari's computer a lump in my belt.

Bethari had far more apps than I did, and some of them looked really interesting. If I'd had more time, I would have liked to investigate MindNote or Roadcraft.

But I'd told Marie I was doing homework. If Koko *was* being monitored, I had to spend enough time using my own computer to make the lie plausible. I made sure the antispyware apps were running, put up the privacy shield, and set Bethari's computer searching for *Ark Pro**, cross-referenced with *Operation New Beginning* and *Inheritors of the Earth*.

Then I flipped Koko open and looked for the easiest remedial history assignment. There was one that was a project on world news. Pick five current humanitarian or economic situations, do a brief overview on each, then select something for an in-depth report, which I could 'cast, write, or display in creative form. If I displayed it to the class and invited criticism, the project would gain more credits toward my performance and sociability standards.

Fine. I started that search and looked at my other little project.

Bethari's computer was asking permission to break into government archives.

What kind of apps did she *have* on there?

I checked that my door was locked, gave permission, and watched Bethari's computer hunt through locked databases like a snake in a rat's nest.

Koko started blinking at me, wanting to know if she should go into sleep mode. I wasn't spending enough time on my homework.

I waved through the results, bringing up what Koko listed as the most urgent disasters facing mankind. I was trying to be quick, but I got dragged in deeper and deeper. Marie hadn't covered anything like *this* in her current affairs and history lessons. I could see why Bethari thought I needed more education.

A fundamentalist revival was predicted in the Republic of

Texico, which was still reeling after the secession of Austin to the United States. I knew the fundamentalist wars had ripped the old United States apart, but I hadn't realized there were people who still wanted a Christian state.

New Zealand Green was violently protesting what it called the theft of the nation's freshwater by Australia's "strong-arm tactics." New Zealand and Australia had been allies for hundreds of years. But now the Australian government was demanding preferential water sales under the closer-economic-relations agreement. "We have guarded New Zealand's shores for decades," the Australian president was quoted as saying. "We are good neighbors. If they continue to take advantage of our need for water with these robber-baron prices, we may have to reconsider what resources we can continue to commit to their protection."

The New Zealand Prime Minister condemned what she called the "brutal attacks of terrorists" on Australian targets in New Zealand but argued that without water, New Zealand's vital agriculture industry would fail. "Do Australians really want to starve us—and themselves, too? Much of the food on their tables comes from our fields."

There were pandemics in Eastern Europe, Asia, and Africa, and supertornadoes in the American South and Texico, and it looked as if France and Great Britain might soon be going to war.

The Ganges had dried up—well, Marie *had* mentioned that, when she'd briefly gone over the North-South Indian War. But the Nile was drying up, too, and there were massive fire events in the Amazon rain forest.

People were still burning fossil fuels, which came as a shock. The cars in Melbourne ran on batteries, and everything was solar-, wind-, or sea-powered, and no one except the military and the very, very rich were flying anymore.

But not everybody had been able to make the switch from fossil fuels, and countries with plentiful oil supplies had managed to offset the cost of switching to clean power by selling oil cheaply to countries that couldn't afford to go clean, or didn't have the infrastructure to manage massive electrical grids.

Wealthy governments had essentially exported their pollution, and now they blamed the polluters, the thirdies they regarded as stupid and backward because they still used their hoarded oil for transportation and electricity generation, because they ate meat instead of raising protein crops (genetically modified, patented, *expensive* crops), because they used coal, wood, and gas to cook their food instead of using clean electricity from their nonexistent solar panels.

The world was too hot, and it was getting hotter. Rising waters were threatening Fiji and Samoa, having, the report mentioned casually, already swallowed Kiribati, Tuvalu, and the Maldives and displaced tens of thousands of people worldwide. Crops that had worked fine in temperatures three degrees cooler were impossible to grow now, increased growing areas in Siberia and northern Canada weren't picking up the slack, and there wasn't enough water anywhere. Refugees crowded on the borders of nations that either wouldn't let them in or threw them into huge detention camps that bred disease, crime, starvation, stress disorders, depression, and despair.

No one talked much about the Australian camps. The media lockout was still in force.

Why the hell was anyone wasting news time on something as pointless as what clothes I wore?

I had thought the future was *better*. Marie could talk about her wife with no fear, and Bethari had been worried that I might object to her scarf because I was from the past, when anti-Muslim prejudice had been the norm. Most people used public transportation, cars ran on batteries, new houses were built underground to save energy, and the humanure toilets that Dalmar admired were in widespread use.

And the Australian army was going to bring dead soldiers back to a second life.

Bethari had told me about the No Migrant policy and the prejudice against thirdies like Abdi, but I hadn't understood what was happening or just how grotesque the situation was.

I hadn't wanted to understand.

With shaking hands, I shut Koko down, knowing it wouldn't help. The news would still be there.

Bethari's computer beeped at me.

Caught up in a world in crisis, I'd actually forgotten what it was doing, and I fumbled to turn off the alarm. Then I saw the big red-framed warning.

BREACH DETECTED. ADVISE CLOUD SEPARATION.
TRACE 41.7% COMPLETE.

But I couldn't disconnect just yet. Bethari's computer, with its very clever programming, had found what I was looking for.

It was called the Ark Project.

The screen displayed that name and a list of addresses, but everything else was heavily encrypted; I probably had only that much because of a lazy coder somewhere. But there was nothing wrong with the other security protocols. Lots of other very clever computers were currently turning *their* very clever programming, and their much more efficient processors, toward finding where the search had originated.

Racing the trace, I dove frantically into the data. Most of the addresses were in the Northern and Western Territories, but there was one in Victoria—in fact, it was in Williamstown.

Close to the army base. I didn't think that was a coincidence. I stared at the address, willing myself to memorize it. Pens and paper didn't really exist anymore, and I couldn't trust any device I might write the information on.

ADVISE IMMEDIATE CLOUD SEPARATION.
TRACE 96.2% COMPLETE.

"Fuckity fuck fuck fuck," I said calmly. Then I grabbed my rusty iron statue of the lady in the sea and beat the crap out of Bethari's computer.

The computer's pliable material resisted, wrapping around the statue and trying to disperse the force, but I hammered it on the ground, hoping to open a crack somewhere. There might have been a less drastic way to separate a future computer from the online world, but I had no idea how to do it, and no time to find out before the trace got through the proxies and triangulated my position. Marie's address would be a very clear indication of the inquiry's source.

"Stop it, stop it!" I said, and hit harder. Even underground, with the thick earth walls, I was worried that Marie might hear. "Home, play 'Revolution,' volume eleven!"

The house computer obeyed, routing the song through the room's speakers, and under cover of the reverberating strings and heavy bass, I brought the statue down again with all my might.

The iron lady's head flew off.

But the computer's surface had finally cracked. I grabbed my bottle of water from the nightstand and poured it into the gap. There were a few sparks, and the screen died.

I thrust the entire mess—statue, water bottle, and all— under my bed.

John sang that it was all gonna be all right.

"Easy for *you* to say," I muttered, and flopped, spread-eagle, on my back.

"Tegan?" Marie's light voice called through the noise. "Are you all right?"

I checked to make sure everything was well hidden before I replied. "I'm fine! Come in!" There was anger burning inside me, a hot, tight feeling that would not give way to tears.

Marie evidently saw it on my face as she pushed open the door. "Is something wrong?"

"No. Just . . . Why is the world so terrible?"

"I don't know," she said. "You have . . . a faith. Does it help?"

"I have faith in a life after death. I don't think that means we get to make this life awful."

"We can try to make it better," she said tentatively. "That's always been my aim. Are you sorry that I brought you back to this time?"

I thought about it. Yes, the future was much worse than I'd thought. But the past had been bad, too, and I hadn't even considered leaving it. There had been love for me there, and music, and joy. And here I had Marie and Bethari, and a chance at all those things. "No. Not really. I like being alive."

Marie's smile was glorious. "I have a surprise for you," she said. "It just arrived."

She leaned down and picked up a guitar case, holding it out to me in both hands.

I sat still for a moment. "Really?"

"You can't possibly use a school guitar for music tomorrow," she said, then laughed. "Well, I know you could, but I wanted to celebrate your first day, and this seemed like a practical gift."

The case was smooth and black, made of something that looked like bumpy plastic but felt like cool, sturdy metal to my fingers. I laid the case on my unmade bed, slipped the catches with worshipful fingers, and caught my breath, gloating, at the treasure inside.

She was an acoustic-electric, with the classic shape, a soft brown-gold body, and a short black neck. She was nestled in the plush red cushioning like a queen in a pile of velvet pillows.

I lifted her out and slipped the strap over my shoulder. She was a twelve-fret, and the neck was slim enough for my short hand span. I positioned a few chords without strumming, checking the slip factor and reach. The strings were made out of some material I didn't recognize, but I liked the give under my fingers—not too sloppy, not too tough. My calluses had vanished during my long sleep, but I'd build them up again.

I plucked the thin E string and listened as the high, pure note rang out. It had a lovely solid tone. My old guitar, McLeod, had been a third- or fourth-hand Ovation and an absolute delight, but I thought I might grow to love this guitar more.

She must have cost Marie a mint.

"I talked to some people," Marie said. "Is it all right?"

"It's unbelievable," I breathed, sliding my fingers over the pickguard—more mahogany, inlaid with some sort of shell. "She's beautiful. Thank you so much."

"Do you want to play it?" she asked.

I did. More than almost anything.

"After dinner," I said, and put my guitar back in her case. My fingers couldn't resist one final swipe over the polished wood, but I managed to tear them away.

I couldn't close her up in the dark again, though. I left the case open on my bed, breathing in the air under the earth.

Apart from anything else, she'd help conceal the messy truth hiding under my bed.

With Koko in my pocket and Abbey the guitar beside me, I traveled alone to school the next morning. Gregor was driving, and I could feel him watching me.

It was no part of my plan to provoke suspicions. So before I got out of the car, I said, "Thank you, Gregor. For stopping the Inheritor. You saved my life."

Alex, who was an accomplished liar, had taught me as best she could. Keep it simple, she'd said. It sounds more sincere.

Gregor's teeth flashed. "You're welcome," he said, sounding entirely too pleased with himself. "All part of the job."

Which job would that be? I thought, but my face stayed, I hoped, in the same grateful smile. I was still wearing it when I got out, to be escorted by Zaneisha past the crowd of journalists waiting for me.

"Why are you so happy, Tegan?" yelled one of them.

Hah. If only they knew.

I was hoping that I'd have time to find Bethari before music, and maybe even enough privacy to talk about what I'd found— and to apologize for destroying her computer.

But Abdi was waiting just inside the entrance. He was still gorgeous, those light eyes striking in his dark face. He still looked completely uninterested in me.

He had a flute case in one hand, though. That was new.

"I'm supposed to show you to music," he said.

"No need," I said politely.

"The teacher told me to show you."

"Well, that's fine, but I know the way," I said, sharper this time. Zaneisha had made me memorize the building plan and every escape route.

I glanced at her for confirmation, but she was no help at all. She and Abdi could have an expressionless face-off.

Except that Abdi's bored blankness had broken into open annoyance. As I turned back to argue the point, he grabbed Abbey's case from my hand and took off.

"Give her back!" I snarled, and raced after him. Had it been my wallet he'd snatched, I would have tackled him. Unfortunately, he was holding something much more precious, and I couldn't risk him dropping her. While I dithered, he dodged through a slalom course of students coming the other way and started down a flight of stairs.

Mistake. I took a deep breath and swung myself over the edge. I heard students gasping behind me, but I twisted and landed square on the bottom step, facing Abdi as he came to a halt, inches from my nose.

Okay, it was a stupid stunt. Jumping onto stairs is far more dangerous than onto flat ground, where you can easily roll to take the impact. But I'm light, and I land well, and it definitely got Abdi's attention.

I snatched Abbey away from him, cradling her tenderly. "What is *wrong* with you?"

"People are staring," he said tensely, and then walked through the door. I caught snatches of instruments being tuned.

He'd led me right to music, just as he'd said he would.

People *were* staring. "That's not *my* fault," I told Zaneisha, who had caught up with us and was resolutely avoiding eye contact.

I hoisted Abbey a little higher and stepped into the classroom. What a great start to the day.

≈ ‡ ∞

When I'd asked Koko for information about my music teacher, I'd been flooded with it. Kieran—one name—had a blunt nose, dark curls streaked with blond highlights, and an incredibly impressive record. He was a Wurundjeri man who'd been a session musician, a solo artist, a producer, a soundtrack designer, and, in semesters when he felt like it, a teacher at Elisa M, his alma mater. I couldn't imagine anyone more different from Just-Call-Me Eden. Kieran's students were all quiet and disciplined, seated in a semicircle, straight-backed on stools with table attachments.

No one would be napping in his class.

There were instruments and equipment at the back that I longed to get my hands on and at least two recording studios elsewhere in the school. Koko could do a lot of basic production for me, but a real studio was still the golden apple of the recording world.

However, I wasn't going anywhere or touching anything until Kieran let me. And right now, perched on my own stool in front of them all, I wasn't sure that he'd even let me stay in the class. Now that I'd met Kieran, I could sort of see why Abdi had obeyed his instructions instead of my wishes.

So far, under the guise of "getting to know my new student," I'd answered questions about my training (one guitar lesson a week was clearly horrifying), my practice hours (not too shabby, thank god—but I'd had to admit I hadn't really practiced since I'd woken up), and my performance credentials (apparently playing for old people's homes didn't count).

By the end of the interrogation, I was more hiding behind Abbey than holding her, and the line of sweat down my back owed very little to the warm classroom.

"Well," he said finally, "I can see we have some work to do."

I nodded, thoroughly cowed. Abdi must have been *loving* it, but I didn't dare take my eyes off Kieran to check.

"Who are your favorite musicians?"

"The Beatles," I said. "Ani DiFranco. Nina Simone. Bruce Springsteen. I like, um, Janis Joplin, Vienna Teng, Janna van der Zaag, and..."

Some of my classmates were nodding, which was a pleasant surprise. I should really have expected it—they were musicians, like me. Of course they'd be more informed than Bethari on the obscure music of the last century. But they didn't seem terribly excited by my choices.

I cast around for something from this day and age. I'd listened to some contemporary stuff and liked much of it, but it was all falling out of my head now that I was under pressure. "Um, that bhangra-punk group—what are they called? Brighton?"

"Birmingham," someone supplied.

"Right, I like them," I said. Feeling like an idiot, I retreated to familiar ground. "But the Beatles, definitely, are my all-time favorite."

Kieran nodded. "All right, Tegan. Play us something by the Beatles."

My fingers tightened on Abbey's case, appalled. Now? In front of everyone? "They don't really...I mean, they're songs, you know? It's not compositional; it'll sound weird without singing."

"Then sing."

I shook my head, pushing my voice past the lump in my throat. "I can't, not really. Backup only." I tried a weak grin.

Kieran wasn't smiling. "Music is risk, Tegan. I want you to open yourself to the possibility of failure. I'm not judging you on the quality of your performance—only on your willingness to try and your ability to access emotion."

My classmates were watching carefully, waiting for me to get over my fear and begin, so they could get a feel for who I was and what I could do. They'd decide in that moment whether I deserved to be there or if I was only at Elisa M because the government had told them to take me.

And then they'd tell the whole world what they thought. I recognized several of Soren's cronies and wondered what a good famer could do with an exposé on my talent—or lack thereof.

Abdi wasn't watching, though. He was holding his flute case on his lap and staring at a point above my head.

"Okay," I said, and pulled Abbey out of her case. She got a few raised eyebrows—she really was a beautiful guitar. I checked the tuning and snapped a capo on the seventh fret. "Okay, but I warned you."

No one seemed to recognize the tune as I picked out the first notes, which tightened my throat again right before I had to sing. So I lengthened the introduction a little bit, playing around with that bare premelody, and then gathered my courage, opened my mouth, and gave it my best shot.

It was a disaster.

I'd chosen "Here Comes the Sun" because it has a simple voice part and I knew it very well. On the other hand, the guitar part has a lot of complicated time signature changes, making it a rhythmically impressive piece. I definitely wanted to be impressive.

And in a way, it worked. My playing was fine.

But even on the simple melody, my voice cracked and warbled; I hadn't been lying about my singing. Worse, and more unforgivable, I didn't catch the feel of the song. I didn't sound like someone full of hope, at a glimpse of spring and a new beginning. I sounded exactly like a schoolgirl forced into a reluctant performance before her peers. I was mechanical and flat and soulless.

Hardly the performance of someone accessing emotion.

I was trying not to cry as I struggled through the final line of the first verse, singing that it was all right, when it most definitely wasn't. Soren's friends were flicking little glances at one another and moving their fingers surreptitiously over their computers. I absolutely couldn't cry. The humiliation would never end if I did.

In the brief moment between the first verse and the second, Abdi stood up and tucked his flute under his stool.

People gave him sideways looks, but he ignored them as stonily as he'd ignored me.

Then he squared his shoulders and sang.

His face looked mildly disgusted, as if he wasn't quite sure why he was doing it. But his voice was absolutely pure, and it filled every corner of the room with warm longing. I promptly dropped back and let him take over the melody, joining in on the chorus bits for extra volume.

We rocketed through the long bridge, my fingers hitting every shifting beat.

I still don't know if it's because Abdi was so good that he was able to anticipate my moves, or if it was because I was so desperate that I was instinctively following his cues, or something else altogether, but in the space of that bridge, we somehow achieved the kind of mind-reading synergy you get with someone you've been making music with for years. Owen and I had it. Owen and Dalmar had it. Dalmar and I didn't have it, but we would have gotten there eventually.

But Abdi and I made it happen right away. So when he nodded at me at the end of the bridge, I knew he was going to leave me on my own for the final verse.

My voice still wasn't pretty, but my singing was bright and strong, instead of faint and unemotional. I sang about ice melting and clear skies and sounded like I *meant* it.

And then Abdi picked me up for the final chorus, his

beautiful voice sliding around my creaky one. I strummed through the outro, and we were done.

It wasn't until we finished that I wondered if it had really been appropriate to choose that particular song. People here were probably happy about long winters. The sun was the enemy, not something to welcome. But the silence didn't seem angry—just faintly puzzled. And maybe a little bit awed. Soren's friends were busily tapping away, but they didn't have that air of triumph I knew to be wary of.

"Did you two work this out before class?" Kieran asked.

I shook my head.

"No," Abdi said.

"Then...all right. Thank you, Tegan." He waited a breath, and then added, "Thank you, Abdi."

That didn't sound like a teacher giving rote thanks to a student; it sounded like a fan thanking someone he admired. Which is when I remembered that Abdi hadn't sung a note in public since he'd arrived in Australia.

No matter how much money he'd been offered or how many glittering stars had requested duets, he hadn't sung for them.

But he'd sung for me.

CHAPTER EIGHT
Revolution

Three weeks before I died, Dalmar had asked me why I liked the Beatles so much.

"Best musicians of their century," I recited, as I had many times before. "And ours. And all the ones to come."

"Yeah, but *why*? You think that lots of Paul's melodies are saccharine and some of John's experiments are horrible and Ringo—"

"Ringo is perfect," I warned him. "Don't say anything about Ringo."

He grinned at me, the wide flash of teeth that always made me feel shaky and warm. Even in our garage "studio," that smile belonged to a star. "You say things about Ringo."

"I'm allowed. I love him most." I fiddled with Owen's guitar strap. "Have you seen my dopey brother?"

"He's in the kitchen, trying to get money out of your mum. There's a live gig at the Corner—"

"Oh, the pig! If he wants money, he can get out of bed and help her at the markets, like I do!"

He shrugged. "Really, why the Beatles?"

"They changed the world," I said. "And they changed themselves. I mean, there are lots of reasons I like them. They were amazing composers, and they reformed pop forever, and they gave young people a voice. But they also realized they'd made terrible mistakes, and they tried to reform themselves. Like, John, he hurt a lot of people—"

"He hit his first wife," Dalmar said. "And he cheated on her."

"Yeah. He had a lot of anger, and he took it out on people. And doing those things was bad, the sort of thing that's bad forever. You don't get to take that back; the best you can do is change yourself and never do it again." I tightened my hands on the guitar strap. "I just...I need to believe that people can change, Dalmar. The world's so horrible, and I'm scared that no one's going to care enough to do anything about it, and I really need to believe that they can." It was the first time I'd ever said it to anyone else.

"The Beatles give you hope," he said softly.

I nodded. I didn't dare look at him. "You give me hope, too," I said. "Well, you know. On your better days."

"You're not so bad yourself, Tegan Marie Mary Oglietti."

"I should never have told you my confirmation name," I said, and looked up. He was staring at me, and for a moment, I saw uncertainty in his eyes.

But that was absurd. Dalmar was never uncertain about

anything. It was one of the reasons I'd been in love with him for years, without hope or expectation.

He moved closer to me, and I felt my heart contract. "Tegan Marie Mary Oglietti," he said softly, like a prayer.

And then, of course, Owen crashed in, having scammed forty dollars off Mum, and dragged Dalmar off to the gig, while I sat in the garage and practiced until Alex turned up and we hit the old sewers for some urban exploration.

It makes me wonder, now. What if Owen hadn't come in? What if Dalmar had said what I now know he'd been planning to say right then? What if he'd kissed me, in the garage that smelled of old socks and the pine air freshener Owen loved?

We could have had three weeks, not one day. If I'd been standing a little to the left, if the sniper's aim on the Prime Minister had been better, we might have had a lifetime.

But "what if" and "might have had" have never been any real use to anyone.

Hope, though. That's still important.

≋ ‡ ∞

I didn't look at Abdi for the rest of the class—surprisingly easy, with Kieran giving me the hard word on filling in the gaps in my education. He made me take a battery of tests before he conceded that my sight-reading wasn't totally abysmal and my knowledge of musical history—up to a hundred years ago, anyway—was almost up to par. He loaded Koko with a bunch of music references to get me up to date on the last century and told me to pick two other instruments to start learning— preferably a percussion and a wind.

But there were no further hints that I didn't belong in Kieran's class. And when he let us go, Abdi and I, through unspoken agreement, lingered. Zaneisha stood near the door, doing her best impression of a human statue.

"Thank you," I said, without looking at Abdi's face, and jumped off my stool. "After I—I mean, that was really pretty cool of you."

"I don't like bullies," he said.

"Yeah, well, apparently that's just part of the deal, and I'm going to have to get used to it."

"It's not something you get used to," he said, and I looked up at him.

"About yesterday—" I said, and he made a cutting gesture with his hand.

"Bethari talked to me, about this Dalmar. Do I really look like him?"

"A little bit," I admitted. "But not a lot. I screwed up, and I'm sorry."

"He was Somali, she said. From Somalia?"

"Yes."

"I'm Somali from Djibouti," he said.

"I know," I said. "I looked you up. You're a popular guy on the tubes. Lots of information."

He smiled, then—a small, guarded smile. There were a few stubbly hairs at the corners of his lips that he must have missed shaving. I felt something tingle down my spine. *Stop thinking about his mouth, Tegan Marie.*

"But the tubes didn't tell you I liked the Beatles."

"That was a surprise," I admitted. "Are you a big fan?" *Oh god, please make him say yes.*

The smile grew. "Did John ask the Queen Mother to rattle her jewelry at the Royal Command Performance?"

I nearly collapsed with relief. The questions boiled out of me like rice from an overflowing rice cooker. "What's your favorite album? Do you listen to the solo stuff? What's your take on the Yoko question?"

"*Revolver*, some of it—not Wings—and what's the question?"

"Whether she was a scheming money-grubbing bitch who broke up the Beatles or the woman who brought John the most happiness and therefore should get credit for being the best helpmeet."

"Um," he said, eyeing me carefully. "An artist in her own right who married another artist and managed his money because he was very bad at it? The Beatles broke up because they were fighting more days than they were playing."

"That is the *right* answer," I said, and beamed at him.

He smiled back. "My turn. What's your least favorite song? Do *you* listen to the solo stuff? And how much of their work can you play?"

"'Revolution 9,' and I've listened to it all, but Ringo's All-Starr stuff is the best, and I can play nearly everything."

"Are you joking?"

"No. Some of it I need tabs for, though. Oh, we have to do

something from *Revolver* together. Can you play guitar? Your voice would be great for 'And Your Bird Can Sing.' Or 'Good Day Sunshine,' though I don't know; maybe people would want the harmonies there, and I definitely can't manage them, though Kieran's saying that with training I'll get better and—"

"I can't sing," he said, and this was so clearly a total lie that he amended it immediately. "I mean, I don't sing."

I thought about saying *I understand* or *It's up to you* or anything else that was empathetic and accommodating, but what came out of my mouth was, "Well, you're really good."

He didn't seem offended, though. "Thanks."

"Like *really* good," I said. "Why did you stop?"

"Everyone asks that." The smile was gone, his lips in a rigid line, and I was sorry I'd asked. But not too sorry to wait for the answer. "When they 'cast me singing … it was big. I don't want all that attention. They want to use it; they want to use me—"

"That I can understand," I said. "I hate it, too."

He shook his head. "Do you *know* what people say about thirdies?"

I flinched. "Yes."

"The Talented Alien thing, it's like they think they rescued me, you know? Like I should be grateful they were so *kind*. But the truth is, someone from home who can show firsters that we're not stupid and corrupt can be a spokesperson. My family … my community. It's wrong, and it's stupid, but they need someone firsters trust."

"So no singing," I said.

"No. I'm good with the flute, good enough for this class.

They can't complain. I miss singing, but I won't perform for them."

Inspiration struck. "Well, hey, do you want to come over to my place sometime? I can guarantee that no one's going to get through the door that my security team doesn't want there. I don't have Ringo's stuff—I couldn't afford it—but I have the Beatles collection. And maybe Bethari could come. I'm trying to teach her—"

"I can't be friends with you in public."

The flat statement hit me in the stomach. "I see."

His light eyes were rueful. "You're a big deal. You attract a lot of attention. And as soon as someone sees me going to your house, or getting into a car with you, or something like that, it'll be very public." He hesitated. "But we could be friends privately, perhaps."

"Like some sort of secret friendship affair?" I said.

He winced. "That sounds bad, doesn't it?"

"Little bit," I said. "Okay. You don't want to do public. Well, sure, I get it, but I'm not going to do private. I've got my principles, too." *And my pride*, I nearly said. Far too much pride to let him know that he'd hurt me.

It was really petty to feel bitter about someone deliberately avoiding the kind of attention I found so difficult to deal with. But I'm really petty sometimes.

Bethari, bless her, chose that moment to call me.

"I'm on the roof!" she said in my ear. There was a small pause that I chose to read as significant. "We can talk."

Right. Secret projects and a man bleeding out in a church

should definitely demand more of my attention than a smart, cute, talented guy who didn't want to be seen with me in public.

"See you in class," I said, and swept out the door, Abbey held proudly in my arms.

≈ ‡ ∞

The main building's rooftop was a garden run by the first-year students; Elisa M put it in all its publicity materials. I'd scoffed at the pictures; from my experience with similar programs back home, I'd expected it to be a scrubby thing with shallow, unfilled holes and empty chip packages blowing around dying trees.

But this looked exactly like the tubes had said it did. Soft fake grass on the walkways and lounging patches, but in the beds, real grasses and shrubs, so much green massed together that it made me gasp. There were paper daisy bushes, just beginning to bloom pink and yellow and white. There were snow gums, genetically modified to grow in this heat, and water gums and two long rows of tall Illawarra flame trees covered in hectic crimson blossoms. Most of the plants were natives, I thought, hardy and water-conservative, but I spotted a couple of lemon trees laden with fruit, and I could smell something that hinted at an herb patch farther on.

The whole thing was all watered with the school's gray water and grown in compost mixed from food scraps and humanure.

And in the middle of all that color waited Bethari, wearing a long gray dress, a purple-and-gold headscarf, and gold sandals.

She was also wearing a huge grin.

"You heard," I said. It wasn't a question.

"The news is *everywhere*," Bethari said. "All over the tubes. Big music nodes, news sources . . . you have *no* idea. Abdi Taalib sings with Tegan Oglietti. All witnesses agree it was an amazing performance. Is there a significance in choosing a song from her era? Will they form a band? Can she make him sing again? Will they get together, go back to Djibouti when his visa runs out, and have eighty zillion babies?"

"The Beatles aren't from my era," I said. "Not even the same millennium."

Bethari ignored this petty detail. "And here I am," she said. "In the center of the storm, and I can't say a *word*."

"Not one," I said. "And that's why you get the good oil. Yes, he sang. Yes, he's amazingly good. No to the band, no to singing again, and definitely no to the babies."

"They'd be very cute babies," she said. "Don't you think so, Zaneisha?"

"I have no opinion on babies," Zaneisha told her. "Tegan, please stay under the shaded area."

"You'll burn like toast," Bethari said cheerfully, and tugged me over to a bench under an Illawarra flame tree. Zaneisha stayed by the entrance—out of earshot, if we kept our voices down.

"I think she's worried about another Inheritor turning up," I

139

said. "Or maybe Carl Hurfest hiring a jet pack to get more shots of me."

"Jet-pack fuel is very expensive. He's settling for showing that 'interview' with you over and over again, with additional commentary from music sources."

"I *hate* him."

"About the Inheritor who died... do you want to talk about him?"

Of course I did. But Bethari's chin moved left and right, and I followed her cue. "Not really."

"Oh, good, because I came up with the perfect distraction! Let's talk about Dalmar."

I was trying not to show my confusion, but it was difficult. "There's not much more to tell."

"Don't be shy. No one can hear us." She winked and took her hand out of her pocket. There was a small object blinking a steady green in her palm. "Surveillance interference," Bethari said, tone switching from wheedling confidence to crisp and businesslike. "I borrowed it from Mami, so I'm sure it works, but if they *are* listening, we'll only get away with the 'but we wanted to talk about sexy times in private' excuse once. What's going on? And where's my computer?"

"I broke it," I said. "Do you have a spare?"

"Yes, but—wait, you *what*?"

"Sorry. It seemed like the best idea at the time."

Bethari opened her mouth, snapped it shut again, and folded her hands deliberately in front of her. "Start from the beginning," she suggested. "And don't miss a single detail. I am *very* interested in how you came to that conclusion."

I told her everything.

By the time I was done, she was looking more interested than angry, a frown creasing her forehead.

"It's a shaky lead. All you have is a name and an address."

"And a dead man," I reminded her. "I'm pretty sure Gregor killed him just to shut him up about the Ark Project."

"That's a little more substantive," she conceded. "And when you think about it, it is strange that they brought *you* back. Even if they're having trouble finding the right kinds of bodies, wouldn't it make more sense to practice on more modern patients first? I mean, I like you a lot, but you didn't exactly come equipped to handle this century."

I shrugged. "Apparently, most people donating their bodies to science these days specify that they don't want to be used for revival research. They want the bits to be used right away, I guess. And of course people who do want to be revived want to belong to themselves after revival."

"So you think they used you because your donation form was so vague, they could hold on to you afterward?"

"I'm sure that's part of it," I said. "But the Inheritor implied this Ark Project has something to do with me."

"And how did *he* find out?" Bethari said. "And why do they even care?"

"Exactly." I tapped my fingers on my knees. "I have a lot of questions."

Bethari spread her hands. "Okay. I guess I forgive you for smashing my computer. Even though I had just updated my contacts and archives."

"I'm sorry," I said humbly. "Aren't they backed up on your house computer?"

"Well, yes. But some of my apps aren't, because they are the kinds of things that might make Mami ask questions. I'll have to re-create them. So, when are we visiting this mysterious address?"

"We?" I asked. "Bethari, look, your mother's military. Are you sure you really want to risk—"

She rolled her eyes. "Come on, Tegan. I'm a journalist hacker. You don't really think I'm going to let you have all the fun yourself?"

I laughed. "I guess not."

"Good. Your bodyguards and the surveillance across the road might be a problem, though. I've never tried to evade people paid to watch me, and your place doesn't exactly have a lot of escape routes."

My brain was ticking over. "You live in Williamstown, right? Do you have an underground house?"

"I wish."

"No, that's good. I assume friends in the future still stay over at each other's houses from time to time?"

"Sure."

"Okay. It's Friday night. I beg Marie for permission to stay at your house, she says yes, the bodyguards stay outside, and we climb out the window."

"I deactivate the security system, set a program to trip the motion sensors once in a while so it looks as if we're still there, and *then* we climb out the window," Bethari corrected. "You've done this before?"

"Alex and I did it all the time. She had a lock-out curfew at the foster home, so she'd sleep over with me, and we'd sneak out together once Mum was asleep."

"I think I would have liked your Alex."

"I think you would have, too," I said, and felt my throat close up. Bethari patted my shoulder and let me pull myself together.

"Are we done with the stuff we don't want to talk about publicly?" she asked after a few moments.

"Yeah, I think so."

Her hand twisted, and the green blinking light went out. "Really?" she said innocently. "In a fountain? That had real water in it? Tell me more about the strange wastefulness of your past-timer sexual practices."

"You're so gross," I said, and Koko beeped to let me know I had an incoming message.

It was from Abdi. The message itself was blank, with not even a subject line. But he'd attached every single piece by Ringo and his All-Starr band. All the songs I hadn't been able to afford.

I sat there, staring at the list.

"Why are you smiling?" Bethari asked.

I shoved Koko back in my pocket. "No reason," I said. "I didn't know I was."

≋ ‡ ∞

Marie was delighted when I proposed the sleepover. I could see her ticking off boxes in her head—Subject Engages in Voluntary Social Behavior after Witnessing Potentially Traumatic Violence—but she was also giddy with excitement on my behalf. She dropped extra money into my account for game purchases and added a ton of suitably unhealthy snacks to our shopping delivery.

Colonel Dawson was less pleased.

"Unacceptable," he said, standing in the kitchen with his arms crossed. He'd arrived just as I was packing. Apparently this kind of outrageous behavior required a personal visit.

"I've given my consent, Colonel," Marie said mildly.

"The security risks alone—"

"Tegan will be escorted there and back. Bethari's mother is more than capable of providing on-the-spot defense should it prove necessary, and it's hardly as if we're going to announce Tegan's location on the tubes. She'll probably be safer there than in this house."

"I should have been consulted ahead of time," he insisted. "You decided this afternoon! Sergeant Washington and Master Sergeant Petrov have to initialize a surveillance base with almost no notice."

"I think it's time we clarified something, Trevor," Marie told him. "I am Tegan's legal guardian. I decide what's in her best interest. I have agreed to some security measures because I'm concerned about her safety, but I am not going to unnecessarily restrict her movements. If she wants to stay one night with a friend of whom I approve, then she can."

Hidden behind the slightly open kitchen door and spying

through the gap, I pumped my fist in the air and narrowly avoided skinning my knuckles on the wall.

"Marie, Tegan remains the only subject who can tell us about experiencing the aftermath of the revival process. She's an extremely valuable—"

"—sixteen-year-old girl," Marie said over him. "Who should be allowed some of the freedoms she enjoyed before her traumatic and untimely death."

Dawson shook his head. "I thought you believed in the vital importance of this project, Dr. Carmen."

"I thought you were above such an obvious attempt at emotional manipulation, Colonel Dawson."

Whoa. Go Marie.

"I think this conversation is over," she continued. "We both have work to do."

The worst thing was that I couldn't see Dawson's face. I had a feeling the picture would have kept me warm on cold nights. If cold nights existed anymore.

≈ ‡ ∞

Gregor and Zaneisha were still exchanging put-upon glances as they escorted me to Bethari's front door. She met me with squeals and ushered me into the living room.

"Mami, this is Tegan Oglietti."

Bethari's mother was a round, sturdy woman with an amused glint in her black eyes. She was still in her uniform and khaki headscarf, obviously having just gotten home from work.

"Thank you for having me, Captain Miyahputri," I said, and handed over the fruit basket Marie had pushed into my hands as I went out the door. "Dr. Carmen says hello."

"You're very welcome, Tegan. Sergeant, Master Sergeant, would you like a drink?"

"No, thank you, Captain."

"Where will you guys stay?" I asked.

Gregor grunted.

"Outside," Zaneisha said. "Are you sure you—"

"Yep."

"You can signal us on your EarRing. At any time. For any reason, if you notice anything strange—"

"What about when I go to sleep? I've never worn earrings to bed before."

"Learn," Gregor said.

Zaneisha scanned the hallway, the ceiling, the floor, and then looked straight at me. "Our martial arts training has been delayed twice," she said. "We are starting tomorrow."

I ignored the way it was phrased as a threat and beamed at her. "That sounds fun."

Bethari was bouncing impatiently. "Come on, Teeg, let's go upstairs!"

"Okay. Bye, guys! Have a good night!"

Bethari laughed as we went up. "That was mean."

I shrugged as Bethari opened her door. "Not my fault they have to stay up all night keeping watch from the car."

"Actually, it kind of is," Joph said. She was sitting cross-legged on the bed. "Geya, Teeg."

I looked at her. Then at Bethari. "Um?"

"Joph's going to stay here and move around. And cover for us, if necessary."

I gave up and sat on the floor. "Cool. Thanks, Joph."

"I did some research into past-time sleepovers," Joph said. "Do we really have to braid each other's hair?"

"I have the only hair long enough for braiding, so let's not bother," Bethari said, unwinding her headscarf. Long black waves tumbled down her back. "Mami's not going to bed for a while, and I have prayer in a bit, so we may as well have some fun while we wait. Anyone got good games? I want to kill some zombies."

≋ ‡ ∞

A few hundred dead zombies later, we were on our way. Bethari had dark clothes for both of us, and I rubbed her dark purple eye shadow all over my face to prevent my white skin from flashing.

"You look ridiculous," she whispered.

"No one's going to see me," I pointed out, my voice just as quiet. "At least, I hope not. You know what to do, Joph?"

Joph yawned. "Keeping watch isn't that complicated. I'll call Bethi if anything goes wrong. Give me your phone."

"Why?" I asked, taking the EarRing out.

"They can probably track you with it," she said. "My parents tried that all the time when I was a ween, until Bethi showed me how to disable it."

"Won't they know if we turn it off?"

"Probably. So I'll just wear it." Joph slipped the phone into the piercing on her other ear. "There. Have fun!"

Bethari's eyes were glued to her replacement computer. "The security screen's going down...now."

I wrenched open the window and started down the trellis, hugging the wall. A few decades earlier, it had probably held roses. But the roses were gone, and what remained was a convenient exit route.

Bethari, for all her apparent skill with digital crime, didn't seem to be experienced at this kind of subterfuge. When we hit the bottom, she started giggling.

"Shhhh," I hissed, and hustled her toward the back wall.

She boosted me up, hands steady under my feet, and then I helped yank her up and over. She landed as lightly as I did on the other side. Cheerleading obviously lent itself well to breaking and entering.

The address was a warehouse in an industrial area, a forty-minute walk from Bethari's house. I made Bethari stop jogging as soon as we were out of the immediate range of her house. It was strange not to have streetlights; they were probably considered a waste of energy.

"People notice runners," I said. "We walk from here."

Bethari made a face of mock terror. "I don't know if my nerves can take it."

"Some fearless journo you are."

"Speaking of! I have a lead on a story, and it's a good one. Did

148

you know that poorer countries get charged prices that they can't afford for patented medicines?"

"Sure. That happened in my time, too."

"Well, it's still happening, and it's, what do you call it? Totally crapular?"

"Craptacular?"

"I love your slang. Yes. Things like Travis Fuller Syndrome and Maldonado Disease kill a lot of people, but they're easy to treat—*if* you have the right drugs. One course of Serbolax will completely cure Travis Fuller, but it costs about twelve hundred dollars."

It took a second, but I converted that to about sixty dollars in my time, or way out of reach for your average person below the world poverty line. "And they don't discount, of course." I was watching the few passing cars. Nobody seemed to be paying any attention to us.

"No. And because they're protecting their patents and the vast amounts of money they can make on them, they don't let anyone make generic, low-cost versions. But people are anyway. They're stealing or reverse-engineering the formula and smuggling in the drugs, or making them right in the countries that need them most."

"Isn't that dangerous? Taking homemade or smuggled medicines?"

"Not as dangerous as spewing up your lungs," Bethari said bluntly. "Travis Fuller is *awful*. Anyway, today my sources confirmed that there are chemists making the medicines in

Melbourne, and I have a lead on a customs officer who lets things slide through. I want to do an in-depth series, talking about why people take these risks, and how the pharma companies are losing their grip on the market."

"Uh-huh," I said, scanning the street for watchers on foot.

"Poor regional governments aren't even bothering to ask them for help anymore; they talk to the smugglers instead. So, of course, the companies are pressuring *their* governments—including ours—to introduce more sanctions and tougher penalties for home chemists who make patented drugs, and—am I boring you?"

"No. This is it." I leaned casually against the wall and jumped when it stung me.

"Hint about the future," Bethari said. "Don't touch private property unless you have a handy friend with a good computer. Though not as good as her former, and much mourned, *other* computer. Let's go around the side."

The gap between two walled yards was barely wide enough to qualify as an alley, and we had to feel our way down the walls as feral cats hissed at us.

Bethari stuck her tongue between her teeth, made me hold her computer, and got to work. In the light of the screen, her fingers gleamed as they moved through minute, intricate gestures.

I suddenly missed Koko, who had also stayed behind with Joph.

"They don't have much security," Bethari murmured. "Okay. Located the closed-circuit camera controls. Just need to branch the broadcast to . . . huh."

"What?"

"Teeg, I hate to say it, but you might have the wrong address."

I turned her computer around to stare at the footage of the warehouse interior.

It was empty.

CHAPTER NINE
We Can Work It Out

"This was definitely the place," I said, staring at the screen. It was showing night-vision pictures of a bare asphalt parking lot, dusty offices upstairs, and a huge, concrete floor decorated by only a few big scrap-metal bins—also empty.

"Well, there's nothing in there now. And the security's totally minimal. It's not what I'd expect to see at a secret facility."

"Could it be some sort of loop? Could the cameras be showing us fake footage when there's actually a whole ton of animals in there?"

"Animals?"

"It's called the Ark Project," I said. "My money's on illegal animal testing of cryonic treatments, but I'm trying to keep an open mind."

"I was thinking a gene bank of extinct animals that they're exploiting for genengineered soldiers, but I might watch too many movies," Bethari said. "To answer your question, no, there's no loop; I'd know. What we're seeing is the actual footage."

"Why would there be surveillance cameras on an empty building?"

"To keep out squatters? I don't know. It obviously belongs to someone. They might just check the feed every now and then."

"I want to go inside."

"Hacking the locks will be more difficult," she said. "I'm not sure that—"

"Shhh!" I could hear the distinctive rumble of a truck approaching. The cats set up their screeching again, and we moved deeper into the alley.

Even back that far, we could hear the gates open.

"Tegan," Bethari whispered. "Look!"

On the screen, the footage of the parking lot showed the gates opening and the truck driving in. The picture on the side of the truck declared it a humanure collector.

"This is *not* a compost-treatment plant," Bethari said.

"Holy crap," I said as a man swung himself out of the passenger seat and dropped to the ground. "Bethari, can you get a close-up?"

She fiddled her fingers in the air. The camera zoomed in on the man's face. I hissed.

"Do you know him?"

"That's Colonel Trevor Dawson," I said. "My keeper. And head of Operation New Beginning."

"He's not in uniform."

Those loose overalls were definitely not approved army wear.

"Wait, what's that?" I said.

Something was happening in the warehouse. One of the scrap-metal bins was moving by itself, rolling away to reveal a large metallic rectangle set securely into the floor.

"A trapdoor?" Bethari said incredulously.

The rectangle rose. It was actually the top of an elevator, about the size of my underground bedroom, but we could see only the metallic back.

"The angle," I said urgently.

"I'm trying, I'm trying. Okay, another camera in the corner… there."

Two large containers were wheeled out of the elevator and into the yard, escorted by four people in equally nondescript black clothing. Dawson had opened the back of the truck and was saying something to one of the escorts, a tall woman with short brown curls.

"Can we get audio?"

"Um, if the cameras have mics, I can try a subroutine.…" She did more magic with her fingers, but Dawson had stopped speaking. The only sounds were the grunts of the escorts and the scrape of the containers as they were gently slid into the back of the truck.

"What the hell is in there?" I wondered.

"I would give all my teeth to know."

Dawson nodded at the escorts, and they all straightened, saluting.

"Dismissed," he said, his voice small and tinny.

"They're all army," Bethari said, sounding distressed.

"We knew they probably would be," I said.

"I know. It's just hard."

We glanced at each other, two army brats in perfect accord. It was uncomfortable to think that our protectors—our families—were up to something secret, and maybe no good.

We were both quiet as the truck rumbled past our hiding place again. The other soldiers went back into the warehouse, and Bethari was watching intently as the curly-haired woman walked to the elevator.

"Black shoe alligator glue," the woman said, her voice clear, and Bethari stabbed the air with one finger. "Password recorded," she said. "Might be useful."

"We are not storming an army installation," I said firmly. "We'll have to lure them out before we can sneak in."

"Definitely," Bethari said. "Let's go home and think about how."

≈ ‡ ∞

We broke back into Bethari's house as uneventfully as we'd broken out.

"Oh, thank goodness," Joph said, sitting up from her mattress on the floor, as I climbed through the window.

I expected her next words to be, *What did you find?*

Instead, she yawned, stretched, and said, "I *really* want to go to the bathroom."

I blinked as she ambled out the door into the hallway. "She's really not very curious, huh?"

"She used to be different," Bethari said, handing me some wipes for my eye-shadow-covered face before getting into her pajamas. "But even now, if you were a new serotonin-producing formula, the questions would never stop."

I laughed and rubbed at my face, watching the purple smudges disappear from the smooth material. "How do these work?"

"I don't know," she said, sounding distracted. "Look. I'm not sure how to put this. So I'll just ask. Are you sure you're straight?"

My chin jerked up. She was sitting on the edge of the bed and swinging her feet. Her head was tilted at the ceiling, as if my answer was the least important thing in the world.

"Yes," I said. "I've never—yeah."

She looked at me for a long, searching moment and nodded. "Oh, well," she said. "It'd never work, anyway. I'm too bossy, and you're too stubborn."

"Plus, we don't screw the crew," I reminded her.

"Except for you and Abdi and your eighty gazillion babies."

"Not happening."

"*Oh, Abdi, your beautiful voice, like a chorus of heavenly messengers—*"

I knew she was just teasing, but I couldn't help the bitterness from seeping into my voice. "Actually, no. He doesn't even want to be friends in public."

"Wait," she said. "Wait, *what*?"

"What?" Joph echoed from the door. "He likes you. He sent you those songs."

"How do you know about that?" I demanded.

"*What* songs?" Bethari said over me. "Have you two been keeping secrets?"

"Not really," I protested. "Just that… after music today, Abdi and me talked a bit."

"Did you, now?" Bethari was sitting upright.

I sighed and told them both about our conversation. "I don't think anyone saw us," I said when I'd finished.

"I know they didn't, or it would be everywhere," Bethari said. "And what's this about songs?" she asked Joph.

"Teeg likes the Beatles. And that drummer who had his own band. Abdi found those songs for her."

"Ringo Starr and His All-Starr Band," I said. "Not *that* drummer, Joph. *The* drummer, yes."

She nodded peacefully. "He didn't have enough to buy them all, so I helped him find the free versions."

"I didn't know you two even knew each other," Bethari said. She was looking more than slightly disgruntled.

"He's smart," Joph said. "I like him. Don't you think he's pretty, Teeg?"

"He's all right," I said, remembering those light eyes looking into mine as we'd made music.

"Oh, I see," Bethari said, looking insufferably smug.

"You have to remember that two months ago I was in love with Dalmar," I added, and then wondered about the past tense. I still loved Dalmar, didn't I? I'd loved him for years when he didn't love me, when I'd thought that he never would. Surely little things like him growing up, having a family, and being dead didn't change that. "Besides, shouldn't we really be talking about—"

I was interrupted by a knock on the door. I was still wearing my stealth clothes so I yanked a sheet up over myself just before Captain Miyahputri poked her head in, hair tousled around her face.

"Girls, you woke me up," she said. "Could you *please* go to sleep and save the gossip for the morning? Later in the morning, I should say."

"Yes, Mami."

"Sorry, Captain Miyahputri."

Bethari slipped out to wash up before sleep, and Joph ordered the lights off.

I pulled on a tank top and sleep shorts in the dark—shoving the incriminating clothing under Bethari's bed—and lay down on my mattress. It shifted around me, redistributing my weight to provide lumbar support.

I stared at Bethari's ceiling. I was expecting to stay awake for a long time, worrying about what could be concealed underneath that warehouse, and what it had to do with me. And I might possibly devote a tiny, insignificant amount of time to what Abdi had meant by the gift of those songs.

But it felt like only a second later when Bethari shook me awake, her golden headscarf gleaming in the sunlight streaming through the gap in her heavy curtains. "Colonel Dawson is here," she said, looking nearly as scared as I felt. "He wants you to go home."

I spent as long as I could getting dressed and packing my bag, trying to calm down. Dawson wasn't a mind reader, but he also wasn't an idiot, and I couldn't afford to give anything away.

While I cleaned my teeth—very slowly—I decided that I should act just like a girl who'd had a slumber party interrupted.

Surly, sleep-deprived, and uncooperative.

So I stomped down the stairs, offered Captain Miyahputri polite but brief thanks, and scowled my way out the door before Dawson could do more than offer me morning greetings.

I slouched in the backseat of the big black car, then glared at Dawson when he joined me.

"What?" I demanded.

"I'm sorry to interrupt your visit," he said. "Did you enjoy yourself?"

"It was okay," I conceded. "Would have been better if I could have stayed for the end. Joph was going to make pancakes."

Zaneisha was driving. I relaxed a little when we swept past the turnoff that led to the army base.

"The fact is, Tegan, an excellent opportunity has arisen. We have a wonderful chance to get your story to the world."

"How do you mean?"

"We've arranged an interview for you with one of Australia's most-watched tubecasters. We go live next Thursday." He smiled in apparently genuine excitement.

My first reaction was relief that he wasn't taking me to some interrogation room to have a long conversation about breaking into hidden databases and trespassing on government property.

My second reaction was pure horror.

"I can't do that!" I said.

Dawson ignored me. "We've had hundreds of offers, of course, but we wanted to be very selective, especially for the first official interview. Your public-approval rating is very high, you know. You make an appealing face for Operation New Beginning." He made a wry face. "The truth is, Tegan, we can feed people all the facts we want, but until you personalize a situation for them, they usually don't care. You personalize revival."

"I don't want to do an interview."

His gray eyes glinted steel. "Now, Tegan, you'll recall that you did agree to make yourself available for supervised media contact."

"But I don't know how," I wailed. "Look what a mess I made with Carl Hurfest before! And I was an idiot in class, twice on my first day! I'll say something stupid, and people will hate me!"

He actually patted my hand as we pulled up outside Marie's place. "We'll take care of that, Tegan. It will all be fine." He jumped out, and I scrambled after him.

Marie was standing in the kitchen, pouring tea into a mug for another woman.

Dawson beckoned me in. "We've hired the best media specialist in the business, Tegan. Meet Tatia."

I stared at the strange woman, and then at Marie, who shook her head ruefully.

Oh, just hell.

≈ ‡ ∞

Tatia was short and plump, and her skin was pale and glowing— I mean, she was actually glowing, an effect achieved through the microwires in her long, flowing gown. Her lips were painted black; her eyes were fitted with purple contacts; her eyebrows were covered in something that looked like silver tinfoil; she wore wrist-length lacy, glittery gloves; and her tight black curls were locked in place, refusing to move even when she bounced to her feet.

"Hello!" she perked at me. "Delighted to meet you, chicken. Let's feed the eyes."

She circled me, making a complete scan of my body. Instinctively, I crossed my arms over my boobs, and she tutted and pulled them down. When she was finished, she tapped a sparkling lacy finger to her lips. "Bones are good; skin needs some work; breasts a little spoffy, but don't worry, there are plenty of designers who owe me giggles—we'll find something! Shame about the lack of height. Now the hair—the hair is feral. Disaster, Teeg!"

"Tegan has been concentrating on her studies," Marie put in. "And on adjusting to unfamiliar circumstances."

Tatia shot her a dark look, then waved her hand. "Of course, marvelous, she's making a fantasmical effort to assimilate. I can certainly do something with that. But we must always make time for style. I wonder, could Teeg and I speak alone?"

"I—" Marie started.

"Of course," Dawson said. "Why don't you both go talk in her room?"

Marie shook her head slightly, but her eyes were resigned. "I'll be right up here if you need anything," she promised me.

Tatia dragged me off as I tried to mentally convey that what I needed was a device to teleport me far away from this situation. Surely they had that kind of thing in the future.

Tatia was unimpressed by my bedroom decorations. "All these old, battered buildings!" she exclaimed. "Not quite the giggle, chicken."

"I like them."

"Of course, Teeg, of course. You prefer Teeg, don't you? Viewers love a nickname; it makes them feel more connected. We'll use Teeg. That Living Dead Girl catch must go. Carl was such a gerty boy to flash it! Well, now we've a chance to ruffle his lemons, don't we?"

I stared at her, and not just because she was using so much slang, I couldn't entirely understand what she was saying. It was the way she'd inspected me, then my room, as if everything she saw were a flawed piece of furniture she needed to reupholster and polish.

"Teeg's mostly for family and friends. I think I'd prefer Tegan or Ms. Oglietti."

"Teeg is better," she said, her face flashing steel beneath the sparkle, so fast I barely saw it. I felt the effect, though; it was just like misjudging a jump and catching a rail with my stomach instead of flying over it. Except I was prepared for that possibility when I tried to jump a rail, and not when a pretty, polished woman kicked me in the gut with a three-word phrase and a smile.

She didn't pause to see if I had further objections; she was off again, talking about skin care and depilatory wands and a million other things I couldn't care less about. It all washed over me, until I heard "speaking skills."

"I don't have any," I told her.

"Oh, I'll teach you all the razzle. We'll rehearse the questions, your answers, and any possible surprises. I don't think Carl Hurfest will toss you a real badger, but you can't ever be certain with him, naughty boy."

"Wait, *Hurfest* is doing the interview?"

Tatia smiled. "Of course. Who better?"

"Anyone!"

She waved the objection away as if it were an irritating blowfly. "He's sent the questions; your replies are on your computer now. Today you'll memorize them; tomorrow you'll—"

"Hey," I said. "*Hey.* You wrote my answers?"

"The army wrote them; I refined them." She laughed, a tinkling, pretty sound. "You don't think we'd just throw you to the sharks, Teeg? No, no, I'll do all the work, I promise. You just have to repeat what I tell you."

"But Hurfest—"

"It has to be Carl, Teeg. He's famous, actually quite good at what he does, and irritatingly incorruptible. But most important, he ambushed you and aired it, and now he'll make public amends. That will silence any number of objections to the operation."

"No."

She smiled, sat down at my desk, and pointed to my bed. "Let's go over the questions now."

"No," I said, louder. "I don't want to be a prop. I don't want to be *publicity*."

Tatia didn't look angry at my defiance. She looked amused, which was much, much worse. "Darling, you can hold your breath until you turn blue, but I'm not going to dodge the whippet. You'll do it my way, or no way. I don't care how stubborn you are. I earn a truly staggering amount regardless of your tantrums. But if you walk into that interview unprepared, Carl Hurfest will eat your risen carcass like the nasty little scavenger he is. And if you don't turn up at all, your face will be utterly broken. Smashed beyond repair. He's probably hoping you won't show, in fact; he can spin news out of that for days."

I didn't move. I barely breathed.

Tatia leaned forward, smile just as slick but, I thought, a little warmer. "Or you can listen to me and beat him. I'd be happy to help you do that because between you and me, I have as much love for that man as I do for a malaria-ridden mosquito." She leaned back again and looked elaborately unconcerned. "However, as I said, either way, I get paid."

I *knew* I was being manipulated, but I still couldn't help grasping for the carrot she offered me. "I can really beat him?"

"Teeg, my chicken, we'll dust him dry."

I had no idea what that meant exactly, but the context was clear. If I listened to Tatia, I could get some measure of revenge on Carl Hurfest. And another benefit had occurred to me: Cooperating with Tatia would show Dawson I was being a good girl, and certainly not someone who would sneak out of a slumber party, go hunting for the Ark Project at an address I'd hacked with Bethari's computer, and then personally witness him up to something definitely dodgy.

I needed to fend off any suspicions he might have to buy time for Bethari and me to find out what was going on.

So I said yes.

≈ ‡ ∞

Okay. Abdi's telling me that we need to move. He's pretty sure they're close to tracing our current location, and we need to get to Place B well before they hit the streets.

I'd like to give a big hello to those of our searchers who are watching this 'cast. Enjoying the show? *I* am.

I know you'll catch us eventually.

But I *will* finish my story first.

CHAPTER TEN
Eight Days a Week

Okay. Hi again.

Sorry about the lighting; Abdi rigged it as well as he could, but we can't take too much power from the grid, and we don't want to give away too many details of our surroundings.

If I wriggle around a bit, it's because I'm sitting in the water dripping off my clothes. It's still storming out there, and the bike helmets did almost nothing to protect us from the rain, though they were pretty damn good at warding off the hail. Abdi got beaned by one big piece that went through an air slit. He's okay; it's bleeding a lot, but the cut's shallow.

The lightning was really scary, but the big danger was not being able to see through the rain. Still, if we couldn't see very well, then no one could see us, either.

Actually, I take it back. I just caught a glimpse of myself in my computer's reflection, and I am not at all sorry that the lighting is so dim. I look like a drowned rat.

Where was I? Oh, right. I said yes to the interview.

≈ ‡ ∞

And so began five days of torment.

It wasn't enough just to memorize the answers they wanted me to give, of course. Oh no, I couldn't be allowed to do something that simple. I had to practice the answers, over and over, until they sounded natural, which was not easy when I had to hit every pause, every glance and smile and solemn nod, right on cue.

Then I had to practice what Tatia called the "impro trees." If Hurfest altered the wording or sneaked in extra questions, I had to be prepared. "No comment" was all right when being accosted by reporters; it was unacceptable when I was participating in an interview I'd agreed to, because it showed I had something to hide.

I've already said that I'm not a good liar. All the prepared answers were technically true—I think Dawson made sure of that—but the gestures and timing and expression practice made it feel uncomfortably like lying, which meant that it took me ages to get it right. And some of Tatia's suggestions for impro trees were downright fabrication.

"But I *did* eat meat," I told her.

"My little butterfly, you cannot—oh, all right, say that yes, you did, and now you deeply regret it, all right? You understand that you were the product of a terrible Earth-hating culture."

"Do you know what's going on?" I demanded. "Rich nations

have been dumping radioactive waste off the shores of Africa for decades, and they're still doing it! Talk about Earth-hating."

Tatia shook her head, looking like a disappointed cherub. "Teeg, my sweet, number one: Who cares? And number two: What is our first rule?"

"Don't lose my temper," I said.

"Don't lose your temper," she repeated, nodding at me. Her eyebrows were metallic blue today, and they flashed as she turned her computer to the next impro tree. "Now, if you're asked about Abdi Taalib..."

I twitched.

"...bench him."

"I have no idea what that means."

She fluttered her tiny glittery hands at me impatiently. "Say that he's your classmate, and you respect his musical accomplishments, but you're not friends. The last thing we need is you being associated with a thirdie."

"We're *not* friends," I told her.

"Less defiant, more dismissive," she said. "As if the thought had never crossed your adorable resurrected brain."

I rolled my eyes, and we moved on to the next possibility.

≈ ‡ ∞

The advertising for the upcoming interview began before I'd even agreed to it, and the famers were flocking like flies to a carcass. Soren was trying to get me to go to a party. Any party. He'd sent three messages to Koko on the weekend, and on Monday he waited in the hall, catching me before I could even get to class.

"Banger at my place next Saturday," he announced. "You'll come, won't you, Teeg?" Then he did a double take. "You look great!"

After a weekend of endless criticism and nitpicking, I was not feeling my best. But Tatia had wasted no time in overhauling my style, and I did look much better. My hair had been trimmed, my clothes had been replaced, and a huge array of makeup—most of which I'd managed to ignore—had been purchased for my use.

I was wearing a retro silver jumpsuit with blue highlights, and platform wedges to disguise my shocking lack of height. Tatia had tried me in heels, but after the third time I'd deliberately fallen out of them, she'd given up and gone for thick soles instead.

"Thanks," I said, and glanced at Zaneisha, who moved forward, forcing Soren to back into the classroom. Undeterred, he followed me to my chair, where Bethari and Joph were already waiting in the seats on either side.

"It'll be a dazzler," he said, hitching one hip casually onto my desk. "I always supply the best stuff, don't I, Joph?"

"I don't supply you anymore, Soren," Joph said. "Last time you gave my breathers to fourteen-year-olds."

"What's the difference?"

"The age limits aren't just there to make parents feel good," she said with as much bite in her voice as I'd ever heard her manage. Bethari shot her a startled look. "There are important differences in hormone loads and brain chemistry. Those boys could have gotten very sick."

"Oh. I didn't know that."

"You should have. It's on every label."

"Will you supply me again?" he said hopefully. "You make the best."

She pursed her lips, noticed Bethari staring, and gave him a vague smile. "Oooh, I'll think about it."

"You'll come, won't you, Teeg? Bethi and Joph, too, of course."

I looked at Bethari, who shrugged. Soren was at least open about my fame being my main attraction. I was going to be in this world for the rest of my life; I'd better start learning how to work it.

"I'm a little busy right now," I said, and tried a smile.

He looked hopeful. "But later?"

"I'll see what I can do," I promised.

Abdi came in then, and I couldn't help the way my eyes darted to him. Soren noticed it, too.

"And Abdi," he assured me, and called across the room, "Hey, Abdi, come to my party on Saturday." He dropped one hand onto my shoulder. "Teeg's coming."

Abdi looked up and saw Soren draped all over me. Something flashed in his face before it returned to his normal polite blankness. "No. Thank you."

Soren rolled his eyes. "Aw, come on, you can climb out of your shell for one night. We're okay with thirdies, aren't we, Teeg?" His hand squeezed my shoulder.

Abdi said nothing, and Soren's voice got louder. "We'd have

to hose you off before you walked in, though. All that thirdie pollution might stink up the place." His gang giggled.

"Get off me," I snapped, and tried to shrug away from Soren's grip.

His hand followed my motion. "Just a bit of fun, Teeg. Thirdie dirt grinds in, you know?"

"It's not funny, Soren. Let go!"

Zaneisha was clearly wondering whether it was time to take steps, but Abdi didn't hesitate, closing the distance between us. "Tegan said let go," he said softly.

Soren took his hand away with exaggerated care. "Like that, is it? Makes sense. Thirdie loves freezie. Why don't you take her home to your seventeen brothers and sisters? You can show her your mud hut and—"

Abdi was fast, but Zaneisha was much faster, deflecting the punch he aimed at Soren and trapping his arm. "Take a walk," she suggested, her voice calm. "If you fight in here, someone could get hurt."

He closed his eyes and nodded. Zaneisha let him go, and I shot to my feet and followed him out the door.

"Hey," I called, but he gave no sign of hesitating. I jogged after him through the thankfully empty halls. "Don't make me chase you down," I said. "You know I can do it."

Abdi stopped. "Go back to your famer friend," he said without turning around. "He can help you with your interview."

"That asshole is not my friend! And I'm not—you can't think I'm doing that interview because I *want* to."

He turned. "What *do* you want, then?"

"To tell you I think Soren's a racist jerk and I'm never going to his parties." I looked over my shoulder. Zaneisha was right behind me, but no one else was around. Yet. "Look, if you want to hide for a while, I know a good place."

I took his arm, and though the muscles were rigid under my hand, he didn't resist when I tugged him into the janitor's closet I'd fled to on my first day. Zaneisha raised an eyebrow but stayed outside when I gave her a pleading look.

It was dark again, of course, but Koko provided enough illumination to show that Abdi's fists were clenching as he stood between the mop rack and a stack of replacement humanure containers. I hesitated, not sure if I should stay or go.

"He hates me," he said. "He hates me for no reason, because he needs someone to hate, and I am here."

I was pretty sure he wasn't actually talking to me, but I nodded.

"He's a stupid, arrogant child!" Abdi shoved the humanure containers. They rocked, threatening to topple. I braced, pushing them back into place. "But people listen to *him*. My mother said people would say things, but I didn't think—"

The moment was too raw. I should have left, and yet I couldn't look away.

He dropped his eyes and took a deep breath, then another. "Thank you," he said after a minute. "Starting a fistfight would have attracted the wrong kind of attention."

"Thank Zaneisha, not me. I was kind of hoping you'd hit him."

He let out a huff of air that wasn't quite a laugh. "If I am charged with assault, I will be deported."

"Oh. Can *I* hit him?"

"I don't think you need publicity, either. Not that sort."

"But it would feel so good," I sighed, and this time his laugh was real. "Thank you for the Ringo songs. I didn't know you knew Joph."

"She's all right. She doesn't bother people. She doesn't gossip."

"How did you get to know each other?"

His face hardened into blankness again. "Just in class."

That was clearly my cue. "Speaking of class," I said, and got up, "I'll see you later."

"Yes," he said. "You will."

But except for a few stray thoughts, I was actually too busy to think about Abdi much for the rest of the week.

≈ ‡ ∞

Okay. He's laughing at me. Because apparently I am sooooo funny.

All right, I might have looked at him once or twice. But I noticed more than a few glances coming my way. It's sort of obvious when someone seated in front of you keeps looking at the back of the classroom, you know.

Hah, yes, who's laughing now?

Anyway.

≈ ‡ ∞

I really was very busy. On top of school, and my psych and physical testing at the base, and the constant media training and critiques from Tatia, Zaneisha had stuck to her promise to teach me martial arts. I got an hour of training every day between school and Tatia.

I'd had this sort of wistful vision of being hailed as a martial arts prodigy and going straight to breaking bricks in half with my hands. My bodyguard squashed that notion at the beginning of our first session, which took place in our kitchen, on the mats she'd laid out there.

Zaneisha put me through a warm-up routine that stretched every muscle I had and made my heart feel as if it were going to pulse out of my chest. Then she taught me how to fall.

Actually, I *was* kind of good at that, if not quite prodigy level. If there's one thing you learn from free running, it's how to roll with the impact of your landing and protect your head. But I hadn't practiced falling backward from a standing position, and it took a little effort to learn how to sit down and slap the mat as I went back.

"Break your fall, not your head," Zaneisha instructed as the back of said head touched the mat lightly. I got her point, annoyed with myself; it would have hurt, had I done it on concrete.

"Three more times," Zaneisha said. "And then I'll teach you some throws."

That was enough motivation to get up again. After being tossed a few times myself, just to make sure I'd got the falling part down, I learned how to throw Zaneisha if she bear-hugged me from behind, if she tried to choke me from the front, and if for some reason I just needed to throw her without any provocation on her part. That one was especially fun.

"Very good," she said. "You should rehydrate now."

I nodded and got myself a drink. Zaneisha leaned against the bench and watched me swallow.

"Have you ever thought of following your father into the army?" she asked.

I sprayed water all over the floor.

She looked as if she was thinking of slapping me on the back, so I waved her away and leaned over the sink, arms braced, until the coughing stopped. "Um," I said. "Well, I've thought about it. But I have, you know, liberal tendencies. And a few problems with authority."

"So did I," she said. "My parents are American. They immigrated here just before the fundamentalist wars. I grew up with no trust for the government—any government." Her eyes were intent upon my face, and I tried not to back away. Besides, there was nowhere to back up to. "I don't deny that society needs radicals and protesters to ask questions of the people in charge. You might be better off in a less structured environment. But the army can be a very good place for people like you and me, Tegan."

I tried to raise one eyebrow, something I've never been able to do very well.

She smiled, warm and bright. "Really. We need people who can think, who can make fast decisions, who care about the well-being of others. And, of course, people who have a certain kinetic ability. Your free running has taught you to think laterally in terms of body motion, and you picked up those throws very fast today. With discipline and comradeship, you could be exceptional."

This was by far the biggest speech Zaneisha had ever made in my presence.

And two days ago, I would have been thrilled to hear it. But I'd seen Dawson drive up to that warehouse in the middle of the night, and my doubts must have been very clear on my face.

"Just think about it," Zaneisha advised.

"Okay," I said. It seemed easiest.

Then Tatia came in, and the next ten minutes were taken up with her horror at the fact that I was actually *sweating*, and by the way, Teeg, chicken, where are your glitter gloves, and my goodness, what have you done with your *hair*?

There was absolutely no time in that week for Bethari to come to my place so we could talk about what we'd seen and how we could further investigate. I didn't trust Koko to transmit or receive a secure message, and at Tatia's insistence, I was attending school only in the mornings.

We couldn't even find some privacy at school, and Soren was to blame. While I'd gone after Abdi, Bethari had ripped the famer up one side and down the other for being a first-class bazza, and Joph had flatly stated that she'd never supply his parties again. The next day, Soren made a couple more overtures of friendship to me, which I ignored with all the contempt I could muster.

After that, Soren gave up on wanting to be my friend and went straight for making my life hell. His cohorts spread out on the rooftop garden, leaned against the corridor walls, loitered on the stairs, and kept up a constant report of my activities to the tubes. It was never quite enough to trip the school's honor code, but more than enough to make me miserable.

The Living Dead Girl is wearing makeup today, but she's put it on all wrong.

The Living Dead Girl is having trouble with basic physics lessons.

The Living Dead Girl stared at Abdi Taalib all through his flute performance instead of taking notes for criticism like she was supposed to.

On Wednesday morning, Bethari and I headed for Joph's janitor's closet as soon as we got to school. But when we opened the door, Soren was there, too, smiling at Joph and making idle conversation about the scents of cleaning products.

"He won't go away," Joph said miserably.

Soren's smile was brilliant. "It's all school property," he said. "I'm as entitled to be here as you are."

"You think you're entitled to *everything*," Bethari said.

He ignored her and wiggled his fingers at me. "Hello, Teeg. You're going to love my next report. The Living Dead Girl loves hiding in small, dark spaces, probably because her mind has been irreparably warped by the revival process—so sad."

"You're disgusting."

"I'm angry," he said, the smile dropping away. "How dare you side with that filthy thirdie over me?"

"Because I have good taste," I said, and stormed off to the classroom, disgust thick in my throat.

Still, he couldn't keep it up forever. He'd get bored, or his friends would want to torment someone else. Bethari and I would just have to wait until the interview was over and the publicity had died down, and then we could work on a plan to find out what Dawson was up to with the Ark Project, and what it had to do with me.

On Thursday, the day of the interview, I missed school altogether, and Tatia called in her team.

I'd thought the previous makeover had been more than adequate, but oh-ho-ho-ho no. The top layer of skin was scrubbed off, any pimples banished, every single hair below my eyelashes stripped away (at least that didn't hurt, but it was deeply obnoxious), and of course I had absolutely no say in any of it.

The hairstylist hummed to himself, added extensions, snipped off bits here and there, straightened bits, curled bits, sprayed me with a dozen things, and then, the crowning indignity, turned to Tatia to ask, "What do you think?"

"*I* think I look like a mannequin," I said.

"A beautiful mannequin," Tatia said. "Reasonable, Jacob." She turned to me and clapped her hands twice. "And now, my favorite part!"

Apparently my makeup was too important to be trusted to anyone else; Tatia brushed and buffed and blended until I wanted to scream.

But that might have cracked my lip color, and then I'd have to do the whole thing over again. "There," she said at last. "Perfect."

I opened my eyes. The girl in the mirror was recognizably me; it wouldn't have helped Dawson's goals to completely alter my features. But everything had been heightened or flattened. My lips were bright red, the cupid's bow of my mouth emphasized. My eyebrows had been left fashionably unplucked but darkened until they were the same shade as my hair. Tatia had put in contact lenses that enlarged my irises and added huge fake lashes, top and bottom. My eyes looked enormous, gleaming dark brown against skin that had been polished to ivory, with just a touch of warm pink on my cheekbones.

All my imperfections were gone. No hairs on my upper lip, no persistent zit just under my left ear. The length of my nose was still physically there—I touched it for reassurance—but some trick of shading and perspective had diminished it to a tiny button.

There was something weirdly familiar about the way I looked, with my black hair molded into smooth waves and collected into the illusion of lustrous curls at the nape of my neck.

I climbed into the costume of a heavy blue tunic and gold leggings, trying to pin down that resemblance.

"Snow White!" I said suddenly. "You made me look like Snow White!"

"Awakened from a deathlike sleep by a handsome prince," she agreed. "We want people to see you as a romantic heroine, not a leech on our national resources."

"Do people even *watch* Disney anymore?"

"There was a revival about ten years ago. That's long enough that the association will be familiar but largely subliminal."

This was just great. The Beatles were obscure trivia, but people could still recognize that stupid movie. It wasn't worth pointing out that I'd been awakened from actual death by a doctor and an army initiative instead of any kind of prince; Tatia was perfectly capable of ignoring these inconvenient facts.

"Now, another question run-through," she said, and I tried not to groan too audibly.

Bethari called me right before the interview, just as my nerves were about to fray completely. I yelled at Tatia until she backed out and left me alone in my room.

"Nervous?" Bethari asked.

"Oh my god, yes," I said. "I'll be so glad when this interview is over and things get back to normal."

There was silence on the other end of the line. "Bethari?"

"I thought you knew," she said. "Don't you check yourself on the tubes anymore?"

"Not since I found that place that talks about where people would take me for our honeymoon. What don't I know?"

"There are rumors that other interviews will soon be announced."

I sat down on the floor. I didn't really mean to—my legs just dropped out from under me. "What?"

"It makes sense. If this goes well, you'll be a public figure. An army success story. They really need one, after all the complaints that they can't keep the northern borders closed. Australia for Australians are calling them cowards."

"Oh, Lord," I whispered. "Give me strength."

"Um, it might just be rumors, but there's also talk about a shadow documentary shot by a live-in crew. Maybe a government-funded Tegan Tour around Australia and to troops stationed overseas."

"Oh, for heaven's sake. Why don't they just make dolls with my face on them and sell them to raise money?"

"Um. If it helps, the profits will probably go to charity."

"You're kidding. You're *kidding* me."

"It could all be random ontedy. People say a lot of stuff on the tubes."

"But you don't think it is."

"Not all of it," Bethari said. "Tegan, you're really valuable to them. People think you're cute. Even when you get things wrong, they think it's kind of sweet, the past-timer messing things up."

"Like a toy," I said. "Like a *pet*."

Someone knocked on the door.

"Go away, Tatia!"

"It's me," Marie's voice said. "May I come in?"

"I have to go," I told Bethari.

"Oh no. Sorry about the worst encouraging phone call ever. Joph and I are watching from her place, and we're wishing you luck."

"Thanks." I signed off. "Come in, Marie."

She slipped in the door. Even though she wasn't going to be on camera, Tatia had insisted on dressing her in a dark red gown accented with glowing microfibers. Marie looked very beautiful, and very uncomfortable.

"He's here," she said. "Are you ready?"

"No. But I'd better go up anyway. Are you going to watch?"

"I'll be standing right behind Tatia and Colonel Dawson," she promised.

I squared my shoulders and felt the heavy fabric move across my body. "All right, then. Let's do it."

≈ ‡ ∞

Personalizing me to my audience required a cozy, home location. *My* cozy home. Professional cleaners had polished Marie's
already spotless kitchen and added a bowl of citrus fruit to the
bench for color and light. The table had been removed, and a
couch had been brought in.

I saw at a glance that the spindly legs and elaborate brocade
upholstery were meant to bolster my image as a fairy-tale
princess.

Carl Hurfest stood to greet me. His eyes gleamed as he took
in my makeover. "Hello again, Tegan," he said, and then paused
deliberately. "Wait, it's Teeg, isn't it?"

Don't lose your temper, I thought, and we began.

CHAPTER ELEVEN
And Your Bird Can Sing

I'm sure anyone who's still watching this has already seen the interview. Maybe most of you just want to know what I was thinking.

The problem was, of course, that I wasn't. I was white-hot with fury, rage burning all the common sense—and definitely all of Tatia's training—right out of my head.

I don't see why I should have to go over it again when you can play the 'cast any time you like, but as I've been told more than once, people need things to be personalized.

They like the inside story.

≋ ‡ ∞

Carl Hurfest started with the easy questions. How do you feel? Are you physically okay? Do you like school? The answers tripped off my tongue. Tatia definitely knew her stuff, and after the first ten minutes, I began to relax into it. Hurfest was sticking, word-perfect, to the questions he'd had vetted.

So when he moved on to the harder ones, looking very grave as he gazed at me, I stayed relaxed and answered well.

No, I couldn't remember what it was like to die. Yes, I'd been confused and disoriented when I ran from my excellent caregivers and into that first press conference. Of course, I was very grateful to the people who had helped me adjust to life in the twenty-second century.

"And what do you think of the world now, as opposed to the one you left?"

"Some things are different, of course," I said.

"The climate?"

"Yes. It was much cooler in my time. The oceans were lower. You could grow different crops in different places."

"Do you eat meat, Teeg?" Hurfest asked, and I felt the faint stirrings of alarm. It was the first question that hadn't been explicitly included on the list. But Tatia had anticipated this one, and I was prepared for it.

"Not anymore. I agree that it's wasteful and destructive."

"You're not worried about it from the point of view of ethical animal treatment?"

I blinked. "I would have given it up at home, if that was true."

"You said home. Do you still think of the past as your home?"

I forced myself to relax and pulled out the bashful smile Tatia had made me practice until my cheeks went numb. "I lived there for sixteen years," I said. "It would be hard not to and, I think, disrespectful to the memory of my family and past-timer friends if I didn't. Melbourne today is my home, too." Behind him, I could see Tatia's nod.

Hurfest smiled in apparent approval. I wasn't fooled; I knew an enemy when I saw one.

"I understand that you have a religious affiliation," he said.

Another of the vetted questions. "Yes," I began. "I'm Roman Catholic, though not at present a member of any particular congre—"

"Roman Catholics believe in the resurrection of the body, don't they?"

"Uh, sure," I said, caught off guard by the interruption, then, "Yes, that's what I was taught."

"And that the body will be immortal and made perfect by God, and the souls of those already dead will be reunited with these perfect bodies?"

I fell back on an all-purpose answer. "My faith is a source of great personal comfort."

He pounced. "Then would you agree with the Inheritors of the Earth that your soul is currently in the keeping of your God, while your current imperfect body is a mockery of his power to resurrect the dead and you should therefore commit suicide to return to his keeping?"

I felt my face freeze into place. "Obviously, I would not."

"Would you agree that this belief doesn't actually contradict Roman Catholic teachings?"

"You'd have to ask a priest," I said tightly. From Tatia's

rictuslike grin and emphatic nodding, I wasn't smiling enough. I tried to force the corners of my mouth up.

"I more or less did. The Inheritors of the Earth derive much of their doctrine from Roman Catholic—"

"But they're not," I said.

"I think we can agree that—"

"You can agree if you like, Carl," I said, almost purring the words. "But I identify as Roman Catholic, not as a member of a sect that broke away from the church sixty years ago. I believe in religious tolerance on every level. The Inheritors are entitled to their theology, but I am not spiritually obliged to live—or die—in accordance with their doctrine."

And thank god that Tatia had included that impro tree in my training. My untutored response would probably have been something similar to, "Those bastards can shut the hell up about me killing myself for the love of God anytime they like."

"What do you feel about the army spending so much money on Operation New Beginning when they've only managed to resurrect one teenage girl?"

"I'm very happy I get a second chance, and I hope our soldiers will, too."

"But it's been billions of dollars, Tegan. You've cost this country an enormous amount."

"I'm very grateful," I said, forcing the words out through my stiff smile.

It made sense that Hurfest was playing this note over and over—it was what had made me lose it in that first "interview." I had been warned about this. But I hated him, and I was furious, and having gotten me to that emotional straining point, this was when he chose to break me entirely.

"What do you think of the No Migrant policy, Tegan?"

Tatia was making a gesture that meant All-Purpose Reply #3.

All-Purpose Reply #3 was, "I think policy should be left to policymakers."

"I think No Migrant is disgusting," I said. Tatia began waving her hands at me so fast, I thought they might detach from her wrists.

Hurfest had perked right up. "Because your resurrection contravenes the stated aims of the policy, which are to preserve Australian resources for Australians? What do you think of the allegations of—"

"I *am* Australian, you dick," I said. "I think it's disgusting because Australia's resources could provide for thousands of starving people, and we're just letting them starve."

Hurfest looked, for the first time, sincerely taken aback. Then he leaned forward, eyes gleaming. "The policy argument seems to be that Australians can't be held responsible for—"

"You wanna bet?" I said. "Australia's been exploiting the developing world for generations, supporting conditions of war and famine and disease, and now we get to feel smug about it and call them dirty thirdies? I don't think so."

"Quite a change of heart, Tegan! Did it come about because of your association with Abdi Taalib?"

I ignored him and twisted to look directly into the bumble-cam. "Do you people even know what's happening?" I demanded.

It's kind of a big blur to me now. Part of me was calmly

watching as everything I'd discovered, every horrible fact and stupefying human-rights abuse, spilled right from my lips. But most of me was in a white-hot rage. The thing was that all these disasters were so obvious; no conspiracies involved. Anyone could have found them in the same search that I'd done. So what was it? Did they not know, or did they not care? Hurfest didn't even try to interrupt, recoiling as the words kept coming.

By the end I was shouting. "I am ashamed of you!" I yelled. "You are not the future I wanted. I can't believe the same stupid shit is still happening. I wanted you to be better! Be better!"

"Stop, Tegan, stop!" someone was saying, shaking my shoulders until my head snapped back and forth.

It was Dawson. Hurfest was being hustled out of the room, his camera with him. He seemed to be caught between yelling more questions at me and protesting his right to free speech, but Zaneisha did not appear to be inclined to listen to objections.

"Escort Mr. Hurfest home, Sergeant Washington," Dawson snapped at her. "And make sure he stays there. Tatia, you can leave."

"Save me from the ones with *convictions*," Tatia said, sweeping out. "Good-bye, Teeg. I knew you'd come to a bad end."

"You stupid, *vicious* little girl," Dawson said, and shook me again.

Marie was tugging on his arms. "Stop it, Trevor!"

His hands sprang away from my shoulders as if I were something unclean. "Why would you do that? Why would you destroy all your credibility?"

"It was the truth," I said.

"Truth! We didn't put you on camera to speak the truth! We needed a pretty face!"

"Well, tough," I snapped. "You got me instead. I guess your little clockwork doll broke down."

"You're going back to the base. Tonight. No more school, no more sleepovers. You will do what you are told, when you are told, and—"

"Colonel Dawson! I won't permit it!"

"Dr. Carmen, don't push me. This little bitch may have just scuttled the operation, do you realize? We haven't gotten the results we promised, and she's obviously unstable." He whirled and leaned over me. "You're going to spend a long, long time underground, Tegan Oglietti." His pupils were huge, dilated with fury.

"Screw *you*," I said, and shoved him with all my strength.

He staggered back a few steps, and I jumped to my feet, meaning to make a run for it.

But I stopped dead.

I was looking down the business end of a very shiny, very deadly looking weapon. Not a sonic pistol. The same kind of weapon that had killed the Inheritor in the foyer of a church.

"*Trevor*," Marie breathed.

"Shut up, Marie. I won't shoot if I don't have to."

"What are you doing?" I said. My hands were at my sides; I moved them carefully up to shoulder height. *Watch the eyes*, Zaneisha had told me, but I discovered it was hard to stop looking at the barrel of a gun. With an effort, I shifted my gaze to Dawson's face instead. It was just as hard, just as inflexible as the weapon. The anger was gone, replaced by a calm certainty, and that was even scarier.

"Kneel down and lace your fingers on top of your head. Dr. Carmen, there are restraints in my briefcase. Get them."

"But—"

"*Get them.*"

Marie gasped and scrambled back. I saw her pick up the briefcase from behind the kitchen bench, then carefully put it down. Her eyes met mine over his shoulder.

I needed to distract and delay him. I needed something that would make sure his attention was on me. "What's the Ark Project, Trevor?" I asked softly.

His eyes narrowed. "Who told you about that?"

"What is it?"

"Humanity's last chance."

My confusion must have been clear, because he let out a harsh laugh. "Do you know what happens when the Antarctic ice sheet goes, Tegan? And it *is* going. The Gulf Stream will enter thermohaline circulation shutdown. In a century, maybe less, we're looking at the beginning of an oceanic anoxic event. Do you know what that is?" He sighed, sounding genuinely weary. "Of course you don't. You're an ignorant little girl, and your politics have always been a pose. Get on your knees, Tegan. I won't ask again."

And then Marie smashed the fruit bowl into the back of his head.

It was clumsy, violent, and effective. Dawson jerked, and the gun went wide.

Even then, we might have been in real trouble, if not for what Zaneisha had taught me. Lunging forward, I twisted the gun out of his grip and delivered an elbow strike to his face. I hit him in the nose and felt something crunch.

He stumbled. Marie hit him again, and he dropped like a stone.

"I'm sorry!" Marie said, and dropped the remains of the bowl. They shattered on the floor, and in the ringing silence we stared at each other.

"I can't believe that worked," I said. "I can't believe I remembered how to do it."

"Zaneisha is a very effective teacher," Marie said brightly, and then stared at Dawson. "What's the Ark Project?"

"You don't know?"

"Tegan, I have no idea."

"Oh, thank god," I said, and stumbled forward to hug her. "It's a big secret military thing, I think. I'll explain as much as I can, but we have to go." My elbow hurt from hitting him. Zaneisha hadn't mentioned that would happen.

"Just a minute." She felt for Dawson's pulse. "He's alive. Oh, good. We'll have to tie him up."

"We should take him downstairs," I suggested.

In the end, we did both. The restraints in Dawson's briefcase went around his own wrists and ankles, and we pushed him under Marie's bed before heading back upstairs to clean up.

I couldn't make myself pick up the gun, but I shoved it under the couch with my foot. I avoided the sonic pistol, too, but I took Dawson's computer, his EarRing, and everything else I could find that might be useful. His wallet had four thousand in cash, which wouldn't get us very far, but was better than nothing. I tucked the plastic tokens into my tunic pockets.

"Is that everything?" Marie asked. "All right, so ... I suppose we should leave." She picked up a fallen banana and stuffed it down the neckline of her gown. "Supplies," she explained.

We didn't run, not quite. We just moved very quickly to Marie's car, and she pulled out into the street before anyone from the house across the road could stop us to make inquiries about why we were leaving without bodyguards.

Marie drove for a few minutes before she started talking, her voice curiously matter-of-fact. "Oceanic anoxia is when there isn't enough oxygen in the water to keep sea life alive. Anoxic events tend to lead to mass extinctions. Trevor must have access to resources I don't; I had no idea the Antarctic ice sheet was in imminent danger."

I was finding it hard to breathe myself. "The planet's dying?"

"Oh no. It's happened many times before, geologically speaking. The planet will keep going quite happily. Humanity might not, though. At the very least, things are going to get a lot worse for a lot of people. My research is beginning to seem quite frivolous."

"What's going to happen to you?" I asked.

Marie took a deep breath. "I've probably lost my job. Now. Tell me what you know about this Ark Project."

≈ ‡ ∞

We discussed it as she drove. It was a huge relief that Marie wasn't involved with whatever Dawson was keeping hidden, but she also didn't have any clue what it could be.

"You didn't hear a whisper of anything?"

She shook her head. "I didn't know that facility even existed. And the containers you describe could have held almost anything. Sensitive scientific equipment, weapons, even enriched uranium, though I'd have to hope they aren't playing with that so close to residential areas."

"What about the name? It could be a reference to Noah's Ark," I suggested. "Or the Ark of the Testimony that held the Ten Commandments."

"That's not much of a clue, either. Army project and operation names can be very obscure, sometimes purposely so."

"So you don't know anything," I said, and slumped in my seat.

"Well, perhaps. You say that the Inheritor man Gregor shot first alerted you to the project?"

"Yes."

"I believe one of the founders of the Inheritors of the Earth was a military man," she said.

I sat up straight again. "The Father?"

"Oh, no. The church was established some decades ago. He'd be very old by now, if he's still alive at all. Still, there might be a connection there."

She pulled the car over outside an apartment block.

The massive concrete structure could have been one of the state housing buildings from my time, but this one had yellow wind turbines on top and a sign out front declaring it to be Mellufius Apartments. There was a crowded bike rack and a tiny garden of wilting grass, lit up with pink lights. Probably housing for corporate cogs who were working too hard to care much about where they slept.

"What are you doing?" I asked.

"I've been thinking about that," she said. "They'll probably find Trevor fairly soon, which means they'll start tracking this vehicle. So I'm going to drive as far as I can before they catch me. And you're going to go somewhere else."

"No!"

"Yes, Tegan. I can try to confuse them for a little while. Enough to give you a decent head start."

I could see the sense in that, but I didn't have to like it. "And what will I do?"

She held up her computer. "I can probably steal you a car from this parking lot."

"Um, I can't drive."

"You can jump off buildings, blackmail the Department of Defence, spy on a secret project, and bring down a professional holding a gun on you, but you can't *drive*?"

"I was always too busy to learn," I said indignantly, and she laughed breathlessly for a moment.

"I'll miss you," she said, and I felt tears spring to my eyes. What would they do to her when they worked out what she'd done?

"Come with me," I said.

"No." She pushed the car door open, and I got out, too. "Can you ride a bike?"

"Sure."

Marie headed toward the rack, kneeling down by one of the bikes. "Do you have somewhere to hide?"

No, I thought, and opened my mouth to say so, but Marie shook her head. "Don't tell me where. It's better I don't know."

Well, all right. I'd come up with something.

"Keep moving if you can. Don't log into any networks under your own name, and get a clean computer if you possibly can. Try to get across the state lines. Change your appearance. Oh, and give me your EarRing. They can track you with it."

"You sound like a spy."

"I've just watched a lot of detective movies," she confessed, and then hugged me again, so tight it hurt. A good hurting. "Don't let them find you." She pressed something cold and hard into my hand: Dawson's sonic pistol. She must have picked it up before we left. My hands shook taking it—it wasn't really a gun, but it was gun-shaped—and I made sure the safety was on before tucking it into my belt.

"I love you, Marie," I said.

I hadn't meant to. It just fell out of my mouth. But her eyes went wide, and she touched her throat. "I love you, too, Tegan. Now. Go."

I went.

≈ ‡ ∞

For the record, riding a bike isn't just like riding a bike when it's a fancy-pants future bike with "helpful" GPS corrections and traffic advice. The first time the bike computer spoke, I nearly pitched over the handlebars in shock, and only a wild swerve and some frantic leg pumping got me my balance back.

The bike also kept calling me Markus.

I felt a little bad about that, but mostly I hoped Markus wouldn't notice his bike was stolen and activate the trackers until well into the morning. I needed somewhere to go, and while I was thinking of where that might be, I needed to get some distance from where Marie had seen me last.

Bethari and Joph had been watching the interview at Joph's place.

I couldn't stay there, but Bethari might have useful contacts from her investigative journalism. It was vaguely possible that she'd know people who would know people who could keep me hidden.

Those people would want to be paid, no doubt, and Dawson's stolen cash wouldn't get me very far, but it was a start.

Joph lived in the Flying Towers, which was a famously fancy building. I told the bike computer to direct me there and whipped around the next left as instructed.

I bumped over the poorly kept roads and felt very nearly happy. Sure, I was cycling through the dark city on a stolen bike, fleeing the Australian army, but it was the first time since my reawakening that I'd been out on my own. It was nearly midnight, and the streets were relatively quiet. The hot air smothered all sounds but my own panting breaths and the metallic slither of my leggings against the chain ring.

As I got closer to the central city, I saw more people. They were walking home after a late shift, or clustered in cafés, or getting legally high in a breathe bar. If I ignored the omnipresent advertising blaring from every bar door, and the clean-smelling air, much nicer than in my carbon-polluted time, I could make believe that I was home.

I was humming, the chorus to "Lucy in the Sky with Diamonds" buzzing over and over again to the steady rhythm of my legs.

The mood didn't last. By the time I got to Joph's building, I'd stopped making music and started ducking my head when people looked at me. The heavy interview costume had collected every drop of sweat, and the contact lenses in my eyes were itching unbearably. I dumped Marcus's bike two blocks from the Flying Towers and walked the rest of the way, forcing myself to a steady, unremarkable pace. The Flying Towers didn't actually fly, just stretched up high enough to imply that they *could*. The apartment building was a dinosaur, an energy-inefficient glass-and-steel monstrosity that flaunted the wealth of the inhabitants like Tatia flaunted her sense of style.

No human eyes watched me enter the lobby, but my skin was crawling under the surveillance I knew was there. A building like this recorded the presence of everyone in it. But it also kept the information to itself, protected behind strict privacy laws and enough money and influence to make even the army hesitate before demanding the records—I hoped.

"I want to see Joph Montgomery," I said to the air. I'd seen enough contemporary movies to know that places like this would have a building computer screening the guests.

There was a pause just long enough to set my every last nerve on edge, and then the lobby computer spoke. "Please enter the elevator to your left."

A section of paneling slid away to reveal the elevator. There were no buttons inside the door. The elevator would deliver me to the right floor, and no other.

I leaned against the shiny wall, second-guessing every choice that had brought me there and regretting everything I'd left behind—Abbey on my bed, Koko on my nightstand, Marie driving into the night, where absolutely anything could happen to her.

Then I took a deep breath and braced myself for what had to come next.

≈ ‡ ∞

Bethari and Joph were waiting by the door, ordering it open before I even signaled the house computer.

"Are your parents home?" I asked Joph.

"Geya, Tegan. They're out; come in."

"We saw the interview," Bethari said. "First, you were *amazing*, and second, what are you doing here?"

"I need help," I told them. "I should probably tell you both that I'm in a lot of trouble, and I could get you in trouble, too, but I really, really need help."

"Of course," Bethari said immediately.

Joph tilted her head, the ever-present vagueness in her eyes abruptly clearing as she looked me over. I felt exposed and vulnerable, and absolutely not above begging. If I had to go to my knees on the plush, expensive carpet, I would.

But I didn't need to. "Come into the lab, Teeg," Joph said, and led me through her home.

≈ ‡ ∞

Joph's lab was behind a triple-locked door. I'd been expecting dust and disorder, broken equipment, and the mess of failed experiments—something more like an alchemist's hideaway.

But Joph was a scientist. The lab was spotless and impeccably organized, racks of drawers were labeled, and equipment I couldn't even guess at hummed in the welcome chill of the temperature-controlled atmosphere.

"This room is on a closed system," she said, sitting cross-legged on the floor and gesturing for me to join her. "No one comes in here, not even my parents, and no one can get through my security."

"*Whose* security?" Bethari asked archly.

"Bethi helped," Joph said.

"That's right, and then you locked me out. I haven't been in here for a year."

Joph looked at me. "What happened after the 'cast, Tegan? And what do you want us to do?"

I took a deep breath, feeling the butt of Dawson's sonic pistol against my ribs. I wasn't any more certain than I'd been on the way up, but I didn't have any choice. I told them everything.

Bethari gasped when I got to the bit where Dawson pulled a gun on me and again at the part where Marie clocked him with the fruit bowl.

Joph watched me with her big eyes, occasionally scribbling a note on her computer, but she was largely silent and still.

"So I was hoping one of you would know someone," I said, and faltered to a stop.

Bethari was frowning. "I don't know. I might—"

"Sure thing," Joph said.

I blinked at her. "Seriously?"

"*Seriously?*" Bethari said.

"Well, it might be a little complicated, but you don't have to worry about that part. I'll get you some clothes, Teeg, and make some calls. Don't touch anything!"

Bemused by her sudden exit, I unclasped the thick belt, carefully laying the pistol on the floor. I could feel myself withdrawing into a cold, tight knot.

"I can't believe this! She's been keeping secrets! From me!" Bethari jumped to her feet and started looking at the lab equipment, obviously dying to disregard Joph's instruction to keep her hands to herself. When she spoke again, her voice was quite different. "Are you all right?"

"I'm okay."

"You don't look okay."

"Fine. I'm totally crap—is that what you want me to say? I

screwed up in the interview; I asked Dawson about the Ark Project; I've lost Marie her job and got her in a lot of trouble, and you guys, too; and I *still* don't know what the army's been hiding or what it has to do with me and Operation New Beginning." Her concerned face was blurring behind a veil of my tears. I dashed them away with the back of my hand. "I'm just kooshy, Bethari."

Joph came back in. "He's on his way. Teeg, are you okay?"

I couldn't even laugh. "No," I said.

"I can give you something to help," she suggested, putting the clothes carefully beside me.

I shook my head and steeled myself. "My brother died," I said. "I mean, everyone died. But he died early, because of drugs."

Joph crouched by me. "Oh, Teeg, I'm so sorry. But these are safe, I swear. Nonaddictive, no bad side effects."

"She's telling the truth," Bethari added. "I mean, I don't take them, but... you really don't look good, and you can't overdose on Joph's stuff."

"No, not like that. Not overdosing. After I got shot, Owen became a crystal addict. He robbed a gas station to buy more, and he got caught. So he went to jail, and there was a prison riot, and he died." I took a ragged breath. "We didn't have anything in common, except music and Mum and Dad and Dalmar. But I loved him and he loved me. He never did crystal before I died. And he died, and Mum lost us all."

Joph made a soft noise and pressed something into my hands. It looked like an asthma inhaler, only it was bright pink with a little blue button on the side. The little cartridge she slid into the top was plain, medicinal white. "You don't have to feel this way. You can feel better," she said. "Push here and inhale."

I hesitated for only a moment. Then I put the inhaler to my mouth and sucked in.

It wasn't a big change. I didn't start seeing things or cooing about how great Joph's hair was. I just gradually felt much, much better. The knot of horror in my gut loosened a little bit, and my shoulders came down from their protective hunch.

Joph beamed at me. "There's a muscle relaxant as well. It's really great, isn't it?"

I nodded. "But I can still move."

"Yep! This one's popular with athletes wanting to increase their endurance before big events. They take a breather, then they can push themselves without stressing."

"Taking a breather," I said. "Cute." I tugged my clothes off, relaxing even more as I dropped the heavy tunic and tight leggings onto the floor. Joph had brought me a flowing bat-wing shift and loose drawstring pants. The hem that hit her halfway down the calf was nearly ankle-length on me. I hitched the pants up under a scarf belt until I was sure I wasn't going to trip, and I stuck the sonic pistol in my belt.

Bethari had given up all pretense of trying to mask her curiosity and was openly rummaging through Joph's cabinets.

Joph watched her for a moment, frowning slightly. When her computer beeped, she took a container from her pocket, extracted a pill, and popped it into her mouth. "My antiandrogens," she said in response to my look.

That wasn't some future slang; I knew what antiandrogens were. In her general Educate and Involve Tegan for Great Justice program, Alex had included a very brief rundown on the mechanics of gender transition.

Joph misinterpreted my expression. "I was born male-bodied," she explained. "These help fix that."

"I know," I said. "It's just...I didn't know you were in transition."

"Huh?"

"Old word," I said hastily. "And that's cool! I was just surprised; I didn't know."

"Now you do," she said.

"I know lots of things," I said. "Lots and lots of things, but none of the right ones." I flopped onto my back, blinking at the soft ceiling lights. "I need to know more things."

"Maybe I should have adjusted the dosage," Joph said. She leaned over and put her fingers to my throat, featherlight. "No, your pulse is fine."

"Serbolax!" Bethari said. She had a handful of bright pink pills, and she was staring at her ex-girlfriend. "Joph, this is Serbolax, isn't it? The cure for Travis Fuller Syndrome?"

Joph looked shifty. "It might be?"

"It's what the *label* says. There are thousands of these pills! It's *you*. The hidden supplier I've been chasing all over Melbourne is *you*."

"That's a big conclusion to leap to," Joph protested.

"Don't you even. How did you—*what?* You're involved with smugglers now? Is that who you've invited to take care of

Tegan? Some criminal with a heart of gold smuggling medicine to thirdies?"

"You might say that," a new voice said.

Bethari swung to face him, her jaw dropping wide.

In the lab doorway stood Abdi Taalib, looking completely unimpressed with me, Joph, Bethari, and the entire world.

CHAPTER TWELVE
With a Little Help from My Friends

Bethari had questions—lots and lots of questions—but neither Abdi nor Joph seemed inclined to answer them. They ignored her until she plopped down beside me in a huff, muttering to herself.

Abdi and Joph were conducting an intense argument in whispers. But it was easy enough to guess the topic of their conversation.

Abdi gestured toward the door, but Joph darted to block his escape. "You promised you'd help me with anything," she said, a bit louder.

Abdi's back was tense. He murmured something, but Joph shook her head firmly. "This is the anything I want help with."

"Come *on*, Abdi! It's Teeg!" Bethari added. "Look at her."

He did, reluctance clear in every line of his body.

I waggled my fingers at him, and he met my eyes for the first time. After a second, he sighed, deflating.

"All right. I'll take you to someone I know, and they might take you to someone else, and that's it."

"That's not a very firm plan," Bethari said.

"They might not do it," Abdi said bluntly. "They're going to be very angry I have endangered the operation."

I stood up. I had so much energy all of a sudden. Joph's drugs were awesome. "Actually, you won't have to bother your smuggler friends at all," I said. "I have a new plan. We'll break into that warehouse and get some answers. We use whatever we find for leverage, to get Marie out of trouble, and make the army let me go and live my own life."

"Blackmail?" Bethari said. She looked as if she wasn't sure whether to be excited or scared.

"I think that's what they call it. Are you in?"

≈ ‡ ∞

They tried to argue with me, of course.

Actually, Abdi did most of the arguing. Bethari was on board almost from the moment I opened my mouth, and Joph gave in after a few minutes. But it took me and Bethari shouting Abdi down to get him to even listen.

"Zaneisha's keeping Carl Hurfest at home, and Gregor was off duty," I said. "Even if Dawson's awake, he won't be found for a while yet. This is our best and only chance. We have to go right now."

"Tegan's right," Bethari said. "If we can record evidence of whatever they've got down there, we might have something of value to trade for Tegan's freedom and Marie. And we know that whatever it is, it has *something* to do with Tegan."

"We don't even know if there's anything there worth recording!" Abdi protested.

Bethari shoved her computer into her pocket. "Gregor murdered a man just for talking to Tegan about this Ark Project. Armies don't kill people to keep unimportant secrets."

"You don't know much about armies," Abdi said, and scratched his chin. "It's too dangerous."

"If you're scared, stay here," I told him with that same Joph-enhanced bravery. I couldn't run from the army, but I might be able to defeat them. "I'm going. Now."

I started toward the elevator, Bethari close behind me. Joph joined us after a few seconds. "We can drive my mother's car," she said.

"What do your parents *do*?" I asked. A two-car family would be paying massive energy taxes.

"Mum's in government. Dad's an actor. It's pretty boring."

"You and me are going to talk about some stuff," Bethari said ominously.

Joph sighed. "I couldn't tell you about the smuggling, Bethari. It wasn't my secret to share."

"But did you have to put on the ditz act?"

"Yes. You know what it's like at Elisa M. Everyone's watching all the time. So I gave them something to watch. And now everyone knows I'm good at what I do, but no one suspects I'm capable of reverse-engineering a patent for Abdi. They just dismiss me as another fluffy chemist who spends too much time sampling her own wares." She shot Bethari a sharp look. "Even you."

I was trying not to slow down or turn around, but I couldn't prevent a sigh of relief when I heard quick footsteps behind us.

"Thank you—" I began.

"You're going to get us killed," Abdi snarled, and refused to speak to me all the way there.

≈ ‡ ∞

Looking back at it, I still think that if I knew everything I know now, I would have made the same choices.

I did the right thing by trying to get answers, although I could have been smarter about how I did it. But there were costs I hadn't considered, and I wasn't the one who had to pay all of them.

≈ ‡ ∞

Joph parked the car several blocks from the warehouse, and we walked the rest of the way. If anything, my nerves were even more hypersensitized than during our first nocturnal visit, but this time I wasn't afraid.

We hid in the same alley while Bethari hacked into the cameras again and declared the coast clear. "I'm putting them on loop," she said. "If there are any cameras underground, they must be on a closed system. But the outside ones are going to show an empty warehouse until we get out."

"If this is such a big secret, why don't they have more security?" Joph asked. "Guards patrolling, or something."

"Because putting a lot of security on something would be a good way to attract attention," Abdi said reluctantly. "It's a risk, but a calculated one."

"Okay, I'm nearly ready to spring the gates," Bethari announced. "You know, Tegan, things are much more exciting with you around."

"Why, thank you."

"You're very welcome."

"Any questions?" I asked. Abdi opened his mouth. "Any sincere, nonsarcastic questions?" He closed it. "Okay, then. Let's go."

≈ ‡ ∞

Bethari tore down the alert system on the gate in a matter of seconds. At her command, it swung open.

"Now, *that* was too easy," Abdi said.

"Not if you're this good," Bethari told him sweetly, and strolled in.

"Leave it open," I warned. "We might have to leave in a hurry." I'd given Abdi my sonic pistol, knowing that my uneasiness with the weapon might slow me down at a crucial moment. Joph had a sonic pistol of her own, and Bethari had some sort of Taser thing that she was supposed to carry for self-defense. I had nothing.

The warehouse door proved to be a little more challenging, having a physical lock rather than an electronic one. Abdi eyed it. "I suppose we could try to break it down," he said doubtfully.

"Let the past-timer at it," I said, kneeling by the door. I'd rummaged through Joph's lab. She had a lot of tools, and a couple of them were close enough to torque wrenches. The hairpins Tatia had used to keep my do in place were very strong and, suitably bent, provided decent rake substitutes.

"Keep watch at the gate," I told Abdi. "Bethari, tell me if anything's happening in the warehouse."

Then I got to work. It would have been much, much easier with Alex's electric pick gun, but I still had the skills that had gotten us into a lot of technically impregnable construction sites and buildings slated for demolition. Locks apparently hadn't changed a great deal in a century.

Twenty minutes later, the fifth pin jumped up, and I felt the door give. Joph signaled to Abdi, and we stepped inside.

"You have to teach me that," Bethari whispered.

Abdi, Joph, and I shoved the scrap-metal bin away and pulled out our weapons. Bethari braced herself in front of the elevator hatch and gestured at her computer.

"Black shoe alligator glue," said the voice of the curly-haired soldier, shockingly loud in the empty space.

Nothing happened. My heart sunk into my borrowed shoes.

Then, smoothly and silently, the elevator rose, and the door opened.

I stepped inside, and the others came with me. We were silent as the elevator descended, clutching our weapons tight.

There was no going back from here.

≈ ‡ ∞

The corridor at the bottom was long, dark, and empty. I said a mental prayer of gratitude. Joph started to say something, but Abdi clapped his free hand over her mouth and shook his head. Computers gave us enough illumination to see, and a door twenty meters ahead was slightly ajar, a shaft of yellow light striking across the bare concrete floor. A second later, laughter came from that doorway.

Abdi inched forward, sonic pistol in his hand, and Bethari slunk behind him with her Taser. He peeked around the door and signaled Bethari back. "Four of them," he breathed in my ear. "Kitchen. Poker party. We can sneak past."

Walking past that door was scary, and the relaxing effects of Joph's breather were wearing off. Opening the other doors along the corridor was even more terrifying. We didn't know who might be waiting inside, or if some sudden noise would bring the guards out to shoot us all down. We found two dorm rooms with two bunk beds each, shower facilities, a storage room piled with supplies, and even a little laundry room with piles of black T-shirts and coveralls. The facility had obviously been prepared for long-term stays.

I was feeling doubtful now. Maybe Abdi was right, ludicrous as it seemed. Maybe there really was nothing to find.

There was only one door left. Like the others, it was unlocked. I saw a big, dark room, ushered the others in, and pulled the door shut behind me. I was focused on the corridor outside, and the silence of the others didn't seem strange until I turned.

And saw what they had seen.

≈ ‡ ∞

The room was enormous, and the glow of our computers illuminated sturdy metal racks that towered above us and stretched out into the darkness. The racks were filled with clear plastic containers, each about the size and shape of a coffin.

There were hundreds of them.

I knew what was inside. We all knew.

Bethari was the first to step forward, holding her computer over the nearest cryocontainer. "It's occupied," she reported, her face expressionless.

I stepped up beside her and peered in at a woman about Marie's age, with pale skin and dirty-blond hair in matted strands. She was naked, but there was no wound visible on her body—just the tubes connecting her jugular vein and carotid artery to the container walls, and a Texas star tattoo on her right hip. Her skin had an odd, waxy sheen, stretched tight over prominent bones.

She looked frozen.

She looked dead.

I stumbled back, and Abdi caught me, wrapping an arm around my waist. "Breathe," he murmured in my ear, and after a moment I nodded and pulled away, looking into other containers. Was this just the place where they stored the volunteers for Operation New Beginning? Had we broken into a perfectly ordinary storage facility?

But they were so *skinny*. I mean, they were all dead, but they really didn't look well.

I remembered the long list of addresses that Bethari's computer had found in that government database, and shuddered. This was just the Melbourne location. Were they all like this?

≈ ‡ ∞

We moved quietly among the silent dead. Bethari was scanning her computer over the cryocontainers, narrating in a whisper, and pausing every now and then for a close-up. She stopped, peered closer at something, and beckoned me down.

"What is it?" I asked, staring apprehensively at the dark-skinned man inside.

"Look at the dates," she said, and pointed at the little screen that was attached to each cryocontainer. "They're all the same day."

She was right. I checked about twenty in the opposite direction, and they all read 8 JAN 2125.

"They all died on the same day?" I said.

Abdi stiffened beside me. "And the same place," he said,

pointing at a three-letter code in the bottom corner of the screen. "HOW. That must be Camp Howard. It's one of the refugee camps in West Australia."

"This one's KEA," I said.

"Camp Keating, in Queensland," Bethari said. "And a different date—17 March 2126." She moved down the line. "Keating, Keating, 17 March, 17 March . . . These must be refugees."

"Refugees can't afford the freezing process," Abdi said.

"So the government paid," I said. "But why? And what killed them? Some kind of disease?"

"In different camps?" Abdi asked. He sucked in a deep breath. "Didn't you say you got a list of addresses connected to the Ark Project, but this was the only one in Melbourne? Where were the others?"

That list of addresses flashed into my head again. "Mostly the Northern Territory and West Australia. A few in Queensland."

"Where the camps are," Bethari said.

There had been over twenty of those addresses. If they all corresponded to facilities like this, that added up to tens of thousands of dead refugees.

Abdi's face was very grim. "Maybe asking what they died from is wrong. Perhaps they died *for* this. Those experimental bodies your Dr. Carmen is working on; where do they come from?"

"They're volunteers," I said. "Like me, that's why they had to use me. I donated my body to science before I thought coming back was a real possibility."

"Are you sure they're all volunteers?"

Bethari and I stared at each other, trying to come to grips with the enormity of what Abdi was suggesting.

"The army wouldn't kill refugees," Bethari said. "I mean, maybe if they knew they could bring them back, when there was enough food for them, when the world was safer.... But Tegan's the only successful revival. These deaths are from before she was even brought back. They wouldn't do that. They couldn't."

"Oh? Why not?"

Bethari stopped, then spread her hands hopelessly. "Because it isn't *right.*"

Joph had wandered down to inspect cryocontainers farther away. She let out a low cry and rushed back to us. "Children," she said. "There are children down there."

"Oh, fuck," Bethari said, and squeezed her eyes shut. "I don't think I can handle dead weens. I just—"

"Give me the computer," I told her, and took it from her hand before she could protest. Joph buried her face in Bethari's shoulder and shook.

Bethari's computer seemed to know what to do without my interfering. I forced myself to look into the containers instead of just recording blindly. Abdi paced beside me. The tiny bodies were thin, with spindly limbs and every rib clear on their chests. "They're so young," I said.

"About six or seven," Abdi said.

"Are you sure? They look younger."

"Malnutrition does that."

I stared into the next container, at the little girl with white skin and dark hair. She could have been my sister. Where had she come from—Armenia? Kentucky? How far had she come, and what had driven her here?

It was almost too horrible to contemplate, and yet I had to think about it. My army had done this. My government, of my beautiful country, had put this child in this box.

Abdi looked over my shoulder. "Do you still want to use this for blackmail?" His voice was very calm.

The horror was subsiding, and rage was rushing in to fill the void, tingling through my entire body. "No. I don't know what's going on, but I think people need to know about this."

"What makes you think people will care?" he said.

"They have to," I said, startled.

"They didn't care before, when this same girl was rotting in the camps."

"But this is different," I argued. My voice sounded weak in my own ears.

"I guess we'll see," he said, sounding skeptical, and then the lights flashed overhead, and we spun to face the doorway.

One of the guards was standing there, eyes wide as she stared at the four teenagers roaming around her top-secret facility. "What the—"

Bethari shot her.

The Taser prongs hit the guard square in the chest, and she gurgled as the voltage coursed through her. She convulsed wildly, limbs flailing as she dropped.

"Go!" Abdi shouted, and we ran out of that room of the dead and bolted for the elevator.

The guards were facing the wrong way, prepared for someone breaking in, not out. Joph shot the next guard, and Abdi got the third, and they fell, inner ears ruptured by the sonic beams. But even with intense vertigo, the soldiers were conscious, and they were professionals ready to fight. One of them grabbed Bethari's ankle as she rushed past, and she fell full-length to the concrete, wind knocked out of her. Before I could react, Joph ran back and tugged Bethari's shoulders, urging her to rise.

The fourth guard's bullet took Joph in the thigh. She screamed and fell on top of Bethari, clutching at the wound. Blood spurted out between her fingers.

"Halt! Disarm!" the fourth guard thundered, pointing his gun at Abdi. The downed guards were staggering to their feet, using the walls to steady themselves. Joph's lips were white with pain.

"Please be calm," Abdi said.

"Are you joking, kid? I'm not messing around. Put your weapons down or I'll shoot."

I shoved the computer into Abdi's hand and stepped forward, covering his body with my own as I pressed him back into the elevator.

"I'm Tegan Oglietti," I said calmly. "The Living Dead Girl. If you kill me, you'll be in *so* much trouble."

The guard hesitated. His hand dipped toward the other side of his belt, where the sonic pistol rested in its holster.

"Go!" Joph screamed, and threw herself against the soldier's leg.

"Black shoe alligator glue," said the voice from Bethari's computer, and Abdi's hand shot past my waist, sonic beam dropping the last guard to the ground. The elevator rose, and Abdi dragged me out into the warehouse, hand firm around my wrist.

I yanked out of his grip. "What are you *doing*? We have to go back!"

"We can't. They'll have reinforcements on the way."

"But the girls are still down there!"

"They're alive."

"So far as we know!"

"Tegan, she said go; we have to go!" He grabbed my shoulders and looked into my eyes. "This is the only proof we have. We have to get it onto the tubes before we get caught. All right?"

The elevator began to descend.

"All right!" I said. We ran out of the warehouse, through the yard, and into the street. There were trucks coming, army vehicles with ominous shapes on their roofs, but we ran through the dark streets, choosing turns at random as we hunted for some kind of safety.

Abdi stumbled to a halt, clutching his side.

"What's wrong?"

"Can't run anymore," he gasped, and gave me the sonic pistol. "One moment."

I dragged him into a side street, wondering what to do. Should I leave him? Upload the footage right now? Did we have time for him to catch his breath?

"Tegan, stay still," someone said from behind us.

It was Zaneisha Washington's voice.

I didn't even look over my shoulder to make sure it was her. I darted left, right, and kinked around a corner, yelling at Abdi to move.

Bless the dark and narrow streets. They were a maze. If I'd been trying to find a specific building, I might have been in trouble, but all I was looking for was escape.

I hit what might have been a dead-end alley for many people. For me, it was a way out. I jumped onto a recycling bin, hauled myself up a brick wall, used a windowsill to hike myself higher, and finally scrambled onto a roof.

When I flattened and wriggled close to the edge, I couldn't see Abdi. Keeping away from the rooftop's ridge, I slunk along it and let myself down onto the next roof. I didn't have to go too far. Zaneisha had him pinned against a wall, and she was talking into his ear.

No backup had arrived, which was weird. I crept a little closer until I could hear Zaneisha's words.

"—need to find her," she was saying, her voice tinged with something very close to desperation. She pulled Abdi away from the wall and shoved him in front of her as she moved down the alley. She had her sonic pistol jammed into his back. It couldn't kill him. But it must have felt like a real gun, a real threat. I caught a glimpse of his eyes, wide with fear, and wriggled back from the edge, trying to reason out the situation.

Moving an unbound prisoner was a really stupid move if

you had backup, and Sergeant Zaneisha Washington was anything but stupid. Therefore, she had no backup. Whatever Zaneisha was doing, she was doing it alone.

Therefore, I might have a chance to extract Abdi and escape with him.

"Tegan," she called softly. "Tegan, come out." She moved her light beam around. I ducked as she flashed it across the rooftops. "You can't get far. Come back with me. We found Dr. Carmen."

I stifled my gasp.

"She's safe, but we really need you to come in and explain. Tegan, she said something about an Ark Project. Is that what that Inheritor was talking about? If you tell me about it, I might be able to help."

I wavered. If she meant it, if she truly didn't know, then maybe she would help us. But it could be a trap. Could I take the chance?

"I don't want to have to call the others in; someone might get hurt. Come with me. I won't hurt you or Abdi, I promise."

I think she meant it. That's the thing that pricks my conscience, like a splinter worked deep into my memory. Zaneisha really thought she was doing the best thing for me, trying her hardest to protect me, even from myself. And if it had been just me, I might have taken the risk.

But she had Abdi. And whether she knew it or not, she had the footage that was our only proof of the Ark Project.

So the next time she flashed her flashlight in my direction, I rose over the top of the roof ridge and shot her in the face.

I truly hate guns. But I was weirdly calm and my hands were steady, and, most important, I had a clear view and a big height advantage. Zaneisha fell. She did it perfectly, breaking the drop with her arms to protect her head and rolling nearly to her feet. Then the vertigo caught up with her, and she staggered, vomited, and fell again, this time with much less grace.

I could hear her cursing as I climbed down, but by the time I jumped off the recycling bin, Abdi had Zaneisha's gun in his hands and was pointing it steadily at her.

"Don't shoot," I told him.

Her eyes narrowed, focusing on my lips. With ruptured eardrums, she probably couldn't hear me. "Don't run," she said as I slipped off her EarRing. Her hand groped for my wrist and gripped hard. I broke the grip with a move she'd taught me herself. "It'll be worse if you run," she insisted.

Zaneisha's computer was flashing a message. I glanced at it and swore. She must have managed to trip the alarm even as she fell that second time.

"They're coming?" Abdi said.

"Yes."

"Let's go."

"One second." I couldn't trust Zaneisha with our precious footage. But I scribbled a note for Zaneisha on her computer and tucked it into her pocket. Maybe she could do something to help Joph and Bethari. "I'm sorry," I told her. "I really am."

Then I turned my back on her and ran.

"Stay," Zaneisha called after me. "Tegan, please stay!"

We got a few blocks away, but while Abdi had obviously gotten his second wind, I was flagging.

He cast a look around and tugged me into another alley, where he yanked out the computer and crouched over it. "We'll upload it now," he said.

I nodded, pressing my hands to the ache in my side.

But he never got the chance. Because that's when they caught us, the people who had been following me, patiently and professionally.

They wore plain linen in pale colors, what I had come to think of as the uniform of the Inheritors of the Earth. There were two of them, and they carried long-barreled weapons that looked like plastic rifles.

"Wait—" I said, and then they shot me.

CHAPTER THIRTEEN
You've Got to Hide Your Love Away

"Tegan. Tegan, wake up. Tegan."

Someone was patting my face. "Don't," I said, pushing the unwelcome intrusion away with hands that felt like cotton wool stuffed into rubber gloves.

"It's Abdi."

"We're alive?" I tried to sit up, but everything swayed around me. "Why is the world moving?"

There were hands under my arms, propping me up. "We're on a boat."

"A *boat*?"

"Do you remember anything?"

I tried to concentrate. "The Inheritors?"

"Yes. They tranquilized us. I woke up just before we got to

the boat. You've been unconscious for a few hours." It was only later that I thought about what that must have been like for him, sitting there with an unconscious girl and not knowing for sure if she'd wake up. At the time, I was too confused to think about anything but my spinning head.

"What's—" I said, and tried to stand up. Which prompted my stomach to crawl up my throat.

Zaneisha's revenge, I thought, and was then so messily sick I couldn't think of much at all.

After a while, I became aware that Abdi was gripping my shoulders, keeping me balanced. He'd helped me over to the toilet—no humanure here, only a chemical toilet in the corner. I retched violently into it. "What's wrong with me?" I asked. "I don't get seasick!"

"I think whatever they shot us with reacted badly with the drugs Joph gave you. Do you know what it was?"

"No. She said it would make me feel good."

"Did it?"

"All the everything floated away. It was wonderful." I considered. "I don't think I could have gone into that warehouse without it. It made me so brave."

"Now you tell me," he said, sounding resigned.

I sat up, clipping my head against his chin. "The footage!"

"They took Bethari's computer. And our weapons."

"Oh god. It's all gone wrong." My stomach convulsed again, but there was nothing left to come up. I spat thin yellow saliva into the bowl, closed my eyes, and leaned back against him. "Where are we going? What's going to happen?"

"I don't know. They wouldn't talk to me. Are you feeling better?"

"Not really." I sat up straight again. "They shot Joph!"

"I know."

I gagged again and sobbed through the heaving. "Oh god. It's all my fault. You warned me. You said I'd get us all killed."

He hesitated. "It was her decision to go."

"But—"

"No. You can't take the responsibility for her choices. She was brave, and you can't take that bravery from her."

"Do you blame me for being kidnapped?"

There was a pause while I threw up again. Then he said, "No."

"Don't lie to me, Abdi," I said. "Everyone lies to me."

"It's tempting," he admitted. "But blaming you wouldn't be fair. I made my own choices. Here." He pressed a water bottle into my hand.

I rinsed and spat, then sipped cautiously. My stomach didn't revolt. "Zaneisha said that if they take you alive, it's so they can do worse things to you."

"Where there's life, there's hope," he said quietly. "I saw your interview, by the way."

"Really? What did I say?" I yawned. "I feel *terrible*. Do you hate me?"

He sounded surprised. "No."

"Oh, good. But you don't want to be friends."

"I think we have to be friends now," he said. He sounded very matter-of-fact. "If we don't have each other, we'll have no one. Have you finished vomiting?"

"I think so."

Abdi lowered me onto the floor, which swayed alarmingly, and went away. When he returned, it was with a blanket, which he draped over me. It was scratchy but warm, and I curled under it, trying to ignore the swooping sensation of the boat rolling back and forth. "We're really friends?"

"Sure."

"So you should sing to me," I said triumphantly.

He laughed. It was a clear, ringing sound, and totally unexpected in that dank, stinking place.

"I'm serious!"

"I know. That's what's funny. We're kidnapped and imprisoned, and you sound so happy that you might be able to make me sing."

"Well?"

Abdi laughed again, softer this time, and then he began to hum. It was "Hey Jude." After a few bars, he began singing properly, his rich voice quiet but clear. After that, he sang "I'm So Tired" and "Blackbird." He was halfway through "Golden Slumbers" when I felt his hands in my hair, gently picking out the pins keeping all the curls in place.

"Nice," I mumbled.

Abdi's hands stopped. "I thought you were getting some sleep."

"Nope."

"Then you should try," he said. "I think we'll need rest."

I thought about arguing, but he was singing something else,

in a language I couldn't understand. It was a soft melody that sounded like a lullaby. Caught between my exhaustion, the drugs, the gentleness in his voice, and the rise and fall of the sea, I fell asleep.

≈ ‡ ∞

Okay. Most of this next part might be a little dodgy in terms of chronology. Some of this stuff I learned later, listening to Rachel and the other girls talk in the kitchens, but it wouldn't make sense to explain that every time, so I'm just going to lump it all in together.

Abdi says that I don't need to underline this, because everyone knows that a life narrative is edited in the telling, even if it's just unconsciously, but I think it's important to be honest.

I promised to tell you the truth.

≈ ‡ ∞

Abdi woke me when we made landfall.

"I think we're here," he said. "Don't do anything stupid."

When the two men came in with their long guns, I managed to behave myself, standing quietly beside Abdi.

"Move out," the shorter one said. "Slowly."

"This is so illegal," I said.

"We follow the laws of God, not man," the taller one said. "Keep your hands in sight, child."

I was pretty sure God had some stuff to say about violence and abduction. "If you're going to kill me, do it now," I said.

Abdi bit out something that I was pretty sure was unflattering and stepped in front of me, pressing me backward, as I'd done for him in the underground complex.

"We will not hurt you, Tegan," the shorter one said earnestly. "You must meet God in your own time."

"Quiet, Conrad!"

Conrad subsided, looking guilty, but he'd said what I'd been desperately hoping to hear. The Inheritors of the Earth had been fairly publicly consistent about what they wanted me to do. As long as they were sticking to persuading me to kill myself instead of taking a shortcut and cutting out that intervening step, I was confident I could handle it.

I mean, it creeped me out, and I was worried about what they might do to persuade me, but I was much less concerned about a weirdo cult that expressly didn't want to kill me than I was about a powerful government that possibly did.

You've got to have priorities.

"You could let Abdi go," I said. Even if we didn't have the footage, he could at least be a witness, and he could make sure Bethari and Joph were okay.

"He could identify us to your police. He stays," the taller guy said, and gestured to the door with the butt of his rifle. "Move."

We moved.

Outside, it was evening, shading into night. We'd spent most of the daylight on the water.

The Inheritors' compound was a collection of low, neat

stone buildings nestled in a small bay, with high, forested hills rising from the grassy plain. It was noticeably cooler than Melbourne had been, though still hot by my standards. There weren't many places in Australia on the coast that were cooler than Melbourne.

"Are we in Tasmania?" I asked.

"Hush, child."

I opened my mouth to argue, but then I saw the cows.

Actually, it would be more accurate to say that then I *smelled* the cows.

They were being driven out of the milking sheds, what looked like a hundred of them, all mooing and pooing and generally looking one short step more intelligent than sheep.

"But people don't keep cattle anymore," I said.

"We do," Conrad said. "We are the Inheritors of the Earth. Masters of the fish of the sea, the birds of heaven, the cattle, all the wild animals, and all the creatures that creep along the ground."

"And God said, 'Be fruitful and fill the earth,'" I said.

"And subdue it," Conrad finished, and smiled at me. "It's good that you understand."

"I understand that you abducted me and made me throw up," I said cheerfully. "I hope God forgives you, because I sure won't."

His face fell. We walked up a low slope to the biggest stone building with the highest roof. I looked around, trying to get my bearings. It was pretty useless—I hadn't even been to Tasmania in my own time, and it was a big island. About all I could say was that we were on the coast somewhere.

There were boys my age and younger in the milking sheds, taking care of the milking machines. They weren't in loose-fitting linen like the men who'd abducted us, or the man Gregor had shot in the church, but T-shirts and jeans. I hadn't seen blue jeans in a while.

"You must sell the milk," Abdi said conversationally. "And the beef, to those gourmands who still eat it."

"Rich hypocrites," the other man grunted.

"Be kind, Joseph," Conrad said, and I wondered which of them was in charge. Or if neither was. These people were really weird. When I'd gone to Mass regularly, there'd been people there who kind of freaked me out the same way, as if they weren't entirely in this world. Some part of their heads always seemed to be somewhere else, thinking about things I couldn't imagine.

The guns were very real, though, so Abdi and I kept walking.

The biggest building turned out to be some kind of combination meeting hall and cafeteria. It was absolutely packed with people sitting at long tables, from old poppas and nonnas to the babies some of the women were holding. I noticed that most of the people seemed to be white, but not as many as I would have expected from communities like this in my time. "Racial purity" clearly wasn't one of their things. It was hot inside, and the big fans lazily cycling overhead didn't do much more than move the air about.

They were all dressed in jeans, except for some of the older women, who were in long dresses, and a couple of the older guys in those linen robe things, and they were all looking at us, hushing one another as they craned to stare at the strangers.

Conrad gestured us to a door at the back of the room. We'd have to walk past all those staring people to get there.

I felt Abdi hesitate beside me.

"It's a performance," I said under my breath. "Just a show." If I could do a live interview with the horrible Hurfest, I could do this. I conveniently ignored how that little adventure had ended, lifted my chin, and began to walk.

I'd wanted to pretend they weren't there, but I was looking around too much for that, so instead I held eye contact with a few people. One dark-haired girl actually let out a small scream when I did, hiding her face behind her friends. Abdi was looking straight ahead as if they were beneath his notice. Between us, we must have looked pretty fierce, even though I was wearing ill-fitting borrowed clothes spattered with my own dried vomit, and Abdi had patchy black stubble sprouting on his chin and scalp.

Then we were through the door that Conrad held open. He shut it behind us, and for the first time in a while there were no guns pointed in our direction.

Escape wasn't an option, though. For one thing, I could smell something that made it clear just how hungry I was. For another, the woman waiting for us was huge, so big and muscular that I almost didn't notice the girl in jeans hovering behind her.

The woman sported cook's muscles, like my mother. She

had the same sort of smell about her, too, of herbs and flour, and the scent made me inhale sharply. But unlike Mum, who liked shorts and colorful tops, this woman was wearing one of those long dresses under a spotless apron. She looked us up and down and grunted. Then she moved away, and I saw the smaller table behind her. There was a big loaf of bread in the middle and bowls filled with something that was steaming hot.

"Sit," she said, and we sat. There was definitely meat in the bowls, along with diced vegetables and a thick gravy. My mouth got in the way of my principles by watering uncontrollably. I swallowed before I started drooling.

"We say grace," the woman announced, and bowed her head over the food. The girl quickly followed her. I said a quick prayer myself, though it was more a plea for help than an expression of thanks. Abdi, when I opened my eyes, was looking at me dubiously.

The woman pushed a plate of bread toward us. "I'm Mrs. McClung, and this is Rachel. We know that unbelievers abjure the full bounty of the Lord, but we cooked this good meal, with the grace of God, and you will eat it with no complaint."

I almost laughed in her face. The Inheritors of the Earth must have been the only people in the country who didn't know that, as a past-timer, I was a filthy meat-eating Earth hater.

But it was Abdi who was the real star of the show. Without blinking an eye, he picked up his fork and popped a chunk of beef into his mouth. "Good," he said around the mouthful.

Mrs. McClung's eyes nearly started out of her head. Rachel

stifled a nervous giggle. She looked a little older than me, and I envied her long, light brown hair. No one had stuck her in a chair and argued for three hours about which extensions to use. Lucky, lucky her.

I stuffed a forkful of stew into my mouth, knowing it was that or hysterical giggles as I began to lose it. Abdi was right, though; the stew was freaking delicious.

"What herbs are you using?" I asked.

Mrs. McClung's eyebrows rose. "Never you mind."

"I taste tarragon and rosemary," I said. "And something else, something warm. Cumin?"

"Paprika," Rachel said, then looked guilty.

"Oh, of course. Hungarian?"

"Smoked," Mrs. McClung said grimly.

"Deeee-licious," I said, and speared a piece of potato. Potato is nearly always the best part of a stew. I rolled the bite around in my mouth, enjoying the richness of the meat sauce. Mrs. McClung might be a zealot-cum-prison-matron, but she was an excellent cook.

I ate until my stomach felt round and tight, tearing off pieces of bread and dunking them in. Rachel refilled my bowl twice, looking impressed and faintly gratified. Abdi ate more slowly, flicking his eyes at the room as he chewed.

I had no idea what he was looking at, but it turned out he was searching for something that wasn't there.

"Where are the computers?" he asked.

"We don't use those things here," Mrs. McClung said,

somewhat smugly. "We're good, old-fashioned folk here, free of the outside world's contamination."

Some of the buildings, Rachel told me later, were over a hundred years old, older than the Inheritors as a group. But the newer buildings were built in the same style, with big windows and old-fashioned electrical wiring. They turned their lights and appliances on with switches instead of talking to a house computer, and they had no Internet at all: no 'casting, no Ear-Rings, no news.

To me, it was weird, but close enough to familiar. To Abdi, it looked like something out of a history 'cast.

≈ ‡ ∞

To be honest, until we talked later, I didn't have a really strong idea of what Djibouti was like—though I knew it was more complicated than mud huts. I'd kind of been envisioning the Djibouti of the future with a similar level of technology to my Melbourne of the past. But it wasn't. Medicines might have been limited, but Djibouti's geothermal energy was plentiful, and computers were cheap. Djiboutians didn't typically get the best upgrades and the fanciest applications, but all but the very poorest citizens had a computer or access to one, even if it was fifty tech-generations old.

Abdi's own family was far from poor. His father owned a small shipping company that did a brisk trade throughout the Red Sea, and his mother was a politician with huge popular support. They took holidays in Arta, where it actually got cool at night, and lived in a big house with its own generator and plenty of servants. (He glossed over that a bit, but I was pretty sure he hadn't made his bed himself until he got to Australia.) Abdi was given his first brand-new computer when he turned four.

His parents had made it very clear to their children that they were fortunate, and that one of the consequences for that was service to those who weren't. Abdi's older sister had completed an engineering degree at the University of Ilorin in Nigeria and went home to work on an irrigation-system update for Djibouti's limited arable land. His older brother was halfway through a medical-technician apprenticeship. Abdi had expected to follow in his mother's footsteps and go into law, then politics.

And then a curious firstie 'caster had wandered past Abdi's cousin's wedding and caught Abdi singing on camera, and the wealthier parts of the world had taken note of his voice. When the Elisabeth Murdoch Academy offered to sponsor Abdi through the Talented Alien program, the family had discussed the opportunity at length. It had been a difficult decision. Abdi was brilliant and studious and spoke four languages. He could get a law degree from the University of Ibadan or the University of Khartoum. He could go to Cairo or Kuwait City or Paris.

But an education in impossible-to-reach Australia at an elite academy and a law degree from a university there might give him even higher standing on his return. His fame had been undesirable and unlooked for, but it could be made to work for him and his homeland. He would certainly encounter prejudice in Australia, but the contacts he made there could be very valuable.

The family talked it over but could come to no consensus. It was up to Abdi to decide.

Even back then, he might have been thinking how else he could help his people. No one in Abdi's father's household was likely to die of Travis Fuller Syndrome; they had the money and influence to get almost everything they needed for themselves. But Abdi had been eight years old during the first epidemic, and eleven during the second. By the time he'd turned fifteen, nearly a third of the kids in his flute classes—the poorer ones—were dead from a disease that could be fixed with four little pink pills.

Abdi knew the risks. He didn't want to disappoint his family, and having representatives in Djibouti who firsters would listen to was important. But getting badly needed drugs back home was even more so, and he could trade on his father's name to shipping contacts. He made a few discreet inquiries and waited.

Barely a week after he got to Melbourne and settled in with the family with whom he was boarding, he'd been approached by someone he only ever described as "my friend." Abdi's friend knew that Abdi was going to Elisa M and of Joph's reputation as a chemistry genius. Abdi talked to Joph, and she agreed to manufacture the necessary medicines for nothing more than the price of replacing the materials. She took on the ditz role, increased her sales of recreational drugs in order to pay for the extra equipment she needed, and handed Abdi the drugs in the janitor's closet.

Four little pink pills per person. And Abdi took hundreds every week to "his friend."

I know that a lot of you think I'm a hero. Abdi isn't showing me all the messages, because I need to concentrate on what I'm doing, but every now and then, he'll pass one to me when he thinks I need cheering up in a bad part.

But Abdi and Abdi's friend and Joph and everyone else who helped get those drugs to the people who needed them are the real heroes. They've saved thousands of lives.

Those aren't the lives you want to hear about, though, are they? Those stories have been available to you for decades, and you haven't been listening. It's my story you're hitting in unprecedented numbers. It's the Living Dead Girl you think is—

Okay. I'm being bitter. It's not that I think my story isn't worth your attention, obviously. But when I'm done, or while I'm still talking, I encourage you to look a little wider.

≋ ‡ ∞

Anyway, like I said, we talked about that later. That first night, we were separated right after the meal. Conrad came in and told Abdi to go with him.

"We do not allow young men and young women to sleep in the same quarters," Mrs. McClung said.

Abdi looked back at me and made a gesture I thought was supposed to be reassuring. I didn't feel very reassured; my only friend in a strange place was walking out the door.

Rachel led me to another of the stone buildings. It was full

237

of three-tier bunk beds and chattering girls. They didn't exactly stop talking when I came in, but there was a pause, and then their voices went hushed and secretive. All the beds had individual curtains, and little shelves built into the headboards, so everyone had some privacy and personal space.

Rachel held out a long cotton nightgown. "You may wear this."

I took it and glanced at the other girls. Some of them looked boldly back, then turned to their friends to gossip. "I guess I'm big news," I said.

"We do not often see strangers," Rachel told me. "Were you ill?"

I blinked at her, then rubbed my head. "Oh, my hair? No, the doctors took it off when they began the revival—well, I guess I was ill, sort of. You know about me, right?"

She nodded. "The Father told us. You are the one brought back to life against God's will."

"The Father's pretty confident about speaking for God," I said grimly.

"Of course," she said, looking faintly shocked.

"Where is he, anyway? I thought he'd have come to tell me to shoot myself by now."

"He is out among the unbelievers, doing God's work," she said, and pointed to one of the middle beds. "You may sleep there. I will be on the bottom, and Sharron sleeps on the top."

"I'm not really sleepy," I said. "I slept all day, after the drugs you people gave me."

"This is when we sleep," she said. I just couldn't get a rise out of her.

The other girls were climbing into bed, still whispering to one another. The dark-haired girl who had hidden her face from me in the big hall climbed up to the top bunk, still averting her eyes. Sharron, I presumed.

"But I'm not tired," I said.

"Then you will probably stay awake," Rachel said. "Perhaps you should pray."

The weird thing is, she wasn't being mean. She said that as if I was being given a really great opportunity. She smiled at me and slid into the bottom bunk, closing the curtains.

I stood there, holding the nightie, wondering if it was some sort of subtle trap. Putting a girl above and below me was their version of security protocols? I could be out of there whenever I wanted.

But where would I go? I was a city girl. I had no idea how to go about surviving in the bush. There were tiger snakes in Tasmania, and I didn't fancy death by neurotoxin. There were bushfires, and treacherous terrain. I had nothing to eat, and only a limited notion of how to find safe food in the bush. I doubted if I could get to the boats, and even if I could, I wasn't going to try my luck at sea.

They didn't need to chain me to the wall. The whole island was a prison.

Also, I had to take Abdi with me, and I had no idea where he was.

Well, that would be my first mission the next day, then. Find Abdi. Gather supplies. Make a plan.

The lights went out. Apparently, they were really serious about the sleeping-time business. I groped my way up the ladder and got changed by feel.

I lay awake in the dark for a long time.

CHAPTER FOURTEEN
The Ballad of John and Yoko

Morning was a shock.

"You have to get up," Rachel said in my ear, and I swam back to the surface of sleep. I had the fuzzy feeling that this wasn't the first time she'd tried to wake me.

"Too early," I said, and curled into the sheets. The next time her hand came to shake my shoulder, I snarled at her—lips pulled back to display my teeth, narrowed eyes, hissing, the whole shebang. I got a brief glimpse of her shocked face, and Sharron behind her, looking more impressed than scared. Then I was back in the black depths.

What eventually woke me was water, cold and poured on the back of my neck. My eyes popped open as I jerked upright, hit my head on the bunk above, and swore.

There was a collection of gasps from the girls gathered around me.

I glared at them all. "What time is it?" From the pale light, I had an awful feeling.

"Dawn," Rachel said, confirming my suspicions. "We must prepare breakfast."

My immediate response was to tell her to go screw herself. I didn't fancy my captors getting free work out of me—passive resistance was much more my style. Even the army hadn't made me do *chores*.

But the army had wanted me alive. These people would probably be thrilled if I starved myself to death.

Kitchens meant access to food. Food meant enabling our escape. And I might see Abdi at breakfast.

"Are you coming, or do I have to fetch Mrs. McClung?" Rachel asked. Her voice was even, but I recognized a threat when I heard it.

"I'm coming," I said, and climbed out of bed. I followed Rachel to the bathroom section at the back of the dormitory. There was a proper shower, thank goodness. I washed fast and rubbed vigorously at my hair with a well-worn towel. My clothes had been replaced with jeans and a long, baggy T-shirt, as well as a cotton hat with a wide brim. And sturdy, rubber-soled sandals to replace the too-big sneakers I'd borrowed from Joph.

My feet were grateful, even if the rest of me was dubious.

Rachel waited for me. "Before we go to the kitchen, I will guide you around our home," she said. "You will see our way of life is righteous, and it may encourage you to embrace God's truth."

I was pretty sure that it was going to take more than cow patties and communal living to make me kill myself, but she was offering me a perfect opportunity to scope things out. And indeed, Rachel showed me nearly everything: the school, the boys' dormitory, the houses where married couples and small children lived, the place for the elderly, the chicken run, and the Father's office. I wasn't allowed to go in, of course, and when I suggested a stroll by the dock, she shook her head. "That is not permitted."

"Where's the church?" I asked. We were making our way down from the school, which was high on a slope.

"The whole world is our church," Rachel said. "God is with us always."

"Huh. Seriously, no computers?"

"They are filled with the wickedness of the outside."

"Or, it's hard to keep your brainwashed, isolated kids both brainwashed and isolated if they have access to entertainment in the real world."

Rachel laughed. "This world is very real, and we don't lack entertainment. We play soccer. We play music. And there are handcrafts and games." She smiled, shy and secret and beautiful. "I like chess," she confessed. "Do you play?"

"Music, not chess," I said. "Why do you care? You want me dead."

Her eyes widened as if she'd forgotten that for a moment, and then she continued the tour without any more personal talk. Me and my big mouth. I might have made the first steps toward making her an ally if I'd been able to keep silent. After that, it was all, "This is where we wash clothes" and "This is where we grow vegetables." The last stop was the milking sheds, or rather, the bunker underneath the concrete slab floor. "This is where we shelter during bad storms," she said.

I eyed the cramped quarters, with camp beds stacked up on one side and cans of food on the other. "Cozy."

"The children do not enjoy their time here," she said. "But it keeps us safe."

"Safety is important," I agreed. I sympathized with the kids. Spending a day in there waiting for the weather to clear would not be fun times.

We went back into the fresh air—well, as fresh as you get near milking sheds. The boys were just sending the cows out again.

Abdi was with them, right in front of me.

We stared at each other for a split second, and then my arms went around him without me even willing it. He was squeezing me just as tight. I might have been shaking a little bit—it was only when I saw him that I'd let myself think about all the things I'd been worried about.

"I'm glad you're all right," he said in my ear.

"Me too," I told him. "Can you sail?"

"Yes. Can you get us food and water?"

"Maybe. Tonight?"

"Tonight."

That was all we had time for before Rachel tapped my back.

"That is not appropriate," she said firmly. I squeezed again and let him go. He was more muscular than I'd thought. The flowing fashions of the future really obscure a lot of body detail. He looked different in jeans.

I helped the girls serve breakfast—toast and bacon and scrambled eggs. Real bacon, too. The soy stuff just doesn't taste the same—sorry if that shocks you.

"You have pigs?" I asked Rachel. I hadn't smelled them.

"We trade with others."

Mrs. McClung handed me an overflowing plate when service was done. "Eat."

"Can I help cook lunch?" I asked.

Her eyebrow popped. "Yes."

Great, I could try to grab some food for our escape. I went with Rachel into the big mess hall just as the boys came in from the milking. She sat beside me and ate with a neat efficiency I tried to copy. Something about the bacon started to disagree with my stomach about halfway through breakfast, and I remembered that going from a vegetarian diet to one with meat could mess with your digestion. I found out later that Abdi had passed an uncomfortable night after that beef stew. He stuck to toast and butter that morning, but I wasn't that smart. I moved to the eggs instead, but since they'd been cooked in the bacon grease, it wasn't much better.

After breakfast, everyone stood up, and a man in a linen robe led them in prayer. Abdi and I stayed sitting, which either was the right thing to do or no one cared. Then Rachel beckoned to me.

"We have school now," she said. "But you're to study scripture and consider God's will for you."

"That sounds very exciting," I said.

"It probably won't be," she said, looking puzzled. I wasn't sure she had much of a sense of sarcasm.

Abdi and I followed Rachel up the hill to the school. Conrad was waiting in a small room. There were a couple of desks there, with a Bible and a notebook and a real ink pen on each one. That they were putting us together was the first good surprise. The second was that the school also had a real bathroom, with a toilet that flushed. That was such a pleasure that it almost made up for my upset stomach.

We spent the rest of the morning in that classroom—except for the periods I spent in the bathroom, really regretting the bacon. We couldn't talk much, because one of the adults was always with us, but they didn't seem to care if we were really studying scripture. We scribbled notes to each other and managed to work out a time and a place to meet that night, and Abdi confirmed that the boys' dormitory had the same security precautions as the girls' (as in, none at all).

After that, Abdi put his head down on the desk and went to sleep. He looked much, much younger with his face relaxed from that blank expression he wore in public. I actually did read some of the Bible, flicking through for bits I remembered, in case I needed to support an argument later. They probably wanted me to realize that I was an abomination, since raising the dead was strictly up to God, but instead I was reassured that I was loved and treasured.

Then I napped a bit, too. I woke up quite suddenly at one point, drool pasting my cheek to the desk, and caught Abdi looking at me with an odd expression, as if he was making some complex calculation that involved me. It annoyed me because I thought he'd already worked out we had to get along if we could, and I couldn't think what other calculations he had to make.

"What?" I said.

"Nothing," he told me. "Go back to sleep."

Well, I wasn't responsible for whatever weird things he was thinking. I turned ostentatiously onto the other side of my face.

When it was time to prepare lunch, Rachel came for me. I spent a long time peeling vegetables and stirring stock and incidentally listening to a lot of gossip. When the soup was simmering, Mrs. McClung put her big fists on her hips and looked me over.

"It's good to see you embracing God's role for you," she said, but her tone said *I'm watching you, missy*. She hadn't let me anywhere near the knives, even when I'd offered to chop the onions, but I'd managed to stuff two ends of bread and a couple of unpeeled carrots into my pockets, covered by the long T-shirt.

"God's role for me is treating others as I would like to be treated and not judging others lest I be judged," I said, looking as humble as I could, which wasn't very.

She looked suspicious, but she couldn't exactly argue with scripture. I waited until her attention was diverted. Then I told Rachel I needed to use the bathroom and went back to the girls' dormitory to do it, hiding the food in my pillowcase.

That mattress was so soft. I lay down for a few minutes and woke up when I heard shouting outside.

It was late afternoon, the sun about three-quarters of the way through the sky, and I had very obviously missed lunch.

The older boys were playing soccer, shirts versus skins, using their sun hats weighed down with rocks to mark the goals. A few of the girls were clustered on the sidelines. At first I thought they were watching in admiration, and then I saw Sharron bouncing a ball from knee to knee and realized that they were waiting for their turn.

"I looked for you," she said. "Mrs. McClung said to let you sleep."

"Oh," I said. "Thanks." She nodded, and turned her attention back to the ball.

Abdi was playing on the skins team.

He really was much more muscular than I'd thought. His biceps were nothing to scoff at, and the hard, lean planes of his stomach made something bounce around a little in mine.

His team wasn't doing very well. The goalie let two through in short succession, and he was replaced by an older boy with better hands. He was a better strategist, too; he called the players into a huddle around the goal and then sent them on their way. There was some complicated passing, and then a knot of boys opened to reveal one in its midst, one foot poised on the ball. The shirts team pounded toward him, but he took his time, gauged the distance, and kicked.

The ball flew true between the other team's sun hats. Abdi joined in the cheering of his teammates.

I cheered, too, and at the sound of my voice, he turned to me.

He was smiling, bright and triumphant. Not that little curled-up wary smile, but a full grin that made his eyes crinkle and dimples crease in his cheeks.

At the sight of that smile, I felt something click in my head.

Do that again, I thought.

And okay, you've been watching me talk about this all along and you've been going, *When exactly is Tegan going to realize she really likes Abdi Taalib?* Honestly, I'm not even sure it was then. I might have worked it out on some level when I shot Zaneisha to save him, or when he sang to me in the boat. But when he smiled at me and his whole face lit up with joy, that was the point I couldn't ignore that I was head over heels for him.

I wanted him to smile again. I wanted him to smile always.

And then I thought, *Oh no.*

Because even if, by some extraordinary chance, he liked me back, it was pretty much the worst timing in the world.

So I went back to the kitchen to help Mrs. McClung with dinner. She told me off for missing lunch and made me eat a sandwich, then, apparently appeased by my apologies, put me to work slicing vegetables. I stole more carrots and a small, sharp knife, and thought about Abdi the whole evening.

≋ ‡ ∞

Before dinner, everyone watched a DVD in the mess hall.

The movie was *Lilo & Stitch*, which is a movie about an alien who finds a family in Hawaii. Apparently, part of the Disney revival a few years ago was that some people really got into vintage methods of consumption, like DVDs, and the Inheritors of the Earth grabbed as many of them as they could during this period. Without computers, their choices for entertainment were kind of limited.

Abdi's face during the whole thing was amazing, by the way. He says that when the French soldiers were pushed out of Djibouti, they left a lot of stuff behind. So some people in Djibouti still have DVD players and he'd seen DVDs for sale in the central market, but he'd never actually watched one.

I slipped out of the hall before the ending, where the alien talks about how he's found his little, broken, good family, and stood in the evening air, watching the moon rise over the sea. Abdi came out after a few minutes. I felt his presence prickle along my skin, and I tried to look normal as I turned around.

"Hi," he said. He was shivering. "Aren't you cold?"

"No."

"It's freezing." He started rubbing his arms. He wasn't faking it; he had goose bumps.

"It's got to be seventy, seventy-two degrees."

He smiled, looking a little wistful. "In Djibouti City, it's over ninety every day. Melbourne summer is like Djibouti winter."

"Wow. That's really hot," I said. Were we honestly talking about the *weather*? "Listen. If you get a chance to escape without me, you should take it."

He nodded. "You too."

"I can't sail," I said. "If it comes right down to it, it has to be you."

He gazed down at me, and I thought he was going to say something else. I couldn't stop watching his mouth.

"It is a nice evening, God be praised," Rachel said behind us.

Abdi let out a noise that might have been a groan.

"It's okay," I said, and seized the opportunity to test something I'd been curious about. "Hey, Rachel, you believe in the sanctity of life, right?"

"Of course."

"So what would you think, hypothetically, if someone were killing lots of children?"

Rachel looked shocked. "I would think they were a very wicked person, far from God's grace."

"You'd want to stop them from killing more children?" I pressed.

Abdi didn't say anything, but his face was very expressive on the subject of me shutting the hell up right away. I ignored him and focused on the Inheritor girl.

"Well, if I could," Rachel said cautiously. "Aiding the weak is an act of charity, but ultimate judgment lies in God's hands."

"And if you couldn't stop them yourself, you'd want to make sure other people who could were in a position to know about the murders?" Abdi made an abrupt motion, which I evaded by stepping away.

"I suppose so. I don't understand, Tegan. Why are you asking these questions?" She obviously didn't have a clue about the Ark Project. It was probably only the higher-ups who knew. The man who had died, and maybe Joseph and Conrad. Definitely the Father would know. I was itching to have a serious talk with that guy.

251

"Oh, no reason," I said blithely. "Abdi and I were just having a philosophical discussion."

"It seems a brutal topic of conversation," she said disapprovingly. "Do you not wish to simply enjoy God's bounty this evening? Why must you consider these awful things and destroy your peace of mind?"

For a moment, I experienced a point of double vision, looking at her and seeing myself. I'd never been quite as oblivious as Rachel was, but I didn't have her excuse of being raised in isolation. Given my own way, I'd have happily ignored everything that was going on around me and pursued my own goals, both in the past and in the future. But Alex had dragged me with her to protests, and Dalmar had talked passionately about justice and change. Bethari wanted to destroy the No Migrant policy, and Abdi and Joph had taken real risks to fight murderous pharmaceutical practices.

Thinking about and fighting some of the world's multiple horrors had made my life more painful. But it was a much larger life than I would have lived otherwise.

"I'm really glad I know you," I told Abdi.

He looked puzzled, but I turned to Rachel before he could make any reply. "I'd better go back and help serve," I said, and smiled. Her frown cleared, and she smiled back.

The Inheritors of the Earth were divorced from reality, perhaps even more than people like Soren, who had wrapped himself in a blanket of willful ignorance so he wouldn't have to deal with the truth. Most of the people in this community were deliberately kept away from even being able to investigate for themselves.

But some of them knew that refugees were being stuffed into cryocontainers and frozen in huge warehouses all over the country and, for whatever reason, had chosen not to make that horror public.

Abdi and I needed to escape for bigger reasons than either of us.

So what did it hurt if Rachel spent the night thinking I was being obedient and submissive? We'd be gone in the morning.

≈ ‡ ∞

The first part of the escape went off without a hitch. I stayed awake very easily after my afternoon nap, singing the *Revolver* album to myself three times after lights-out. It was hard to coordinate an escape without any way to tell the time, but during our "study session" Abdi and I had decided on that as a reasonable method that would give the Inheritors plenty of time to go to sleep. When it was time, I dressed by feel and climbed down one-handed from my bunk, with the stolen food crammed into my pillowcase and the knife tucked into my pocket. I held my breath, but Rachel didn't even turn over, and no one woke up as I wafted out the door. They worked hard, those girls.

It was beautiful outside, the half-moon making everything shades of silver and gray. I went down the slope very carefully—I'd wrapped the knife in a strip of sheet so it wouldn't cut my leg, but falling over a loose rock with it in my pocket was probably still not a great idea. Abdi was waiting by the entrance to the underground bunker. He must have sung faster than I did. He was shivering again, and I thrust my nightie at him.

"Here," I whispered.

He took it, but didn't put it on. "It's white," he whispered back. "Later."

I could see his point. A moving white figure would stand out on that moonlit night.

But no one was watching. There wasn't a single light in a single window.

We went toward the dock, and, glory of glories, there were two boats there. Abdi pointed to the farther one, and we crept toward it, lowering ourselves down the side of the pier. My shortness proved a problem, and Abdi had to help me, his long hands cool at my hips.

I picked the lock on the cabin door with my last hairpins and some swearing. Abdi looked at the banks of navigation equipment and nodded in satisfaction. "I can work this," he said.

In retrospect, our biggest mistake was thinking that because the Inheritors were mostly trusting and nice and religiously minded, they were also stupid.

The second Abdi put his hands on the equipment, all hell broke loose.

It was even worse than the time my computer had blared advertising at me. The advertisers had been after my attention, after all. It had been noisy and disorienting, but they hadn't wanted to hurt me. The burglar alarm was a blast of sound so loud, I thought someone had shot me with a sonic gun. But where a sonic gun would have deafened me immediately, this noise went on and on.

Abdi grabbed my arm and yelled something, but I couldn't make it out. I yanked away from him, cringing down with my palms pressed to my ears. He bent down, hands outstretched, eyes intent on mine.

And then the light bombs went off.

We were both blind after that, me because I hadn't known to close my eyes, and Abdi because he'd tried to cover my eyes instead of protecting himself. Sobbing with the pain of it, I curled in on myself. Nothing had ever hurt like that before.

And that was how they found us, crunched in tight balls of misery in the cabin of their boat. I was so grateful that the noise had stopped that I was almost happy about the strange hands that picked me up and hoisted me over a shoulder like a sack of potatoes.

My vision returned quickly, though my head still throbbed. Abdi was being dragged behind me, an Inheritor holding each arm as he stumbled along. I nodded, trying to convey the message that I was okay.

But I wasn't so sure. My hearing still hadn't come back.

The man carrying me stopped and swung me down, taking my arm in a firm grip. We were near the milking sheds, and I had a nasty suspicion that was quickly confirmed, as we were marched down the stairs into the storm bunker.

Conrad was one of the men with Abdi. He said something to

Abdi, who shook his head and motioned at his ears. Conrad sighed and spoke to the other men, who set up two camp beds on opposite sides of the room. Conrad pointed Abdi to one and me to the other. Apparently the gender-separation rules could be bent but not broken for abductees who tried to run away.

Then they left. The heavy door closed behind them; I felt it more than heard it, the vibrations moving through the concrete floor. I stared at Abdi from across the room, seeing my own uncertainty reflected in his face.

The lights went out.

I shot to my feet, moving in Abdi's direction. I was locked up in the silent darkness; we'd lost our best and probably final chance to escape, and I couldn't stand it alone.

I was barely halfway there when I bumped into a warm body and flung my arms around him. He hugged me back, tight and strong, and I clung to him, almost grateful for the dark that hid my weakness. I couldn't see or hear, but I could feel and smell. Abdi smelled like dirt and cheap soap and something that might have been the garlic from the pasta at dinner. His hands trembled as he smoothed them down my back. He rested his chin against my forehead and said something; I couldn't hear it, but I felt his lips move against my hair.

I reached up to stroke his face and felt light stubble prick my fingers. He stilled, and I felt him shudder against me.

When he kissed me, it was desperate and hungry and very, very sweet.

I clutched at his back with fierce fingers, thrilling at the way he held me so tight. Abdi Taalib didn't think of me as the Living

Dead Girl, or a lost soul, or some sort of figurehead to be pitied, celebrated, or despised. He wanted Tegan Oglietti; he wanted her to kiss him.

A cynical part of me said that it was just because we were sense-deprived and scared. I told that part to shut up, and concentrated on the rest of me, which was very happy indeed.

Sometime later, as we sat on the bare stone floor, Abdi kissing a line of little explosions down the back of my neck, I realized that sound had come back to me. He was murmuring my name between each kiss.

"Abdi?" I said.

I could feel his response even before he answered. "Yes?"

"Oh, thank god, I thought the hearing loss might be permanent."

"No. The burglar alarms are designed for temporary sense deprivation." He hesitated. "I'm so sorry, Tegan. I didn't think."

"Neither did I," I said reasonably. "We were both stupid to think it'd be that easy."

"I should have checked for an alarm. I knew better."

"Really?"

He laughed. "Of course. It's common tech. What, did you think I grew up rubbing sticks together to make fire?"

"No. I didn't really think about it," I said half truthfully.

"Hm," he said, exploring down my sides. His hands hesitated. "What's this?"

"My knife!" I'd completely forgotten about it, too miserable during the alarm assault, and then too thrilled in the dark. "Lucky they didn't search us."

"They searched me," Abdi said. "I think they don't take you seriously."

"Idiots," I grumbled.

He laughed softly. "Well, look at you. You're short and delicate. You've got pale skin that looks like it might tear in a strong wind and big, dark, innocent eyes. I bet they think you're breakable."

"Hey, I have muscles!"

"Oh, I know," he said, and I felt the heat rise in my cheeks. "But these are people who are so certain of how things *must* be that they don't pay any attention to how they really are."

It was a good point. "I keep thinking about it," I said softly. "It's hard to believe that people this nice can't see that it's wrong to want me to kill myself."

I felt his shrug. "Religious fanatics."

"It's not the religious part that worries me. The God I believe in wouldn't want me dead, but I don't know if I can convince them of that. I wish I could figure out how they even knew about the Ark Project."

Abdi's voice was genuinely horrified, and not for the reason I would have suspected. "You really believe in *God*?" he said.

"Well, yeah. I don't know why you're so surprised. Most people believe in a higher power of some sort."

"Fifty-four percent is hardly most."

"Of course it is. More than fifty percent. Most. And anyway, I read it was more like seventy percent."

"It doesn't count if you don't attend services," he said.

I poked him in the ribs, hard. "It definitely counts. Anyway, wait, you saw my interview. I said I was Roman Catholic right there!"

"I thought that was for the audience," he said.

"I thought *most* people in Djibouti were Sunni."

"Well, I'm an atheist, like my father," he said, looking stubborn. "And I thought you were smarter."

"Um, gross," I said, and then had to explain the meaning of *gross*, though I'd thought it was pretty clear from context.

The rest of the argument went as these arguments tend to go, from "You can't prove that something doesn't exist" to "If there's no positive proof, there's no reason behind faith" to "Religion is an amazing force for good in the world" to "Do you *know* what forced Islamic and Christian conversion did to Africa?"

Once you start talking about gay people being executed, and female genital mutilation—*not* an actual Islamic practice, I'm just saying—and missionaries deliberately impeding measures to prevent the spread of HIV, there aren't many ways for the conversation to get good again, especially when neither of you can finish it by walking away. We edged away from each other, sulking silently, and occasionally saying, "If you'd just—" or "If you'd think about—" and then stopping before we finished the sentence.

It was lonely, there in the dark.

"Hey," I said finally. "Are you awake?"

"Yes," he said guardedly.

"How did you grow up?"

There was a pause and some shuffling sounds, and then a

long body lowered itself beside mine. "I'm the third of four children," he began.

We talked for a long time, sitting on that bare floor, wrapped in each other's arms. We talked about our families, our home lives, what we'd done in the past and dreamed of for the future.

And, of course, we talked about the Beatles. Abdi had become a fan when he'd heard a sample from "Blackbird" on an ad for shoes. He'd chased down the reference and discovered it was from a song over a hundred and fifty years old. There were more songs, by the same people. He'd streamed pirated versions, then paid for the legal downloads. He made his younger sister listen, and she became a fan, too.

"They always meant hope to me," I confessed. "It's stupid but—"

His fingers were tracing a pattern down my arms. "I think I see. I feel that way about La Belle Nuit—do you know them?"

"No."

"They live in Scotland. Their singer is Djiboutian. She sings mostly in French, but some Arabic, some Somali. Very beautiful songs, and she's a wonderful vocalist."

"I don't understand any of those languages," I said, embarrassed. "Well, a few words of Somali."

"From your boyfriend." It wasn't a question, and his hands went still on my arms.

"My ex-boyfriend," I said, and twisted around to face him. Not that I could see him any better that way, but it seemed appropriate. "I loved Dalmar. But I'm here, with you." It was true, I realized as I said it. My love for Dalmar had been real, and beautiful. And it was still there, partly. I didn't think it would ever completely disappear. But it had diminished under the stresses of the last weeks and months, like a shore eroding under the constant pressure of the waves.

I wasn't ready to put words to my feelings for Abdi yet, but they were there, warm and bright, like a new flame. Only time could tell if the fire would burn too hot and fast, or die for lack of fuel, or be steady and strong. But I wanted to have the time to find out.

"You're here with me because we got kidnapped by cultists while running from the army with footage that could blow open a government conspiracy," he pointed out, but the tension in his body had eased.

"Details," I said.

Abdi laughed. "Well, I can teach you some French and Arabic, if you would like."

"I would like. What's Arabic for 'nose'?"

"It might depend on the dialect. I would say *anf*."

I touched his nose with my fingertips. "And what's the word for 'mouth'?"

"*Fam*."

I traced the outline of his lips, feeling the corners stretch and curl as he smiled. "And what's the translation for 'kiss me'?"

"*Boseeni*," he replied, his breath warm against my skin. It seemed a shame not to close that gap.

After that, I discovered that language lessons held less interest than the other things Abdi could teach me.

CHAPTER FIFTEEN
Across the Universe

We woke up when the lights flickered back on, squinting painfully at each other through the glare. At some point during that long night, we'd found our way to Abdi's bed and dragged it back over to mine. Lying on the camp beds wasn't the most comfortable thing ever, but it beat the heck out of sitting on concrete.

And, okay, not that it's any of your business, but no, we did not go all the way. Neither of us had any form of protection handy, and the whole thing was so weird and new. We weren't ready.

Besides. As much as I liked the touching and the kissing, it was the talking that was most important that night; it gave us the most comfort and support. We talked about everything, until Abdi couldn't even mumble replies to my slurred questions, and I followed him into sleep.

Everything, that is, except what we were going to do in the morning.

But morning, or its artificial equivalent, had come, and we had to deal with our situation.

"I should move the bed back," Abdi said quietly. "I don't want them to separate us."

I nodded and combed my fingers through my hair, trying to get it in order while he shifted the evidence of our nighttime tryst.

The Inheritors of the Earth came in, five of them, all men, Conrad leading them. He eyed us both.

"Can you hear me?" he said, slow and loud.

"Yes," I told him, and he nodded, looking relieved.

"Food and water will be brought to you," he said. "In the meantime, if you need to relieve yourselves, come with me."

You've probably never been escorted to a toilet, with one guard waiting outside the door and another outside the tiny window—I know, because I climbed up to check. I can tell you, it's not much fun. It was good to see daylight and breathe fresh air, but other than my escorts, I didn't see another living soul; they must have warned everyone else to stay inside. Here and there, bumblebees swam lazily through the air.

I would have liked them, but they reminded me of the flock of bumblecams that had haunted me, which, in turn, made me think about Bethari filming the ranks of frozen refugees. I was desperately afraid for her and Joph, and was pinning all my hopes on Zaneisha having the ability and inclination to do something to help them. Abdi and I couldn't do a thing unless we escaped, and I was running low on ideas of how to accomplish that.

There was a chemical toilet set up for us behind a privacy screen when we got back to the cellar. I guessed that it might be a while before we got to go outside again.

Rachel brought food down to us on a tray. Cold roast beef sandwiches, a couple of apples, a pitcher of water.

"How long are we going to be down here?" I asked.

"I'm not supposed to talk to you," she said, and then blushed, looking stricken.

"We won't tell," Abdi said, giving her his small, careful smile. I bristled a little bit, then hauled myself back.

Rachel was looking troubled. "Those children," she said. "Those murdered children. Are they real?"

"Yes," I said softly. "They're real, and they're secret. The Father knows, but he hasn't told. We want to make sure the secret is known, Rachel. That's why Abdi has to escape. I can stay. It's me you need."

She jerked away and joined the men at the other end of the room.

"Too far," Abdi said critically.

"Worth a shot," I told him, and bit into my sandwich.

When Rachel came back to collect our plates, she was biting her lip. "The Father is back," she whispered. "I heard Joseph tell Mrs. McClung that he wants to see you after you've eaten."

I should have been afraid. I know that now. But at the time, I was eager to have it out with my mysterious foe. Maybe I could persuade him to tell the world about what we'd found. He wasn't a supporter of cryonics; surely he wasn't in favor of freezing refugees.

Abdi's expression didn't reflect my anticipation. "Be careful," he said.

I smiled at him, and Rachel looked modestly away from whatever she saw in my face. "I will," I told him. "I mean, really, what can he do?"

You'd think that by that point, I'd have learned to stop asking those kinds of questions.

≋ ‡ ∞

The Father was shorter than I'd thought.

Other than that, he looked just the same as he had in the tubecasts: dark eyes, pale skin, a strong, clean-shaven jaw. His hair, which had been covered by a hat in the 'casts, turned out to be an indeterminate brown.

The thing that a tubecast could only faintly convey, though, was the sheer power of his presence.

I felt it like a fist in the face when I walked into his office, my Inheritor guards on each side, and those dark eyes fastened intently on mine. I'd thought Tatia had strength of personality, but the Father had her beat without a fight.

"Tegan Oglietti," he said, each word measured and precise. "Are you ready to return to the grace of God?"

"If by that you mean top myself, no, not so much," I said. I'd wanted to sound brave and angry, but in the face of his charisma, I sounded childishly petulant.

The guards made shocked noises behind me; the Father waved them out with a trace of amusement around his mouth. The door closed with a thunk; there'd be no escape that way. I was very aware of the knife in my pocket, but that was a chancy last resort. It would be better to persuade him to see my point of view, if I could.

The Father placed his chin on his folded hands and regarded me. I leaned back, as nonchalantly as I could, determined not to break the silence first. But he was accustomed to this sort of power play, and I wasn't very good at being patient.

"How did you know about the Ark Project?" I said. "The Inheritor who Gregor shot—he mentioned it. You knew, too, didn't you? What does it have to do with me? Why did you want me to know about it? And why haven't you exposed it?"

He said nothing.

"They're killing people! Doesn't that bother you?" I was trying to sound reasonable, but sarcasm crept in. "I guess it's okay, since you want me to die."

"You are already dead, Tegan."

"I *was*. Now I'm alive. Isn't that the part you guys object to? If you don't think I was really brought back to life, then you've got no reason to hate me."

"We do not hate you, Tegan. We object, in God's name, to the abrogation of his holy privileges, and those of his son. Without God's grace, no true resurrection is possible. Thus, you are not truly resurrected. Your every breath is a mockery to the God with whom you claim to hold faith."

"I *do* hold faith," I said. "It's you who's got it wrong. Look, maybe you don't understand. I can explain the revival process; you'll see that it's pure science, not—"

"Tegan," he said, interrupting me so firmly that I actually shut up. "It is you who doesn't understand. Would you like to learn about the other half of the Ark Project?"

My argument caught in my throat. *Other half?*

"Yes," I said, almost whispering. "I would."

≋ ‡ ∞

Unlike his flock, the Father used computers.

This hypocrisy shouldn't have surprised me—he had to have made those tubecast appearances *with* something, after all—but when he opened the wooden cupboard to pull out his equipment, my jaw dropped. Another computer was balled into the corner, and after a moment, I recognized it. Bethari's computer, the one with the footage.

"That's mine!" I said. "What happened to 'Thou shalt not steal'?"

He ignored me, settling back into his chair and opening the computer. "Why do you think you were brought back, Tegan? Do you think it was out of mercy? Did you think they took pity on your youth and beauty?"

"I think they wanted to test the science, and my donation form let them study the aftereffects," I said. "I'm not naive."

"You are," he said, and spun the computer so that I could

see. "Why would they test on you? You know they already have thousands of bodies upon which they can practice their debased corruption of a miracle."

My breath caught. Of course they did. If they were freezing refugees anyway, why not carefully shoot them first and use those bodies to practice reviving trauma victims? There was absolutely no reason to use me in particular.

"Your father was a military man, was he not?"

The abrupt change of subject caught me by surprise. I said nothing, but he kept going, unperturbed by my silence. "So was mine. He was a general when the Ark Project was first proposed at the highest levels of government. He retired soon afterward, but he maintained his contacts, even as he rediscovered his faith. A few of the Inheritors of the Earth have always known what this earthly authority intended. Several of our young men have made great sacrifices, joining the enemy forces to maintain our watch over their efforts."

"You sent spies."

"The word is inappropriate to soldiers of God." He whipped the computer around. "This, Tegan, is the Ark."

It took a moment for my eyes to make sense of what I was looking at—some sort of vast structure in a hollow space, like a massive silver egg, partially cracked open. There were girders and plating and machines. And people, tiny as ants against the immensity of the structure.

"This is the prototype of a starship," the Father said. "It is being built in a secret military installation beneath Mount Ossa, right here in Tasmania. If all goes well—and my sources suggest it goes *very* well—it will be rebuilt in space. This first stage is nearly complete."

I gaped at him.

"The Ark Project is designed to send people from Earth to colonize other planets, similar enough to ours to sustain human life. But these will be long journeys."

"Centuries long," I said, stunned at the scope of it.

"Perhaps thousands of years. No one lives for so long unaided. And the governments of this world have little trust; they will not believe their followers can bring up successive generations to be obedient to their vision. What if they forget their mission? What if they lose their science, grow to believe that their entire world *is* the starship? No. Better to freeze your elite colonists. Have some awake at given times to crew the ship. Have them sleep when their shift is done. Inch closer to the new world. And once they arrive, wake the sleepers in the hold, to labor on the land."

It was nightmarish. It was sickening. And it was all too possible.

That's how the British had set up their Australian colonies, after all, with waves of indentured laborers, prisoners compelled to work out their sentences in a land so distant it might as well have been another planet.

And today's refugees were all *illegal* immigrants, breaking the laws of Australia simply by being here.

The government and army could do it. If they threw out the last two hundred years of human-rights progress, they really could.

The Father spread his hands when he saw the understanding in my face. "And they will never give a thought to the blasphemy they have created. Now, tell me, Tegan Oglietti. Why did they raise *you*?"

"Because I'd been dead for a long time," I said. It was unfolding out before me, like a composition I'd heard only in fragments. Now the whole score was becoming clear.

"Yes," he agreed. "A hundred years dead, and they raised you, healthy in body and stable in mind. Or healthy and stable enough, at any rate, to proceed. You see? There was no need for us to interfere until *you* were revived."

It finally explained the mystery I'd pondered, why they'd bothered with someone prepared for cryorevival so long ago. It explained the battery of psych tests and intellectual tests—even the way they'd let me go to school. They wanted to see how well I could adjust.

And I'd performed for them like a trained dog.

Operation New Beginning had nothing to do with dead soldiers. It had never had anything to do with dead soldiers. It was about allowing the elite, the powerful, and the wealthy to escape to a new world, from the mess they'd made of this one.

I stared at the Father, and I hated him for telling me the truth at last.

"I thought you cared about the sanctity of life! You say you don't kill people, but you just let all those refugees die!"

"They would have died anyway, of starvation or disease." He shrugged. "Or perhaps lived, according to God's will. It is bringing them back to a semblance of life that desecrates God's sacred will, and that blasphemy I must expose. I have always had faith that my father's fears were well founded."

"Marie said they couldn't make starships," I said. "She said the technology wasn't there yet, that the ships would cost too much, that people wouldn't stand for their governments' doing it."

"Indeed. So they have done it in secret, because they are full of hubris and greed," he said, and laid both hands flat upon his desk. He did it with terrible gentleness; I could see he wanted to slam them down, and the self-control it took him to be soft scared me even more than the anger he was suppressing. "They do this, because they are not *content* with the one world God gave us to rule over."

"How do you know?" I demanded.

I was remembering Trevor Dawson's face when I'd challenged him.

What is the Ark Project?

Humanity's last chance, he'd said, and ranted about ocean anoxia.

The end might not come for some time. But this project had started over sixty years ago. They had been looking to the future, to their children's escape route.

Humanity's last chance.

Maybe it was just a way to justify the project to himself; maybe it was the only way he could cope with knowing what he was doing. But what if he was right?

"What if they're doing it because this world is dying? You've got a computer. You must have seen the climate news, the drying rivers, the rising oceans. You know that things are getting worse, not better."

"God will not allow it," the Father said. "The world will end as the prophets predict, not by any tools of man."

"How stupid *are* you?" I demanded.

The Father hit me in the face.

It was an open-handed blow, almost contemptuous, but with enough force to snap my head around. I was completely taken aback, with no chance to put my basic training into motion. *Zaneisha would be ashamed of me*, I thought. I got to my feet somehow, and stumbled to put my back against one of the side walls, fists up in case I needed to use them. The Father sat there watching me, his anger carefully put away again. It wasn't fake. He genuinely hated me, blasphemy in person, mouthing defiance against him. But he'd pull the rage out and use it only when he needed to, like a weapon.

A *weapon*.

I still had the knife in my pocket. It was all I could do to stop myself from grabbing for it. He was bigger and stronger than I was, and it was too chancy. I needed to wait for an opportunity. I shifted my weight and felt the knife move against my thigh.

"So," I said softly, "you want me to kill myself because you want to prove I'm unstable, is that it? You want to scuttle the Ark Project by proving that someone from a hundred years ago can't make it?"

"I want you to reunite yourself with God," he said. "I will reveal with your body the blasphemy these secularists seek to perpetuate. And when I do, my people under the mountain will rise up and destroy the Ark starship."

"You're going to use my dead body as a signal for sabotage? Why don't you just leak the news?"

"It is God's will," he said simply. "You are the first; you must return to him."

I laughed, but there was no humor in it. "I am so tired of being *used*. The army tried to do it, Tatia tried to do it, and now you're trying to do it. I'm a person, not a symbol, not property, and not a prop. If you want me dead, I can't stop you, but I won't make it easier for you, either. Dirty your own fucking hands."

"Murder is a sin," the Father said flatly. "And you are not a person. You are an empty shell mouthing excuses in an attempt to delay the inevitable, and I will not allow you to continue." He raised his voice, pitching it to the office door. "Bring in the boy."

My heart squeezed painfully as they brought Abdi in, Conrad and Joseph on either side.

"Tegan," Abdi said, his eyes going straight to my face.

"I'm all right," I lied, ignoring the stinging in my cheek.

"Say your good-byes," the Father ordered, and allowed himself a smile at my outrage.

"What?" Abdi demanded.

The Father ignored him. "My followers have been much too kind to you, Tegan Oglietti, misled by their soft hearts." Conrad and Joseph shifted, looking abashed.

"This is what will happen now," the Father said. "You will be imprisoned underground. You will be given sufficient food and water to maintain yourself, no more. You will speak to no one, hear from no one, see no one, for there will be no light for you. Once in a while, I will come, and ask if you are done with this charade of life."

I could hear my heartbeat in my ears, a muffled drum. I'd fight it. I could hold out. Maybe Abdi would escape and lead a rescue, maybe Rachel would have a crisis of faith and help, maybe the army would storm the compound and release me.

The Father's voice was very soft and utterly relentless. "And how long do you think you can last?"

Not long enough, I thought dully. The army thought I had escaped, and they knew I had no reason to trust the Inheritors; they'd never look for me here. Rachel was too loyal to her people to assist me, and they'd be watching Abdi closely. There would be no rescue from outside. There was no way to fight from the inside.

I could resist the Father for a time. But eventually I would give up.

And giving up, I would die.

"Now say good-bye to your friend. Forever."

With an inarticulate yell, Abdi Taalib, that caring, studious musician, flung himself across the Father's desk and tried his very best to strangle him with his bare hands.

It was a futile effort; Conrad and Joseph were shocked but acted swiftly, pulling him off the Father and giving him a couple of punches to the head for his trouble. But they were fully occupied trying to deal with Abdi's frantic struggles, and the Father was leaning back in his chair, watching him with wide eyes. It had probably been a long time since anyone had tried to smack him around.

For that moment, no one was looking at me. Abdi had given me the opportunity I needed.

Slipping the little knife from my pocket, I moved behind the Father and placed its sharp point against his throat. He froze immediately, but the others were still fighting.

"Stop," I said. It didn't entirely sound like my voice. "Stop, or I'll kill him."

≈ ‡ ∞

I promised to tell you the truth.

And the truth is, I think I would have done it. I'd never felt that kind of hatred before, not for Dawson or Tatia or Carl Hurfest. Not even for the sniper who accidentally shot me on the steps of Parliament House.

But I felt a killing kind of fury for the Father, who told people God said I wasn't a person, who refused to recognize that I had a story of my own, who let refugees die until it suited him to intervene. If things had gone wrong, I would have slit his throat with no hesitation, thou shalt not kill be damned.

I don't know whether Joseph and Conrad could see that, or if they just weren't prepared to take the chance. They immediately stood away from Abdi, holding their hands up in plain view.

"Abdi, can you find something to tie them with?"

"Uh," he said. His eyes were wandering slightly.

"Abdi!" I snapped. "I *need* you."

He pulled it together. "Tie them up. Right."

"This is foolish," the Father hissed.

"Try the cabinet," I said, ignoring him. Well, half ignoring him. I might have pushed the knife in just a little deeper. The Father sucked in a breath and shut up. "Bethari's computer is in there."

Abdi shoved the computer in his pocket and rummaged around until he came up with some sort of flexible metallic strips. Conrad and Joseph both looked resigned as he made them kneel and wrapped the strips around their wrists and ankles.

"Please," Conrad said. "Please don't hurt him."

"That's going to depend on you, isn't it?" I said. "I don't owe you any favors. You were going to lock me underground!"

He flushed and looked away. I didn't have a lot of sympathy. He might have felt bad about it, but he'd have done it.

Abdi tied the Father's wrists, too, and then looked at me. "The boats?"

"Yes. I think he'll be able to turn off the burglar alarm, don't you?"

"I do," he said, and glanced at the Father. If anything, he looked even less forgiving than I felt. "I should take the knife. I'm taller."

That made sense. I let him take control of it, sliding out from

276

under his hand. I grabbed the Father's computer, with its footage of the starship, took a deep breath, and looked around the office. There was nothing else we needed, and speed might be our best ally. "All right. Let's go."

I stuck my arm under the Father's and heaved, counting in time with Abdi. It was awkward, but we got him out of the chair and into the doorway.

"If you come after us," Abdi said, looking directly at Conrad and Joseph, "if we run into *any* trouble, we'll cut his throat and push him over the side."

"No, no," Joseph whispered. "No trouble."

We'd have to trust their fear. I closed the door behind us, and we set off. Once outside, Abdi moved the knife to the Father's back. I was absolutely certain he couldn't reach the heart with that small blade, but it didn't matter. The Father could hardly run, encumbered as he was, and this way we wouldn't murder him by accident.

Besides, whatever curfew had been placed on the other Inheritors was still in effect. Cows were wandering the high pastures untended, and the buildings were quiet. There were more boats in the harbor, fishing boats that must have been brought in.

"Where is everyone?" I asked, and Abdi pushed the Father's wrists up his back until he answered.

"They are in silent contemplation of God's will," he gasped. "You hell spawn!"

Abdi shoved his wrists higher.

I smiled. "It doesn't matter what he calls me, Abdi. He's a stupid, insignificant person under the delusion he speaks for God."

The Father choked on his own rage. I helped Abdi get him down onto the boat deck, and then it came to the moment of truth.

I don't think the Father was a coward, exactly. But I think he weighed his options and decided God would rather have him guiding his flock than dead at the hands of a thirdie atheist and a soulless husk. He deactivated the burglar alarm, and the computer banks hummed into life at Abdi's touch.

"All right," Abdi said absently, and guided the boat free from its berth. I grinned at the movement.

"And what are you going to do with me?" the Father asked.

"Can you swim?"

"And if I said no, devil's child? Would you toss me in to drown?"

"Maybe," I said. "Can you swim?"

"Yes," he growled.

"Take us out a little way, Abdi," I said.

"I'm coming up with you," he said, and his voice brooked no argument. In the end, I sawed through the Father's wrist bindings with my little knife, and we both shoved him over the rail before he had time to recover. The sound of his belly flop was immensely satisfying.

I watched, for a little while, just to make sure he hadn't lied. He *could* swim, with a strong freestyle stroke that would get him back to shore all right. He would definitely call for help, maybe mobilize their fishing fleet to follow us. But we had a head start.

Abdi had gone back into the cabin, and I followed him, clinging to the back of his chair as we picked up speed. "Will we get caught?" I asked.

"This boat's got some heavy-duty electronic shielding," he said. "And the navy isn't worried about people breaking into the mainland from the South."

That was true. It was the North that caused the problems, the North where refugees were crossing in increasing numbers. Not in fancy cloaked vessels, but in anything that would float. And as a reward for their bravery and perseverance, they were caught and held in the camps.

It was the North where they killed those people, storing them in cryocontainers and waiting for a time when they could be resurrected to a new and distant world—if they could be resurrected at all.

It was a beautiful afternoon, the sun glinting on the water. I didn't want to break the peaceful silence, especially when Abdi put his arm around my waist.

But I had to.

"Abdi," I said, "let me tell you what the Father said about the Ark Project."

≋ ‡ ∞

After I'd shown him the footage of the starship, Abdi was silent for a long time.

"The refugees could be volunteers," I said weakly. "They could have chosen this to get out of the camps."

"Seven-year-old refugees, choosing between the camps or freezing. Some volunteers." He shook his head. "The only real difference is that these slavers won't have to worry about their cargo dying on the way."

I winced at the starkness of *slavers*.

He noticed. "You want to use another word? 'Pioneers'? 'Explorers'?"

"No," I said. "It's just...they've done it all before. Take condemned people and ship them to a new land to work. Send poor kids over to make up labor shortages. Oh, and kill or drive off the people who are already on the land and steal their kids, too. Tell yourself that it's all for the best, that you're making a bright new future." I swallowed hard against the bile in my throat. "I just thought...I thought we'd learned better. I thought we'd stopped making this sort of horrible mistake."

"People are still people," he said gently.

"I know. You're right. But I...my dad was in the army. They told me I was helping soldiers. My guardian, Marie, she has no idea about any of this; they were using her, too. I feel sick."

Abdi put one arm around my shoulders and steered with the other. "I'm sure your father was a good man," he said steadily.

"He was. He wouldn't stand for this. We have to get the word out. I can't believe there won't be any change, if people just *know*."

He tugged me in a little tighter and tucked his chin over my head. "You're optimistic."

"I have to be," I said. "Or why not just give up? Protest and people speaking up has worked—it honestly has, in so many ways. Equal marriage, gender rights, religious tolerance— some things have really changed for the better since my time, Abdi. This could change, too."

"I've seen too much to take that on faith," he said. "But, Tegan, I hope you're right." After a second, he began to sing "The Ballad of John and Yoko."

Awful as it might seem, I started to laugh. Harassed by the press, trying to get away for some time together, spreading the word about peace—John and Yoko hadn't had it easy, even before John took off for his months-long Long Weekend of debauchery.

But they'd still been able to joke about it.

I sang along, and for once, I didn't mind that my voice was rough and creaky. Me and Abdi, we sounded good together.

I don't know what's going to happen with us, to us. But we had that, at least, and it was much more than nothing.

CHAPTER SIXTEEN
Come Together

Running from the warehouse, we'd planned to upload the footage as soon as we could. But with no one out to get us right away, we had time to spare. The first priority was to check on news of Bethari and Joph.

For once, Soren came in useful. The headline story of his 'cast was still the absence of his four classmates.

"He says we're all on vacation," I said, scanning the accompanying transcript. "Soren knocked on Ms. Miyahputri's door, and some guy was house-sitting. He implied I'd had a nervous breakdown, and you guys were going with me while I recovered in the country somewhere."

Soren, of course, was delighted by this news and talked about it at some length, complete with excerpts from my interview with Hurfest, dwelling lovingly on the bits where I'd appeared the most upset and furious.

"I really hate that guy," Abdi said, leaning over my shoulder.

I nodded, tapping my fingers against my thigh. "This isn't good news," I said slowly. "But at least it's not bad, either. No reports of finding their bodies in a ditch."

Abdi nodded and did something to the boat controls. "Do you want to upload the footage now?"

"I was thinking about that," I said. Seeing the interview extracts was an unpleasant experience, but it had given me an idea. "Let's try something else."

≋ ‡ ∞

It was a seven-hour trip to the mainland, and Abdi stopped arguing with me at about hour two, having gone from outright opposition to making sensible additions that gave us a much greater chance of success. We studied the maps on the boat computer. Instead of going straight for Port Phillip Bay, we headed for a much quieter destination along the Great Ocean Road, near the small township of Kennett River.

Despite my confidence in our plan, I was nervous. So many things had already gone wrong.

"Weather's not good," Abdi said as we got closer to the mainland, eyeing the boat computer. "There are supercell storm warnings."

"That sounds bad."

"We'll make it there well before it gets serious," he told me. "It's actually good; there should be fewer boats on the water."

"But you can manage the boat all right?"

"I've done this before," he said, not for the first time.

"Not in Australia."

"The Red Sea is a challenge," he said. "Bass Strait is easy." He paused. "Easy-ish. Relax, please? Trust me."

I did. I just didn't trust the weather. By the time we got close to land, the sea had gotten noticeably rougher and the wind was blowing hard enough to make me hold tight to the handgrips when I went on deck. The bay itself was sheltered enough, with a nearly deserted sandy beach. Abdi kept a sharp eye on the depth gauges as we went in, sonar guiding him through the rocks. There was a chunking sound as he dropped the anchor.

I eyed the beach. It looked depressingly far away. "That's it?"

"That's it. Close as we can get with this keel. The currents should be all right, though."

"Augh," I said, and started taking off my shoes and pants. The T-shirt could stay on, but swimming in jeans wasn't something I wanted to try.

Abdi stood still and stared.

"Oh," I said, remembering that our nighttime explorations had been in that solid dark. "Uh, so, yeah, should I do a little dance?"

"No, this is good," he said, and pulled off his own outer clothes.

Abdi in underwear. Mmm.

The actual swim was about as unpleasant as I'd thought it would be, even with Abdi taking the job of towing our supplies behind us. My eyes stung, and salty water went up my nose, and every time seaweed brushed me, I was convinced it was a shark. And sure, the oceans are warmer than in my time, but that doesn't translate to actually warm. I was shivering by the time I found sand under my probing feet, and my fingers were clumsy undoing the knots Abdi had made on the tarpaulin wrapped around our things.

"I think I like the Red Sea more," Abdi said.

"Would you show me someday?" The question popped out before I could think, and I immediately wanted to grab it back, but Abdi tilted his head, smiling.

"I would like that," he said softly. "If I can, I will."

I hugged him, wet body to wet body, and neither of us mentioned how unlikely it was that I'd ever visit those faraway waves.

Putting on dry jeans over wet underwear was not the funnest, but the important things were the two computers, safely wrapped in our clothes, and the little knife, which I stuck back in my pocket.

We trekked up the beach to the highway and waited behind a pile of rocks. This was the most uncertain—and most morally dubious—part of the plan. But we needed transportation, and we didn't have much choice.

It always seemed to come down to a lack of choice.

Abdi spotted the car before I did, moving smoothly down the long highway toward the distant city. The white van looked similar to a builder's van from my time—with the exception of the solar panels on the roof instead of ladders.

I ruffled my already ruffly hair. "Do I look pathetic enough?" I asked.

"Pout more," Abdi suggested. "You look cute when you pout."

I smiled, but it was wobbly.

"I can do it," he said.

"I'm smaller. Less threatening." Before we could argue further, I jumped over the rocks and ran toward the approaching van, waving my arms in frantic patterns. "Help me!" I called. "Oh god, please, please help me!"

The desperation wasn't feigned. We could try it again, but every missed opportunity would decrease our chances of the plan working. The van slowed to a halt, and I didn't have to fake my relief, either. "Oh, thank you! Thank you so much! Please help me!"

The driver opened his door and jumped out, his blue eyes filled with concern. "Are you all right, ween? What happened?"

He was alone. He was old, a few white hairs still clinging to his bare scalp, the skin nearly translucent with age. And I held my little knife to his wrinkled throat and said, "Please don't move."

He froze. Abdi jumped the rocks and pulled the EarRing, very gently, from the man's ear.

"I'm sorry," I said, as Abdi went through his pockets and pulled out his computer. "I'm so, so sorry, I really am."

"There's money in the glove box," he said. "Take it. Please don't hurt me."

"We need the car," I said miserably.

"Please don't kill me. I have grandchildren your age."

"We won't kill you, I promise. Just don't fight."

Abdi climbed into the van and looked at the dashboard. "Bring him over here, Tegan."

"Please," I said, and pushed him very gently toward the open door.

"Voice code, please," Abdi said.

The man leaned over and mumbled something at the steering wheel, and Abdi coaxed the engine into action.

"You're Tegan Oglietti," the man said suddenly. "I thought you had a breakdown."

"No. The army's trying to keep secrets."

Abdi shot me a pained look. "Sir, there's a town about an hour's walk down the highway. We'll leave you water; all you have to do is follow the road. Maybe someone will pick you up before then."

The man was looking at Abdi square in the face, no longer quite so frightened. "What's your name, son?"

"Abdi."

"Well, Abdi, I'm Jack Harrison. I don't know if you've been paying attention to the weather reports, but there's a superstorm coming in from the east and I don't walk very well. If you plan to leave me out in the open, you may as well cut my throat now and get it over with."

"I'm really sorry," I said. "Those rocks there should give you some shelter."

Abdi bit his lip. "Tegan, I think we have to take him with us."

I stared at him. "He'll try to take the car back. We could lose everything, for good this time."

"These storms are dangerous, Tegan. No one might drive by in time."

"Abdi, this is important! We can't risk screwing it up *again*."

Mr. Harrison was silent and motionless, only his shifting eyes following our faces.

Abdi looked directly at me. "I guess Dawson thinks what he's doing is important, too. Worth making some sacrifices for."

"That's not fair!"

"Isn't it? I think this is how it starts, Tegan. You make a decision that might hurt someone in pursuit of something that helps a lot of people further along. And then you make worse and worse decisions, and then you're willing to sacrifice more people—"

"I am not Trevor fucking Dawson!" I yelled. My hand was shaking on the knife, and I pulled it farther away from Mr. Harrison's throat in case I accidentally hurt him.

Abdi waited.

"All right! Bring him, then."

Mr. Harrison's hands were trembling, too. "Thank you," he whispered.

"We'll have to tie you up," I warned him, and made Abdi take the knife while we got him into the back of the van. I was getting really good at securing people. "I'll ride in the back with you," I said, and put the knife on the other side of my seat, well out of his reach. He followed it with his eyes.

"I really wouldn't," Abdi said, leaning in. "If anything happens to Tegan, I will be angry." He climbed into the driver's seat. After a moment, the van started gliding down the road.

"Where are we going?" Mr. Harrison asked.

I wasn't prepared to be that trusting. "You'll see when we get there," I said, and settled in for the long drive home.

≋ ‡ ∞

The Father's computer had even more spy apps than Bethari's. Despite the address being private, we managed to find it with very little trouble, and Abdi parked the van outside a pretty suburban house much like Marie's. Small upstairs, probably huge downstairs. Solar panels. And a garden. Funny, I hadn't thought he'd be a gardener.

I raced through the rain that had started to fall in heavy drops, signaled the door, and waited. This bit, at least, might be fun.

He didn't make any pretense of nonchalance. The door swung open immediately, and Carl Hurfest stared down at me. "Where have you been?" he demanded.

"That's a long story," I said. "Really exciting, lots of action and drama. Wanna hear it?"

"Get in, quick."

"Just a second." I signaled the van, and Abdi came out, guiding Mr. Harrison before him.

Hurfest's eyes narrowed as he saw the strips of cloth tying Mr. Harrison's hands. "What's this?"

"We'll tell you," I promised. "Inside."

≋ ‡ ∞

We told him everything.

We had to; there was no way he was going to give us access to his networks without getting as much information as he could. He was angry enough that we wouldn't let him talk to a few army contacts to verify my story.

"Either your contacts don't know anything, or they do and they already didn't tell you," Abdi said finally. "And if it's the second, what do you think is going to happen? The moment you get in touch with them, the army will be banging down your door."

Hurfest looked unconvinced. "If we don't warn the army, whatever the Father's planned for this starship might go ahead as soon as they know you escaped for good. Are you willing to take responsibility for those deaths?"

"The Inheritors think murder's a sin," I said, more confidently than I felt. But even though he'd ignored the cryostasis of thousands, the Father had been clear that actually causing deaths was a no-no. "They'll make sure no one gets hurt."

Hurfest grunted. "People can find excuses for all kinds of sins if it suits them." He sat back and eyed Mr. Harrison, sitting on the couch with his hands still tied in front of him. "What do *you* think?"

"They carjacked me, threatened me with a deadly weapon, and took me hostage," Mr. Harrison said. "By my reckoning, they're also guilty of trespassing, privacy violation, illegal data access, theft, and multiple counts of assault."

I flinched. Abdi slipped his hand into mine.

"But dead weens in a freezer..." Mr. Harrison shook his head. "Put the footage on the tubes. The police can sort out who's most to blame."

"Stockholm syndrome is so popular this year," Hurfest observed.

"So you won't do it?" I said, my stomach plummeting. "You don't care?"

"Oh, I care. I'm a cynical bastard, but I'm not a sociopath. I can also see the story of a career when it's handed to me on a big shiny plate." He gave me a direct look, and I began to let myself hope again. "Okay, this is the deal. I can bounce the raw data to a couple dozen colleagues as coming from an anonymous source. Between them, they'll verify what they can and spread the story. Barring a massive natural disaster or one of the big nations declaring war on another one, in half an hour, it'll be the only thing anyone is talking about."

"But?" Abdi asked. "I think there is a but."

Hurfest nodded. "But it's not going to be enough," he said. "In a week, they'll all be talking about something else."

"But it's the facts!" I protested. "We can prove it; we have the footage we filmed in the warehouse; we have the Father's records of the Ark Project and the footage of the starship—it's all true."

"That won't matter," he said. "Trust me, Tegan, it won't. If you want to get through to people, if you want to make them understand why this is important, it needs to be personal. It needs a human face."

"Dawson said the same thing. He said I was the face of Operation New Beginning."

"You are. Which is why it has to be you. A journalist reveals a military conspiracy and human-rights abuses—big deal, journalists have been doing that for centuries. Only rarely does it make a difference. If the Living Dead Girl discovers that she's been betrayed and tells the world about it, it might be a different story."

It was such a little thing, after everything we'd gone through. But he wanted me to talk to the whole world—not rehearsed, not with Tatia's guidance and lots of makeup to hide behind. Just me, by myself, telling everyone my many faults and mistakes. Exposed, with everyone watching me.

"I don't know how to do this," I whispered.

Hurfest sat back and spread his hands. "I'll send the data anyway. But I'm telling you what'll happen if that's all we do."

Abdi squeezed my hand. "Start from the beginning," he suggested. "Tell them where you came from. You can do this."

I thought of Marie, who'd driven off to lead them away from me. I thought of Bethari, who'd never hesitated and backed me all the way. I thought of Joph, who'd been bleeding and screaming at me to go.

"Okay," I said. "I'll do it."

Hurfest nodded. "I thought you would."

It made me feel better to realize I still didn't like him or his smug, self-righteous face. But just because I was doing what he wanted didn't mean I wasn't doing the right thing.

It took him no more than a minute to send the data and turn off his EarRing and computer, as a zillion bells and whistles started. "Colleagues wanting to talk to me direct," he explained. "They want access to my source. Come on, we can get a secure signal from my bedroom. It'll be easier if we aren't all watching you talk. Abdi and I will work on finding a place to move to when they trace the signal." He looked at me. "You know they will trace the signal, don't you? They'll find you eventually."

I nodded.

Abdi went with me as far as the bedroom door and kissed me softly on the threshold. "You can do it," he said again.

I kissed him back. My throat was too tight to speak, but I squeezed his hands in mine. Then I let go and sat cross-legged at the foot of the narrow bed, while Hurfest hunted out a clean computer and signed me in to a newscasting service, bouncing the signal through half a dozen bases.

"The storm's starting in earnest," he said. "That ought to buy you some time."

"When you're ready," I said, trying to sound composed, and Hurfest gave me a silent three count with his hands.

I think I saw a glint of respect in his eyes before he withdrew.

I'm still not sure where the words came from. I thought back, that's all, to my first lifetime, to my last day. Where else would I start but at the beginning, with my name?

I leaned in and spoke, hoping the computer was picking me up properly. "My name is Tegan Oglietti," I began. "One of my ancestors was a highwayman, and another was a prince."

≈ ‡ ∞

And now you know.

293

≈ ‡ ∞

There was some trouble when they tracked the signal to Hurfest's house, and we had to flee, stealing bikes and riding through the storm. We let Mr. Harrison go when we went, and Hurfest stayed behind to slow down our pursuers by giving them false information about our direction. I hadn't expected that of him. I guess you never know about people.

Even dying down, the storm was pretty rough, but we made it to a safe house Abdi knew of that had belonged to one of the medicine-smuggling teams. They must have all been alerted and cleared out when Abdi went missing, which is how I was able to tell you about him and Joph being involved. We broke in and set up there.

But we're not going to get away again. We knew they were coming, too close to evade, and I only needed the time to finish. I can hear them outside now. I don't know what else I can tell you.

Maybe I should go back to the beginning again. I'm Tegan Marie Mary Oglietti. I was beloved of Dalmar; befriended by Alex; tolerated by my brother, Owen; and cherished by my mother.

But that was in my first lifetime, and I don't think I'm done with my second.

The Beatles sang that all you need is love. It would be nice if that were true. But, like everyone, they wanted a lot more than love alone; they wanted wealth and glory and freedom and peace. They wanted to travel; they wanted to investigate their spirituality; they wanted their children to be happy and safe. Love is a good start, but we need more than that to get through.

My mother's last words to me were, "Now you can go and save the world." I died before I could. Some legacy I left you, huh?

But I give you this legacy, too: You can make a difference. You can help.

Not by yourself, not just one person. But I've been talking for a long time, and Abdi tells me there are nearly a billion people watching right now, one-tenth of the entire world. There are people boosting this signal in Samoa and Nigeria and Euskadi. There are people commenting and 'casting back. There are over two dozen nodes set up to verify the Father's evidence and half a dozen more already planning expeditions to Mount Ossa to force the people there to open the doors. The reporters who used to bug me at school are ignoring the media lockout lists and are heading to refugee camps and those hidden warehouses all over the country. Government representatives are getting hard questions from their constituents. They're all denying any knowledge, which is a pretty good sign they can be pushed into doing something about it. Someone's started a fund to defend us, and it's already raised a lot of money. Someone else has started the Free Tegan campaign before I've even been arrested. Others are trying to find Bethari and Joph, hacking away at government databases.

It's really bright outside, and they're shouting stuff at us.

Oh, the bastards. They brought Marie. She's out there now, telling me to give myself up.

I don't know what's going to happen to me. The secret's out, and there's no reason to kill us, but on top of everything else, I broke the supervised-only media clause in my contract pretty thoroughly, and I still belong to them. I'm going to need a really good lawyer, or I don't think they'll ever let me go again. I hope Joph and Bethari are all right. I hope Zaneisha can forgive me when she knows why I ran. I hope Mr. Harrison and Carl Hurfest didn't get in trouble. And if they hurt Abdi, I don't know what I'll do.

But I'm giving myself up now. Without Marie, I'd never have met Abdi or Bethari or Joph, and they wouldn't have made it possible for me to discover the secrets of the Ark Project. Without Marie, I would never have escaped from Dawson.

Without Marie, I could never have told you this story.

It's my turn to help her, if I can, and so I have to go.

Thank you for listening.

Good luck.

Good-bye.

Acknowledgments

My first thanks go to the beautiful city of Melbourne and the lovely country of Australia, my home for four and a half years. You're not perfect, but when you're great, you're amazing. I wish you a much better future than the one imagined here.

I'd like to thank my incredible editors, Susannah Chambers, Alvina Ling, Eva Mills, and Bethany Strout, for all their assistance, especially when the deadline loomed and I had the absolutely genius idea to replace forty percent of the plot with "something else, I promise it'll be really cool." Thanks also to the Little, Brown crew for many things, including beignets and karaoke, and the Allen and Unwin crew for many things, including gossip and Friday-night drinks.

I started listing the names of the awesome people who made me welcome in Australia, and then I went on for two paragraphs, so I'll just say: You know who you are, and thank you all. For material assistance, hand-holding and cluebat-wielding beyond the call of friendship, I want to thank Robyn, Carla, Melanie, Willow, Avery, Deb, Tessa, Tracey, Keith, Gina, and the Shame-In ladies. My particular thanks to Sefakor Dokli, Willow, Guria King, and Chally Kacelnik for their comments on this multicultural cast of characters—all remaining errors are mine alone. Barry Goldblatt is an excellent man, and a good host, and a great agent.

Finally, I would like to thank the Beatles, and especially Ringo Starr, who has always been my favorite and is the source of that thing I have for drummers.

Tegan and Abdi's adventure is far
from over....

Turn the page for a sneak peak of
WHILE WE RUN,
coming in spring 2014.

Cadenza

Even in the sound-insulated waiting room, I could hear the noise from the event hall. I'd thought the public's greed for this kind of function might have been sated, but Tegan's tour had apparently whetted their appetite, and they were ready to see her triumphant return.

But not as ready as I was. When Tegan came through the door, I was on my feet so fast Diane actually reached for one of her hidden weapons.

Normally, we wore similar clothing—sharp-cut shirts and pants, impeccably tailored. Tegan was nearly always in blues, me in greens and yellows. We had to look serious, after all, like responsible young people championing a bright future. But tonight was supposed to be a glittering event, with President Nathan Phillip Cox here to lend his blessing to the fund-raising efforts. Tonight I was wearing a sleeveless chrome vest over dark trousers, an elaborate gold cord tied around my upper arm like the black one Ruby Simons had worn.

And Tegan looked like a European princess. They'd dressed her in a long white gown, with a shimmer of iridescent dust over her bare collarbones. SADU didn't want to remind people too much of the real, risk-taking girl who had thrown herself off a two-story building to escape a military hospital. At an event like this, it made sense that they'd try to make her look like a fairy-tale figure instead—Snow White or Sleeping Beauty. She was supposed to play the role of a naive ingenue wakened from a deathlike sleep, with the future itself cast as a handsome prince, giving Tegan a second chance at life.

It was a lovely tale.

And much, much safer than the real one.

"Abdi," Tegan said, and walked toward me, swaying gracefully in her heels. Before the tour, she'd still been unsteady, but now she handled her shoes as easily as she did her guitar.

Her minder was right behind her. Lat was youngish, and short, and muscular, and he had a scar through the left cheek that my older sister, who liked swashbuckling stories, might have described as "rakish." His eyes were a solid dark brown that seemed black, and they were as flat and merciless as the eyes of a tiger shark I'd seen in the Red Sea. I hated him almost as much as I hated Diane, and I feared for Tegan in his hands. Her old minder had vanished after Tegan's third hunger strike, never to be seen again. After Lat's arrival, Tegan had very quickly *adapted*.

I put out my hand, and she grasped it tight. This was the

single kind of touch we were allowed. Hugging was too close; we might whisper to each other then. "I'm so sorry," I said, trying and failing to put out of my head an image of the way I'd seen her on Diane's computer—crying helplessly on the ground and begging Lat to stop.

Tegan's hand was thin, but the grip was strong, and her exposed collarbones didn't have that sunken appearance I'd learned to fear. "I understand," she said. "I know you won't do it again. Tonight you'll be perfect, won't you?"

She said it without a hint of sarcasm. That was the worst thing about being constantly observed, constantly exposed; we never knew if the other was being sincere or saying what we thought would keep our handlers happy.

"Joph's coming tonight," I said, watching her face.

Her expression didn't change. "Lat told me. It will be nice to tell her a little about the work we've been doing."

My stomach roiled. Diane smirked. "How was the tour, Tegan?" she asked.

"It was interesting. We went to a lot of places. Canada wouldn't let us in, of course."

Canada maintained that Australia's No Migrant policy was a contravention of human rights and wouldn't allow an Australian citizen to cross its borders except as a refugee seeking asylum. Diane shifted; this conversation was too close to topics we weren't allowed to mention.

"So I performed in a cruiser anchored in international borders," Tegan said quickly. She'd noticed Diane move, too. "It was fun. Lots of sponsors came. How are you, Abdi?"

"I'm fine. I missed you," I said, ignoring Lat's disbelieving grunt.

"I missed you, too," she said. "Planes are much fancier than in my time. Before it was cramped and noisy. And no food. On tour, it was like a restaurant in the air."

My face stayed smooth, no matter that I wanted to curl my lip. "Some people can afford luxury."

"Ahem," Lat said.

"It was an observation, Lat. Abdi wasn't being seditious." Tegan said it with the tiniest hint of irritation in her voice, and I could have wept at this signal that she was still in there somewhere, that this smooth, shiny creature wasn't entirely remade to SADU's exacting specifications.

"Courtesy, Tegan," Diane reproved. "Goodness me, have you lost your manners on tour?"

"Tegan was very good," Lat said, and bestowed a smile upon his charge. She smiled back, her dark eyes lighting, and I hated him a little more.

"Well, no need for her to become lax now! And, Abdi, do you really think such observations are helpful?"

"No, Diane. I'm sorry."

"Good." She touched her EarRing and nodded. "We're up. Walk."

Tegan and I shifted our grip so that we could hold hands side by side and walked the short distance from the waiting room to the stage entrance. President Cox was doing the standard spiel: new wonder, new borders, new phase for humanity. Tegan's hand shifted, damp with sweat, and I could feel the slight tremor. She still had stage fright; she probably always would. Tegan's true love was for the music itself, but they'd warped that into making her a showpiece. I'd always loved to perform; when I was too mired in my head to talk, I could always reach people with music. So they demanded performance of me on their terms, not mine, and had stopped me from reaching anyone at all.

The people in charge had imprisoned us and hurt us, and they'd done it so that we'd fix the public-relations problem they'd so richly deserved.

"Break a leg," Diane whispered, and gently stroked the back of my neck. "And remember what I said about Joph."

Yes. I would have to lie to her.

I would have to look into the face of my one Australian friend and tell her that everything she'd done to help me had been pointless. That her being shot had just been a little mistake, that the frozen children in the cryocontainers we'd recorded had chosen freely and happily to give up their lives here so they could work on a distant planet. If I went onto that stage, I would have to betray Joph, and myself, and Tegan, and I would have to keep doing it, over and over and over.

It would never stop.

It felt as if despair had grabbed my legs and pulled me under the surface of my turbulent emotions, stealing my breath and tightening my muscles. Tegan felt it through her grip on me, and her body language shifted in response. She caught the look on my face and whispered, "Not now."

"... now, I am pleased to present to you the ambassadors for the Ark Project, Tegan Oglietti and Abdi Taalib!"

Tegan stepped forward and jerked to a halt, motionless on the end of my outstretched hand. I knew I had to plaster a smile on my face and walk onto the stage, but my feet were rooted to the floor.

"Abdi," Diane said behind me. It was a command.

"I can't," I said. "I can't do this anymore."

Tegan twisted to face me. "Don't do this to me," she said. "Abdi, please don't! I can't take it!"

Months ago she'd shouted her defiance in their faces. *I'm glad he tried to escape. I'm glad! Hurt me all you want, I hope he does it again!* The Tegan I'd come to know, the girl I'd kissed and fought for, would have screamed it now.

Instead she looked over my shoulder and said, "Lat, I'm being good! It's not me. He's doing it. Don't punish me. Not tonight!"

But there was nothing special about this night. It was just another performance, like a hundred we'd done before, like a thousand more we'd do until SADU decided the Living Dead Girl wasn't useful anymore and found a convenient accident to get rid of her and her thirdie boyfriend. Or, even worse, until we truly became what we only appeared to be, the insides of our heads changing to match the veneer of their perfect puppets.

"It's too much," I said, shaking my head. "It hurts too much, and it'll never stop. I can't do it."

"Please, Abdi," Tegan said. "It'll be fine. Please trust me."

But I didn't trust her. I couldn't.

It was a horrible realization; for six months she'd been my only ally, the only person I could count on to understand how I felt and empathize with my pain—and vice versa. Now I didn't know how much of the strong Tegan I'd loved was still in there. And I couldn't trust what might remain.

Lat bent down by my ear, while President Cox made jokes about stage fright and how shy and humble we were.

"You will move, or I will hurt her in new ways," he whispered, his voice deep and pleasant. "And I'll make you watch it all." He chuckled. "Maybe she'll even enjoy it."

It felt as if he'd wrapped his hands around my throat and squeezed all the air out. They'd never threatened her with that before. I couldn't let it happen.

But I also couldn't continue as I had.

Stretched thin between the two impossible choices, I gave in to Tegan's insistent tug on my hand and stepped forward, into the light of that enormous room and the hundreds of greedy eyes that waited to devour us until we were nothing but empty husks.

Nathan Phillip Cox, president of the Republic of Australia, was waiting to greet us. His face was broad and rugged, a handsome, sturdy kind of face. You could imagine it on the first European pioneers trying to cross the Australian desert or running sheep over the rounded hills. His wrinkles had been superbly tweaked to suggest seriousness, but not sternness, and his crow's-feet proclaimed that this was a man who laughed as often as he frowned. He was laughing now, but the emotion didn't reach his eyes. He'd want to know the reason for our hesitation.

Tegan strode forward to shake his hand, a gesture the

president turned into a one-armed hug. He beamed down at her, a kind uncle, then solemnly shook my hand in a man-to-boy gesture that would look great on the 'casts. The noble firster president of superpower Australia, in common cause with the savage thirdie boy from tiny Djibouti.

Tegan was waving and smiling, happily ignorant of Lat's threat. "Hello!" she yelled. "It's so great to be back! Did you miss me?"

The crowd roared.

"I missed you," I said again, only this time it was part of the script. I didn't have to pay attention; the words spilled out easily, my every gesture rehearsed and fine-tuned.

"Well, I've been traveling the world talking about something really important," Tegan said. "You all know about the Ark Project. You all know about the *Resolution.* You know that we're sending humanity to the stars for the first time. And everyone can be a part of it! Everyone can donate something or spread the word."

"The world is in a slow decline," I said, looking grave. Among the solemn nods and sad faces, I saw pursed lips and heads shaking, and wanted to punch something. This was the one part of our spiel that was true, and it was the part a few people always wanted to deny.

"The first travelers are the brave pioneers of our future," Tegan said. "They're taking on the challenge of finding a new home for humanity! And as soon as the revival process is perfected, we'll all take on the challenge of getting them on their way."

"They had faith that we'd help," I said. "Will you keep faith with them?"

"Will you pledge what you can pledge?" Tegan asked. Her excitement looked so real. Was it real? Had she broken that hard? I felt a flash of curiosity before the intense gravity of my despair crushed it down to the soundtrack of the cheering crowd.

"That's enough politics!" Tegan yelled over the noise.

I held up my hands, the golden cord swaying from my forearm. I was doing everything as perfectly as if Diane were tugging directly on that dangling string to manipulate my movements. Tegan couldn't be punished for this. "How about a song?"

They clapped and laughed, while Tegan was handed her guitar—not the third-hand instrument she'd named Abbey and loved with fierce devotion but a custom-made guitar that had been covered in a white skin of memory fabric, glittering like her dress. She checked the tuning, nodded at me, and began picking the opening notes.

It was "Here Comes the Sun."

They always wanted me to sing "Here Comes the Sun."

From the corner of my eye, I could see President Cox, smiling and nodding along to the beat, and Diane in the wings, looking bored. She was looking at the crowd, scanning them idly.

But Lat was watching Tegan.

His eyes were trained directly on her face, and I felt that fear rise within me again. He'd do it. He'd bend her body to his will. The one thing I'd learned to depend on when it came to SADU is that no matter what we did or how good we were, they would always find a reason to hurt us.

As I looked away, unable to bear the possessive fervor in Lat's face, my eyes snagged on a lump under the president's jacket. Probably ninety percent of the people in that room would never have seen it, but over the last six months I'd become hypersensitized to those lumps and what they indicated.

Cox was armed.

Almost idly, I considered the possibilities. I could finish the song and go over to shake his hand again, grab the weapon, aim for Lat, aim for Diane if I got a second shot....

Cold sweat prickled in the curve of my back as fantasy condensed into a viable plan.

I really could do it. The only drawback, as far as I could tell, was that I would definitely die. And they'd punish Tegan afterward—but I wouldn't be around to watch.

I might be able to save her from Lat, though. Perhaps my death would be able to save her entirely. Questions would be asked; people would want to know what had happened and why. My parents were already unhappy, and with me dead they wouldn't have to step carefully around the need to appease my current guardians; they could cause the outcry I knew they wanted to make. Perhaps the furor would give Tegan an opportunity to escape and tell the truth. Perhaps these Save Tegan people would gain some political traction. Perhaps the Ark Project would be revealed for the horror it was.

I wouldn't be around to see it, but it might happen.

And I wouldn't have to commit that final betrayal and lie to Joph.

That was it, I decided. It would be better if I had a way to warn Tegan, but there wasn't any time for hesitation, and if there was anything of the real, brave Tegan left, I thought she would understand that—she'd always been the one who leaped fearlessly into action. Funny, almost, that I would die in my attempt to do the same.

We neared the end of the song, and I poured joy and power into the final chorus, drinking in my final moments. I would go down singing—that felt right; that was proper. The crowd brightened in response to my sudden effort, and I smiled, my gaze sliding around the room. I felt almost sorry for those excited, happy people, who would soon be scared and shocked.

My gaze caught on a slender girl with short tan hair, pushing her way forward to the front row. She was staring directly at me, her brown eyes lit with the same reckless joy that was rising in me.

I smiled at Joph, wishing that I could say good-bye.

Jump, she mouthed.

I frowned, confused. Joph grimaced and beckoned extravagantly. "Jump!" she shouted, her voice cutting clear across the moment of silence at the end of the song.

And as all the lights went out and the startled murmurs began, I launched myself forward, into the dark.